Lying Love

Carol Reiff

Contents

1. Chapter 1 1
2. Chapter 2 5
3. Chapter 3 9
4. Chapter 4 13
5. Chapter 5 17
6. Chapter 6 22
7. Chapter 7 27
8. Chapter 8 32
9. Chapter 9 38
10. Chapter 10 42
11. Chapter 11 47
12. Chapter 12 51
13. Chapter 13 56
14. Chapter 14 61
15. Chapter 15 66

16. Chapter 16 71
17. Chapter 17 76
18. Chapter 18 81
19. Chapter 19 86
20. Chapter 20 90
21. Chapter 21 96
22. Chapter 22 100
23. Chapter 23 104
24. Chapter 24 109
25. Chapter 25 115
26. Chapter 26 122
27. Chapter 27 127
28. Chapter 28 133
29. Chapter 29 137
30. Chapter 30 144
31. Chapter 31 148
32. Chapter 32 152
33. Chapter 33 157
34. Chapter 34 162
35. Chapter 35 167
36. Chapter 36 172
37. Chapter 37 178
38. Chapter 38 185

39. Chapter 39 190
40. Chapter 40 195
41. Chapter 41 200
42. Chapter 42 204
43. Chapter 43 209
44. Chapter 44 213
45. Chapter 45 222
46. Chapter 46 226
47. Chapter 47 231
48. Chapter 48 237
49. Chapter 49 243
50. Chapter 50 247
51. Chapter 51 252
52. Chapter 52 259
53. Chapter 53 264
54. Chapter 54 269
55. Chapter 55 275
56. Chapter 56 282
57. Chapter 57 287
58. Chapter 58 292
59. Chapter 59 299
60. Chapter 60 306
61. Epilogue 314

Chapter 1

I was standing outside my office in front of the VIP parking lot staring at the expensive cars parked in awe, which belonged to our CEO and high positioned employees. ' gosh! When am I gonna get my own car?' I sighed.

Suddenly someone patted my shoulders and I turned my head towards Chase,who was smiling like a maniac.

"What?" I snapped.

"Tonight he's having a date with Clara, so he has a big smile on his face " said Steve, who was standing beside him.

Well Clara is Chase's girlfriend and they've been dating almost for a year now and this month they also have their anniversary. I like Clara a lot but I do admit that I hate her a bit for the way she acts like she's the only one who knows about everything. Chase loves her alot , The way he adores her, looks at her as if he's seeing a magic. I envy her alot. Even I want someone who will love me unconditionally.

" Let's get going " Steve said pointing towards his car.

Chase and I nodded as we followed him towards his car. Steve had a car not an expensive one but a normal Hyundai car.

It was evening and we were going to our respective homes, well Chase had a motorcycle but today he hadn't brought it so he was accompanying me and Steve.

As we reached towards his car ,I don't know what came over me I asked . "Can I drive your car, Steve, pretty please "

He stared at me blankly ,while I gave him a puppy eye.

"Okay" he sighed and threw the car keys at me and I caught it.

We all three sat inside the car, me in the drive seat, Steve in passenger seat and Chase in back seat.

I started the engine and everybody was silent. I glanced at Steve ,who was staring outside the window and Chase was still smiling.

This silence was getting into my nerve so I started a conversation.

"Guys, soon I'm gonna buy an expensive luxury car for myself " I said while rotating the steering wheel.

Steve rolled his eyes "you've been saying that for months now , you can buy a car like mine, you have a big fat amount in your account. "

"Nope"

"Why?" Steve asked.

"It's been my dream to ride that luxury car, you know that"

"You have so many dreams, which cannot come true" he shook his head in dismay.

"Yeah, I have many dreams like 1. buy myself a luxury car 2. going to time square , New York the sleepless city and shop there and roam around. 3. I wanna go on a world tour............." I kept on listing my dreams and Steve was listening and Chase was zoned out. "And I'll make sure I'll fullfill all my dreams "

"The car which your aiming to buy, only billionaires drive such cars"

"Don't discourage me Steve, dream big and go big"

Steve opened his mouth to answer back but I suddenly took a turn towards a narrow road ,where vehicles don't go often and no vehicles means no traffic.

"Hey where are we going " Steve said in an alarmed tone.

" chill friend, it's a short cut and am saving your fuel and saving fuel means saving money " I gave him a pointed look " so that you can spend your money on your one night stands" I smirked.

"Atleast am not a virgin nor are my one night stands" he said, giving me an equally challenging smirk

I hate this virginity topic. "Not again with a virginity topic"

"You started it " he said nonchalantly

Well I'm a virgin and Steve's a playboy. He can't stand a sight of virgins so he keeps on giving me tips on 'how to be good in beds?' 'How to charm your boyfriend ?' Blah blah......

"Your such a manwhore ,I'll throw you out of the car" I gritted my teeth.

"It's my car" he smirked.

"Ugh" I groaned and gave him a death glare " wait until I get my own luxury car and your not allowed to enter my ca-"

"ASHLEY .LOOK .FRONT " Steve screamed

And when I looked at the windscreen it was already late ,I hit the man and pressed the brake.

We all three had a horrified expression on our face, we got out of the car and saw the man lying unconscious, arms a bit scrapped.

"Ashley, what have you done " Steve and Chase looked tensed.

"I don't think anything happened to him , I wasn't driving at a high speed " I reasoned with full of panic.

"Okay let's take him to the hospital " Chase said.

They both carried him to the car and laid him on the back seat. My hands were trembling so I couldn't drive so now Chase was driving us to the hospital and Steve was sitting in the back seat with that man.

'I hope he's alright .'

Chapter 2

We all three were standing impatiently outside the hospital room waiting for the doctor to come out. The door opened and the doctor came into the view,

"Thanks to God that he don't have any internal bleeding, only he has some scratches on his feet and arms." The doctor said and we all sighed in relief .

"Well is it hit and run case, where did you find his body " doctor asked .

Without hesitation I told him the truth " actually I hit him with his car " I said pointing towards Steve and Steve stared at me oddly like am a lunatic. " but I was driving slowly doctor, he came out of nowhere in the middle of the road "

Doctor stared at me for a while and then said " any way he's alright so no worries "

"Can we go see him doctor " Chase asked.

"Yes " the doctor said and walked away

As we were sauntering inside I asked "why was that doctor staring at me?"

"Because he was thinking, who is this lunatic whose digging her own grave " Steve said pointing towards me and I scowled in return. 'Well am a bad liar '

I turned my gaze from Steve to the guy who was sitting on the hospital bed innocently.

When I hit him with the car I didn't notice his figure due to the panic and now sitting here in the hospital bed he looks strikingly gorgeous, handsome or definition of handsome.. 'OH oh ! Someone is too hot in here'

He had jet black hair slightly disheveled and a beautiful pair of piercing green eyes ,pointed nose and a soft pink lips. He had a tall and a muscular body. He was a perfect Adonis.

"Stop checking him out " Steve whispered.

"Uh?" I was puzzled by his beauty

I cleared my throat and strode towards the bed followed by Chase and Steve. The Adonis was staring outside the window with his cute innocent eyes.

"Hi" I was the first one to talk. He didn't reply

Is he ignoring me or is he deaf?

Okay I tried again " hey, handsome " I waved my hand in front of his face to get his attention. And I got , he jolted and turned towards me, looking at me in the eye.

'Ah! those green eyes '

I'll marry someone who has green eyes like him so that my kids could have those green eyes. I wish even I had those green eyes instead of these brown one.

Somebody cleared their throat and it was Steve giving me a look that said 'stop checking him out '

"Who are you? " the man asked innocently

I blinked "Well man , that's my question, who are you? " I gave him a sweet smile.

He stared blankly at me without answering, again I asked softly with a smile plastered on my face "What is your name?"

again ignored.

"I think he's having amnesia "I joked and chuckled while Steve and Chase gave me an odd look as if am a crazy donkey braying.

But when that guy opened his mouth I jumped like a crazy donkey

"Who am I ?" I snapped my head in an instant towards him, shocked.

"WHAT ?" we three screeched.

"He can't have amnesia, the doctor said there was no internal bleeding " I said to Chase and Steve with a horrified expression.

"True" they agreed. ....

We called the doctor and now doctor was checking him.

" according to the reports he don't have any internal bleeding he's all fit and fine. I can't understand how he's having amnesia " the doctor said and turned towards him "is there any pain in your head"

"Yes , a bit " he said in a painful tone resting his palms on is head.

"I think he's having amnesia " the doctor confirmed.

And I pulled my hair in frustration for the problem that is to come.

Chapter 3

Steve, Chase and I, were standing at the corner of the room afar from the bed where the amnesia guy was sitting, discussing about what to do. When the door opened and doctor came into view,

"You'll can take him home, he's been discharged " the doctor said

"And what about the memory loss doctor " I asked fiddling with my fingers.

"Miss, amnesia is something which cannot be cured , he himself have to try to gain his memory without any pressure "

"And what if we pressurize him doctor "

" Well it can lead him to coma also "

Well I don't have money to pay hospital bills for lifelong.

"Okay when will he get his memory back"

"We can't say that ,it might take days" days was fine with me "or weeks" I paled "or months " I paled and paled " or even years " and now I was a white sheet of paper, palerrrr .

The doctor left after dropping a big bomb on my head.I was trembling when fear overwhelmed me. 'What if it takes years for his memory to come back '

"Hey, it's okay don't worry " Chase and Steve both hugged me sideways seeing my trembling form.

"What are we gonna do, we don't know who he is and who is his family " I sobbed

"We'll keep him with us " Chase said slightly relaxing me.

"You mean you will keep him with you in your house " I asked pointing towards the guy.

"No! No no..I mean I have Clara with me in my house I can't keep him with me" Chase said giving us a pointed look.

Our gaze turned to Steve who was standing there staring at us.

"No!" Steve said

"Why not?" "You can keep him with you and you don't even have a girlfriend " I said glaring at him.

"Because I have my one night stands coming over and I need my privacy " he stated.

Anger swirled through me , " can't you keep your man-whore thing aside for a while and help your friend out" I yelled

"Shh.." Chase hushed me while staring at the no name guy and I followed his gaze and looked at the guy who was staring at us innocently.

I turned my gaze back to them, "Can't he keep his pants zip closed for a while " I asked Chase while glaring at Steve.

"No I can't " Steve whispered.

"Why not" I whisper yelled

But he gave me a blank look which had a meaning.

I gave him a disgusting look. "Ew... your so dirty " my gaze went towards his crotch. "Ew gross, I'm gonna puke now"

"Stop staring at my dick and stop saying ew." He snapped

I gave him a disgusted look,

"Back to the topic, guys" Chase said a bit annoyed.

"It's final, Ashley is gonna keep him with her" Steve stated firmly in an authoritative tone.

"I can't keep him with me "

"Why not?" Steve snapped

"Because I have only one room in my apartment and I'm a woman"

"Oh come on, we are in 21st century and as for the room,you can give your room to him and sleep in the living room, poor guy he's injured and your the one who hit him with my car " Steve gave a pity look to the guy and smirked at me .

'The audacity of this guy to provoke me'

Chase cleared his throat and said "I think Steve is right "

I groaned and raised my chin high in pride and said" fine, I'll keep him with me"

"Okay , we'll talk to him then settle the bills and take him to your home"

We strolled towards the bed and we three stood in front of him as if we were interrogating him.

"Okay " I started "You don't remember who you are , right " He nodded

'Even that nod was so hot, damn!'

Okay, I cleared my throat

'Control yourself Ashley'

"I'm Ashley Grayson and this is Chase and Steve " I said pointing towards them " my boyfriends "

He raised his brows,

" I mean boy as friends kind of boyfriends " I cleared his confusion

His soft pink lips turned into an O as he realized.

"So let's get going , your coming with me to my apartment " he smiled and nodded.

He got up from the bed and started walking but suddenly came to a halt and turned around facing me, " I don't have clothes to wear" he said

I facepalmed inwardly and smiled "Let's keep it as tomorrow's problem "

He nodded and walked further as I was following,Steve tapped my shoulders and said, " time to loose your virginity, young lady " he chuckled

I turned around and smacked his forehead "shut up"

"Ouch!" He smirked " I know you like him, the way you were checking him out every passing time"

I flushed due to embarrassment " shut up Steve otherwise I'm gonna let all your dirty secrets out"

"Okay..Okay , cool down " he chuckled and walked past me.

I inhaled a sharp breath, 'Tomorrow is gonna be a long day ' I sighed and followed.

Chapter 4

Suddenly a loud annoying sound of alarm kept ringing in my ears and I groaned and rolled on my bed to turn that alarm off but- "Ouch " I fell on the floor , flat on my butt and Ouch it pains as hell. Oh God!

"Hey! are you okay?" I heard a melodic voice of the amnesia guy.

I flickered my eyes and slowly opened my eyes and saw him standing there in his yesterday's dress ,black hoodie and black pants and his hair fully disheveled. I was a quite pissed at him for agreeing to sleep in my room as I remembered yesterday's event.

It was night when we returned from the hospital as we all had our dinner in a common restaurant except Chase as he had a date with Clara. "You can take my room to sleep, I'll sleep in the living room " I said

"Okay " he nodded and asked " where's the room " I pointed him my room direction and he went to my room.

I was taken aback ,I thought he would say 'no no .. you take your room, I'll sleep in the living room ' instead he shamelessly agreed to sleep in my room.

Back to the present, I got up from the floor rubbing my back, I forgot that I was sleeping on the couch, actually I have a habit of rolling on my bed.

"Are you alright?" he came towards me.

Well he was stinking so bad without having a bath, can't blame him he don't have clothes to change after taking a bath. So I asked Steve to bring a pair of his clothes. Well today was Saturday, so no work and I was free, so we were going to mall to buy him some clothes to wear, from my savings. I hate spending money unusually but it was my fault to hit him with Steve's car,so I had to pay.

I smiled tightly and nodded.

"I'll go take bath" I said and he nodded

As I was about to go to the bathroom, the door bell rang and I went towards the door to open it and when I did ,it was Steve ,standing freshly out there.

He sauntered in and threw a bag at my face and I caught it. 'How rude of him , throwing bag at my face'

"Here, my clothes are in there" Steve said pointing to the bag

I rolled my eyes at his attitude.

I strolled towards the amnesia guy and handed him the bag and smiled "you go and take bath first " he nodded .

'Good!he was stinking like a rotten fish'

As he went to the bathroom, I went to the kitchen to prepare breakfast,

"Prepare breakfast for four, Chase is on his way " Steve said and I nodded. ....

After preparing breakfast, I was setting the table while Steve and Chase were helping me setting the table. After setting the table we all three sat waiting for him to come outside the bathroom.

The door opened and Mr amnesia came in to the view looking strikingly gorgeous with those wet hair , water droplets falling from his hair to his forehead and to his nose and then to his soft luscious lips ,he licked his bottom lip. 'OH my God! Am gonna pass out with this hot man standing in front of me '

Chase cleared his throat and I looked at them, 'again I was caught checking him out ' Steve was smirking as usual and later on he's gonna tease me for sure .

The seat beside me was vacant, so Mr amnesia came and sat beside me and the smell of my strawberry bodywash was smelling so good on his body,awesome..

"Le.. let's eat breakfast " I stuttered " and then we have to go to the mall also to buy some clothes for him"

And then there was a pin drop silence as everybody started eating their breakfast., I suddenly choked on my own food and started coughing.

"Are you alright, Ashley? " Steve asked Can't he see am choking to death, yet asking me 'are you alright ?' stupid man. I was continuesly coughing pointing towards water but none bothered except Mr amnesia, he passed me water and gently rubbed my back.

A mere touch of him gave me an electrifying tingly sensation, 'It's just a gentle gesture Ashley '

After finishing breakfast we all got ready to leave to the mall.

And I was crying inwardly because am gonna spend my savings on a stranger instead of my car.

Chapter 5

We were standing outside the huge mall staring at the vast building.. "Let's get in" Mr amnesia said and sauntered in followed by Steve and Chase.

I pulled Steve and Chase's elbow and pulled them back and asked. "Can't I borrow some pants and shirts from you'll "

"Oh my God Ashley! Your such a stingy woman, can't you spend some dollars for clothes " Steve scrunched his nose and said in an accusing tone.

"SHUT. UP" I yelled and looked at Chase with a puppy eyes.

"I could have given him my clothes Ashley but he is far more taller than me "

Well that's true. I looked at Steve, he was as tall as Mr amnesia, but I know this traitor, he would never give his clothes.

"Don't look at me like that, I already gave you my one set of clothes and please wash it properly and return it to me, okay?" I just gave him a murderous glare and he continued

"You have a big fat amount on your account, what are you gonna do with that money, take it to your grave along with you "

The nerve of this Steve..

I gritted my teeth and was about to answer when Mr amnesia came, " aren't you all gonna come in"

I was shaking with rage but however I managed to force a smile on my face and said a small yes..

While sauntering in I purposely stomped on Steve's feet, "Ouch " he winced and I smirked.

'You deserved this ,you sick bastard ' I wanted to laugh wickedly but refrained myself as Mr amnesia was present near us.

....

We were in one of the shop selecting shirts for Mr amnesia. I pointed at a orange colored hoodie. "That's nice " I took it out from the rack and showed it to the boys.

"Nah! that looks cheap " both Steve and Mr amnesia said in unison.

'Okay! well it was actually a cheap one '

Steve and Mr amnesia selected some clothes which were quite expensive like white shiny shirt , beige turtle neck t-shirt, black and grey colour hoodie etc

I was the one spending my money but Steve was the one selecting clothes 'So unfair'

So I strode towards the rack and picked one of the check shirt and put it in the trolley.

"Hey that one is cheap" Steve glanced at the shirt disgustedly.

"It's not and I'm paying the bill Steve" I almost yelled.

Steve just rolled his eyes whereas Chase was in his own world and Mr amnesia was standing there staring at us.

After taking shirts,pants and a belt I said, "Go and try them in the trial room" he nodded obediently and went to the trial room.

......

"Ugh" I groaned " what's taking him so long we've been waiting for almost half an hour" well talking to Chase was useless ,he just keeps spacing out , so I turned towards Steve, "Go and check,why he's taking so long"

Steve scoffed " stop ordering me, I'm not your servent,you go and check however he's your man"

I scowled "he's not my man" I huffed angrily and strolled towards the fitting room.

As I reached the fitting room I pulled the curtains without any word and .. 'oh my god!'

My jaw instantly fell to the ground seeing him standing half naked in front of me. He was shirtless showing all of his mouth watering abs and his pants hung low around his waist,belt hanging loose showing a little of his boxers. He had a perfectly sculptured body which any women would love to worship.

His eyes widened as he saw me standing outside the fitting room gawking at him, he instantly covered his chest with his hands. "You" he almost screamed

I turned around feeling embarrassed for gawking shamelessly at his perfectly sculptured body. He didn't had to cover his chest ,he don't have any boobs to cover,well men show their chest.

'He's a Saint type person Ashley'

"So-sorry for pulling the c-curtains " I stammered "I just came here to check that what's taking you so long"

"You can turn around I'm decent"

'You were decent man, you were not totally naked in front of me '

"Well I had so many shirts to try and this is my last one " he said after I turned around pointing to the check shirt which I selected.

And my gosh he was looking so cute....

"Uh..um.. alright, we'll be waiting outside" with that said I quickly sprinted towards my friends.

....

After checking the size of the shirts ,pants and a belt we went towards the bill counter to pay when Steve abruptly stopped walking. But we all ignored him and kept walking.

" We haven't bought any boxer briefs for him"

"Yeah,am still wearing yesterday ones"Mr amnesia said I groaned inwardly again I have to purchase my money for his boxers, damnit.

Well we were in the boxers section to buy him some boxers, Oh my god there were hot men's almost naked pictures with only boxers were hung everywhere as posters.

I think I'm gonna faint with too many hot men around me . I heaved a sigh. 'Why am I like this,damn'

"Yeah I got my size" Mr amnesia said carrying a box of it .

"How do you know that it's your size" I narrowed my eyes and asked.

"Uh.." he hesitated " today while having a bath I checked my size, Ashley" he said hesitantly followed by a weird chuckle. And then walked past me, Steve and Chase followed him.

While I had weird feeling, 'Is he pretending, having amnesia' I shook that thought,

Why would he do that??

Chapter 6

SUNDAY was always my favourite day in a week ,it was always a relaxing day for me, always waking up at noon around 1 pm and then ordering a pizza or a burger for lunch, and especially a day off from my stressful work. I know Saturday is also a holiday but Sunday is different, I like Sunday more than Saturday.

But today, waking up at eight, falling again from that damn couch followed by a stinging pain in my back and now here I am preparing breakfast for him while he's gone for a morning walk.

'my Sunday got ruined thanks to him,ugh'

The door bell rang and I knew who it was.

I sauntered towards the door and threw it open, and there at the threshold was standing the handsome guy, Mr amnesia. All my anger and frustration faded away as I saw his beautiful face.

He was covered with sweat and slightly panting also. I had the urge to flirt with him but I refrained it as he was a gentleman. I moved aside so that he could come in . As he came and saw the the table was set with the food . He turned around and said , " I'll go have a quick shower and come " I nodded and he gave me a charming smile of his that almost melted me and heated my cheeks. Why am I blushing like a lovesick teenager,huh?? ....

After having breakfast he helped me with the dishes. After washing all the dishes ,he went to the living room and sat on the couch and started watching Netflix on my TV.

While I sat on the chair at the dining table and opened my laptop to do some of my office work to kill time.

.... It was already afternoon when I finished half of my office work, I looked at him he was still watching TV. I went towards him and asked " What would you like, pizza or a burger for lunch"

"Anything " he answered without even giving me a single glance.

I ordered two burgers and a ice soda for both of us.

I again glanced at him and saw he was so engrossed on watching TV, that concerned me , I mean not his eyes or anything, but about my electricity bills and TV bills.

Every month I keep a budget and follow it thoroughly so that I can buy a luxury car for myself ASAP. And this month I think my electricity bill is gonna empty my pocket, I mean he watches TV a lot and even switch on AC at night, I don't even turn AC on ,however hot it is just to save my money.

' can't blame him Ashley, he has nothing to entertain himself'

Well true.

Our orders were delivered to my apartment and I gave him one burger and ate another one silently watching him watching TV.

I have to make him turn off the TV, but how??

'Try to make a conversation with him dumbass'

Oh yeah right. I cleared my throat and started a conversation,

"Come on, let's play something, I'm bored" I said as he glanced at me.

" okay what do you wanna play?"

" Let's play twenty questions"

"But I don't remember anything from my past"

"But you can ask me any questions"

"Okay" "Why don't you have any girlfriends I mean girl as a friend "

Even I don't know why I don't have any girlfriends but I kept on thinking how to answer him. "Maybe because girls don't like me?" I said it more like a question followed by a shrug and he just chuckled.

"What are your dreams?" Was his next question.

My favourite question, I love to talk about my dreams.

"I have many dreams"

"Okay , go on I'm a good listener"

So I said him all about my dreams, to buy a luxury car followed by visiting newyork and shopping in time square and then roam around states and a world trip blah blah blah.....

It was almost evening around six we were talking, laughing and making fun of each other. I thought he would ask some personal questions like about boyfriends and dating stuff but he never asked instead he asked about my favourite food, colour etc.

"I still don't have name what would you name me " he asked

I pressed my lips together thinking hard and said "Mr amnesia, nameless, no-name"I laughed and he also laughed richly and then said.

"Hey, it's not funny" he said.

" Okay okay" I tried to cover my grin by coughing and then stood up and strolled towards the kitchen.

"Where are you going?"

"Kitchen" I went to the kitchen and opened one of the cabinet and took out the expensive red wine which my mom gave me when I last visited her home.

"So let's celebrate the temporary naming ceremony event" I squealed raising the red wine bottle and kept the flute glasses on the table. I opened the bottle and poured some red wine to his glass and then mine.

"Cheers" he said and I cheered with him.

"So,what temporary name would you like Mr amnesia"

He pouted and he was looking so cute while pouting. "How about Daniel , Oliver, Alexander, Xavier ......" He continued.

" Jeez they are all old names, how about Stefan" I suggested

Well I know it's also an old name but I have a huge unfading crush on Stefan Salvatore so I suggested his name and he nodded .

" Nice name"

Then I drank my wine but he didn't touch his flute glass at all and atlast I drank his wine and night went on .

After all it wasn't a bad Sunday. I enjoyed this Sunday more than any Sunday.

Chapter 7

I was continuously tapping on my laptop when Steve tapped my shoulders " Pass me that file, Ashley" he pointed towards the file which was near me I grabbed it and passed it to him, while passing I saw a wicked smirk curling up on his lips.

I raised a brow and asked " What?"

"Oh nothing, just wanna know how was your sunday at home alone with Mr amnesia"

"Stefan" I said

"Stefan?" Both Chase and Steve asked with a frown.

"Well I gave him a temporary name yesterday as we cannot just be calling him Mr amnesia, right"

They nodded and Chase got back to his work while Steve was still smirking at me.

" Stefan,huh?your crush Stefan Salvatore's name.you really like him, right" I rolled my eyes at him

"So tell me how was your day with Stefan alone?"

I gave him the sweetest smile " well it was fabulous "

"So did you kiss him? "

"No"I wrinkled my nose "I don't kiss strangers"

"Well he's no more a stranger to you, you just named him Stefan ,your favourite name"

"How was your day Steve ?" I asked changing the subject

"Oh! mine , it was boring in the morning only sleeping,and at night it was fabulous, I went to club and there I found a girl with a hourglass body plump lips , begging to be kissed and her naked form was breath takingly beautiful and-"

"You slept with her" Chase suddenly butted in and asked in a low voice .well it wasn't something shocking, he's a playboy anyways.

"Yeah listen" he was very desperate to tell us" I kissed every inch of her body and kneaded her round fluffy breas-"

"Shut up you shameless disgusting manwhore" I said it out loud and some head turned towards us.

'Oh oh!'

" What's going on there in table four" our chiefs voice bellowed.

We all three put our head down and apologized and started doing our work.

....

I was sitting in the cafeteria munching my burger thinking about my savings, calculating my remaining savings. When I suddenly got an idea.

I took out a blank paper and a pen and started scribbling in it .

"What are you doing?" Chase and Steve,who were sitting across me asked unison.

"I'm making a bill for Stefan, when he recovers from amnesia I'm gonna give this paper to him" I said pointing to the paper.

"But what is exactly in that paper" Chase asked.

"It'-" I was about to tell him when Steve cut me off

"Obviously it's a love letter" He shrugged

"Shut up Steve I'm serious" I gave him a stern look. "In this paper am gonna write ,how much money I've spent on him and when he recovers am gonna ask my money back " I said smiling proudly.

"And what if he's a beggar?" My proud smile instantly disappeared.

"Nah, I don't think so,I mean he was wearing a nice branded hoodie when he was hit by my car" for the first time ever Steve's words were soothing me.

"I mean" Chase started " what if he's thrown out of his house by his girlfriend or parents ,what if he's homeless ,without any job, " Chase gave us a pointed look

Well it can be true , if he's a beggar or homeless guy am not gonna take a penny from him but if he turns out to be a guy with job or even rich I'm gonna ask every money I've spent on him with interest.

....

I was in the kitchen making coffee for me and Stefan, I've been constantly debating with myself to ask him or not and at last taking a sharp breath I thought, 'Let's ask'

I strolled towards him and gave him the coffee and sat beside him while he was watching a movie,

"Can we talk?" I started

"Oh yeah! sure"

"Do you remember anything about who you are and all"

He pressed his lips together, thinking about how to answer me,

"No, not yet"

"Do you think you're a homeless beggar or-"

"No" he replied instantly. Then took a deep breath and calmly said " I don't think so I think I have a home and a job also"

That eased me,okay.

"Do you think you have any girlfriends"

"Why ?" He asked giving me his sweet smile which almost melted me .

"Just curious" I shrugged

"I don't know " he said and continued" maybe yes or maybe no "

After drinking our coffees I went to the kitchen and was thinking,what to prepare for dinner as my fridge was empty. I thought of asking Stefan so I called him,

"Stefan" I called moving towards him but he didn't reply, he was deep in thoughts

"Stefan" I called again but no reply

"Stefan " this time I called louder and tapped his shoulders.

"Stefan?" He asked and I raised a brow at him.

"You forgot, yesterday I gave you temporary name , Stefan "

"No I didn't forget I was just-"

" I know you're worried about your memory loss but don't worry, you'll gain your memory back very soon " I said and he nodded with a smile.

'Poor guy I hope he gets his memory back soon.'

Chapter 8

I was standing in front of my dressing table getting ready for Chase's and Clara's one year anniversary party which there were celebrating in a new club, which opened recently.

I was wearing a black knee length shimmer bodycon dress which hugged my body perfectly. I wore a matching silver stud earrings and was looking at myself in the mirror giving a final touch to my makeup. My shoulder length dark brown hair was left open, I wore my black heels when I heard a knock on the door I averted my gaze and saw Stefan, looking incredibly gorgeous with those white shiny shirt and black formal pants and black shiny shoes which I bought him recently, when Clara invited him to the party.

Actually their anniversary was on Thursday, which was yesterday but they thought of celebrating it today, which is Friday. So that we could enjoy ourselves, partying till late night and however tomorrow is Saturday so no work.

It's been a week since Stefan was staying with me and yet he can't remember anything. How sad

"Ready?" He asked pulling me out of my trance.

"Yeah, just a second " I said buckling my heels.

"Steve is waiting for us"

"Yeah coming " I said walking towards him

....

After waiting for some what for hours we entered the club, as soon as we entered we saw Chase waving at us and we sauntered towards him.

"You look handsome Chase, and by the way happy anniversary " I said followed by Steve and Stefan.

"thank you so much guys" He said as Clara walked towards us.

She was wearing a plain white short dress which was above her knee, flaunting her thighs and the dress was sexy with a spaghetti straps which was falling off her shoulder again and again. Her blonde hair was tied up in a messy bun showing her smooth silky back.

"How am I looking?" She asked rotating herself.

"You look " I quirked my brows " sexy"

"Thank you, Ashley " she said with a bright smile on her face

.

Her gaze averted from me to Steve and then to Stefan and suddenly she gasped, "Are you the one whom Ashley hit with Steve's car" he nodded.

"You've been staying with her since a week, right " she asked again and he nodded again.

"OMG! Ashley your so lucky to have a hot and handsome boyfriend like him"she squealed and now Stefan had a bright smile on his face.

WHAT !

"Clara we don't have a thing between us " I said forcing a smile on my lips.

"What! You and him " she said pointing to both of us " have been staying with each other for a week and didn't develop any feelings for each other" she said embarrassing me.

'CLARA STOP ' I wanted to shout but stayed calm.

" No " I chuckled "we are just friends "

"Oh! my bad, I just have the habit of assuming things,I'm sorry " she apologized.

'THEN STOP ASSUMING' I wanted to say but kept quite.

"No problem " I said smiling weirdly.

"Come let's go and take our seats " Chase said as he started walking followed by Clara and stefan.

As I was about to follow them Steve came and stood beside me .

"You were in cloud nine when Clara asked you him as your boyfriend, right " He smirked.

I rolled my eyes heavenward and pinched him hard in his stomach.

"Ouch"

"Next time think before you speak and I was deep down in hell when Clara asked him as my boyfriend " I said leaving his stomach.

"Oh my God your so violent " he said rubbing his stomach with his hands.

" good,now walk " I said.

....

We were all seated in the VIP section, booked by Chase and Clara, having our drinks and chatting.

"This party is so boring " Clara whined " come on baby, let's go and dance " she said pointing towards the dance floor.

Chase nodded happily and followed her towards the dance floor.

"Wanna dance with me " Ashton, one of Clara's friend asked.

"No, thanks I don't dance" I responded.

"No problem " He shrugged it off.

Zoe one of Clara's friend asked Stefan, " wanna dance with me handsome "

He looked at me and I shook my head in negative.

"No" he said politely

"Come on handsome loosen up" she was insisting him.

"I don't know to dance " Stefan reasoned

"I'll teach you" she said dragging him to the dance floor.

Bitch, can't she understand no means no and leave him alone.

As I expected Stefan was uncomfortable with her and Zoe was clinging on him and almost dirty dancing with him, roaming her hands around his body arms and face ,touching him seductively. He was trying to pull away from her but she was clinging and clinging on him.

ENOUGH...

I stood up from my seat and sauntered to the dance floor towards Stefan.

"Can I have a minute with Stefan?" I asked interrupting her acts.

"Nope, I'm dancing with him" Zoe said with irritation lacing on her face.

"Please" I requested.

"Nope"

AGAIN ENOUGH.....

"Bitch, he's my boyfriend " I snapped

She suddenly stopped her clingy acts and left Stefan. Stefan was looking at me with wide eyes. I dragged him out of her sight and stopped.

"Come, let's dance " Stefan said pulling his hand out .

I playfully narrowed my eyes and took his hand "sure"

We were dancing slowly with his hands around my waist and my hands on his broad shoulders.

" look " I started " I called you my boyfriend because I saw you were uncomfortable with her as she was too clingy and as a friend I thought of helping you ou-"

"I know " he said giving me a ear to ear grin.

After dancing for a while we went back to our seats.

"Come on guys let's play a game " Clara squealed "did or never , if you'll have ever done it you'll will get a shot of tequila and if not then nothing " she said pointing to the waitress who brought two trays of tequila shots.

"I don't remember anything from my past so I'm gonna just enjoy watching you'll " Stefan said,

"Sure, sweetheart " Clara said

"A virgin here " Clara said

Damn..

If I'll lie, Steve is gonna torment me for eternity so I took a tequila and gulped it down my throat. Everybody was staring at me as a piece of specimen except for Steve, Chase and Clara because they knew I was a virgin.

' great! Now everyone knows that I'm a virgin '

and then the game went on with me drinking a lots of shots, I was feeling dizzy and I tripped and was about to fall when two strong arms caught me

"Ashley, are you okay?" Stefan asked

"Finnnee" I slurred

"Come lets get out of here " I nodded

"Ashley can I ask you something? " He asked as we were walking outside.

"Go on"

"Are you really a virgin? "

"What's the problem in being a virgin " I whined

"No not a problem , people shouldn't go and sleep around, I like the thing that your a virgin "

"Really " I smiled and he nodded.

I turned towards him and moved closer to him until our faces were inches apart and again I took a step forward, "Ashley?"

And was about to kiss him when he turned his face to the other side and my lips landed on his cheek.

Then BOOM ,I blacked out.

Chapter 9

I groaned and stirred in my sleep when I felt someone stroking my cheeks softly. I slowly opened my heavy eyelids and saw there was no one, I rubbed my eyes and sat up straight placing my back on the headboard. I looked around and there I saw Stefan standing at the threshold as fresh as handsome.

I placed my hands on my head and groaned aloud

' ahh this hangover'

"Here, drink some tea it will reduce your hangover" he said

He came towards me and bent down to give me the tea and I took it and also inhaled the delicious manly scent. ' he smell so good.....'

I kept the tea at the night stand because it was too hot and looked at him, he was wearing the checks shirt and a denim jeans and was looking damn gorgeous.

I was suddenly worried about my appearance, I looked down at my dress and I was still in my yesterday's black bodycon. Infront of my bed there was the dressing table and looked my image in the mirror and I almost screamed, my make up fully smudged and my hair was a mess while he was standing there fully fresh. Oh god I was even stinking like a rotten fish.

I cleared my throat, "What's the time?"

" It's eleven"

"I don't usually wake up this late" I lied

"No it's totally fine "

Yesterday's every memory came crashing down to me and I looked at him embarrassed, about how I tried to kiss him. Oh god

It's better to act like,I don't remember anything about the last night.

I opened my mouth before he asked me, "Are you blushing?" And now I was blushing profusely with every possible shade of red.

I coughed "no"

"Yes, your cheeks have turned pink "

"No actually my cheeks are always pink, it's natural" I reasoned and shrugged it off

"Oh I see"

"Well , what happened last night I don't remember anything" I said as I massaged my temple.

" Nothing happened , yesterday Steve said me to take you to your apartment while he stayed in the club as he got a girl" that manwhore " so I brought you home and carried you to your room an-"

"In which style did you carry me?" I interrupted

" What?" He asked raising a questioning brow

"Piggy back style or bridal style, which style" I asked desperately.

'Stop being so desperate, Ashley'

"Um, bridal style"

"Oh" I continued " where did you sleep"

"In the couch"

"Did you sleep well"

"Yes" he said scratching his forehead.

'Stop pestering him with questions, Ashley'

I stood up and made my way to the bathroom.

....

I came out of the bathroom and made my way towards the kitchen when I heard him say, "The breakfast is in the microwave"

"You prepared breakfast?" I said as I opened the microwave and saw some delicious pancakes waiting for me. I licked my lips and took it out before moving towards the table. " You know to cook" I asked as I digged in my food.

"Yeah"

"Mmm..this is delicious" I said pointing to the pancakes.

He just smiled " Your hair is wet let me dry it for you or else you'll catch cold" he said bringing the towel.

I nodded in ecstasy and he slowly started rubbing my hair with the towel, while I was enjoying my meal.

After having my breakfast and him wiping my hair, we went to the living room and were watching a movie, it was a very nice movie in which a small boy was lost and the hero was trying to find the boy's family and the hero even made posters of the boy and distributed it to the whole city and watching that, my brain clicked with an idea.

" Hey why don't we make some posters of you and distribute it in Florida" I said , turning to him.

He just stared at me blankly as if he was in some deep thoughts. I tapped his left shoulder and he jolted coming out of his trance.

"Yes" he said and I raised a brow.

"Your trying very hard to search my family." he sighed.

He was looking sad , "Are you sad?" I blurted out and he mumbled something which was inaudible to me.

And before I could ask what he mumbled, he said,

"I have a confession to make"

Chapter 10

"What confession?" I asked with furrowed brows.

"Actually " he started " I never had amnesia I was just...-"

"PRETENDING " I screamed And he looked down at his lap.

"Actually-" he begin and I stopped him by raising my hand.

"Wait, don't speak" I hissed.

I stood up abruptly and made my way to the kitchen, "Where are you going?" He asked.

"I said don't talk unless I tell you to" I shouted.

My phone was on the kitchen counter and I picked it up and dialled Steve's number and he received it on the second ring.

"Hey girl, lost your virginity to Stefan"

"Cut the crap Steve, I have a very important thing to tell you" I said in a serious tone.

"Okay, am all ears"

"No I can't tell it on the phone , come to my apartment now , it's important and bring Chase along with you" I said and declined the call.

....

I was pacing back and forth in the living room waiting for Steve and Chase to arrive while he was staring at me oddly as if I'm a mad woman , actually I am mad at him.

"What?" I snapped

"What?" He furrowed his brows.

"Why are you staring at me like that"

"Because you're beautiful" I blushed a little at his comment but composed myself

"Stop-" I was interrupted with a door bell .

I ran to the door and flew the door open and at the threshold was Steve and Chase, I moved aside so that they could come in.

"What took you'll so long"

"Chase took a lot of time to get ready" Steve said pointing at Chase.

"I was spending my quality time with Clara but you came and said that Ashley is in a serious problem-" Chase said and then pointed a finger at me and continued" and here she looks fine."

"Chase and Steve it's really very important" I said walking towards the living room" this devil -" I said pointing to him.

"So now Romeo turned into a devil" Steve remarked with a sly smile while Stefan was trying hard to hide his grin.

"Shut up Steve" I hissed. Both Steve and Chase went and sat beside him.

I kept my one hand over my chest and the other hand pointing to him, "He decieved me" I said dramatically.

"OMG!" Steve gasped" how could you cheat on her , she had some sought of feelings for you"

"Really?" Stefan had an amused grin.

"No" I snapped " I don't have any sought of feelings for him and Steve will you just shut up and listen to me."

"Yeah go on"

"This selfish , manipulative self centered Bastard , cunning asshole, son of -"

"Will you just stop cursing me and tell them the main point of calling them" he said not so innocently.

'the audacity of this man to tell me to come to the point'

I cleared my throat, "He was just pretending, of having amnesia" I said loud and clear pointing at him and both Steve and Chase gasped and snapped their head towards him and abruptly stood up.

"WHAT?" They both screeched.

"Okay so now let's proceed" I continued " who are you?, What is your name?, Where do you live?." I bombarded questions at him.

"Okay I'll answer all your questions, my name is" I held my breath I was waiting eagerly to see what name he's got " Zyon Rosington"

'Zyon Rosington, nice name'

"And I'm from New York" he said making my eyes go wide.

"Then what are you doing in Florida"

"I came here for a business meeting"

"What do you do for a living "

"I'm the CEO of CTC company"

I along with Steve and Chase were taken aback, "CEO as in chief executive officer" I stuttered

"Yes " he said giving me a small smile.

"Are you a billionaire" he nodded

'OMG! I just got a mini heart attack'

I ran to my room and opened one of my drawers and took the paper in which I've written the amount he has to pay me and also I took a pen out and wrote some extra amount for lying to me . However he's a billionaire, so no worries from taking money from him.

I sauntered back to the living room and threw that paper at his face.

"What is this ?" He asked

"Are you an illiterate?" I snapped

"No, but what is this? I'm not understanding" he wrinkled his nose in confusion.

"It's a bill, that you have pay me , your clothes bill and because of you, my electricity bill skyrocketed this time, I don't care if you call me stingy"

"Okay I'll pay you but my card is in New York , so can you come with me to new York " he asked

And before I could answer him ,Chase asked, "Why did you pretend to have amnesia and stayed with Ashley for a week?"

Yeah even I was curious,

"Actually I had one week of work in Florida and another one week of vacations granted by my father. After finishing my one week work in Florida, I came for a walk on that narrow road thinking of how to spend my vacations, when suddenly you" he raised a finger at me "hit me with a car "

"But that's not a correct answer for our question" Steve said.

"Speaking of that, when I woke up in the hospital bed everything was blank for me and that's when Ashley waved her hand infront of me and I jolted thinking who was she" he continued" and when she said' is he having any amnesia' " he quoted my lines and continued "that time my brain clicked with an idea of how to spend my vacations, so I pretended to have amnesia and stayed with her living a normal life like a normal person and to be honest I enjoyed it, so chill I was here just for fun with no ill intentions" and that bastard just shrugged it off " and also I was pissed at her for driving the car at the narrow road and hitting me with the car like that ,so I thought of punishing her by staying with her and pretending to have amnesia but I didn't want to punish her because she was really very nice to me" I scoffed at his comment of me being nice to him.

" But why did you tell us the truth I mean you could have just lied that you got your memory back but instead you told us the truth" Steve asked

"I felt guilty for lying to such a nice person like her so I thought of telling the truth to her" " And I owe her so much" and then he cleared his throat before saying

" Will you Accompany to New York"

Chapter 11

Steve, Chase and I were inside my room ,locked and we were discussing, whether to go or not go.

"I think you should go Ashley, atleast your second dream is coming true for free, no travel expense ,no staying expenses nothing" Steve said

"I don't think she should go, he just flimflam us and stayed with her for a week" Chase said

"That's what am saying, he stayed with her for a week and didn't harm her I don't think he has any ill intentions" Steve said

"But-" I interrupted Chase and said

" I think Steve is right"

"But how can you trust him " Chase asked

"Come let's go and talk to him then " Steve suggested.

We walked outside the room and sauntered towards him, we three stood infront of him while he was sitting on the couch innocently looking at us like a lost baby.

'He not innocent, Ashley' my subconsciousness reminded me.

"Why do you want me to accompany you to New York" I asked glaring at him.

"You, yourself said that you want your money back " he waved that paper infront of me and continued " and I loved the way you treated me in your house and I think I owe you, so I'm asking you to accompany me so that I can help you fullfill one of your dreams"

I averted my gaze to Chase who shook his head disapprovingly and then I averted my gaze to Steve who had a bright smile and nodded approvingly.

I thought for a while, I stayed with him for a week, I don't think he's any harm for me ,I mean he's a gentleman, a man with morals.

So without any second thought I said "Yes I'll come with you to New York"

Zyon right, was his name, smiled brightly "Give me your phone" he asked me.

"What?"

"Give me your phone I have to call my secretary"

I gave him my phone and he dialled a number and his secretary on the other side received the call.

"Gregor, come to pick me up tomorrow at ten "

Gregor said something

"Okay I'll see through it " Zyon said and then declined the call and gave my phone back to me.

"Tomorrow at 10 we are leaving, so get ready" Zyon said with a smile.

I nodded and made my way to the kitchen and quickly unlocked my phone and saved Gregor's number in my contact list, what if I need his number for any emergency in New York.

' or what if he's a handsome secretary like every handsome billionaire got in a billionaire book'

....

It was almost night, Steve and Chase bid their good nights and left, now I was all alone with Zyon.

He was sitting on the couch, deep in thoughts.

"What are you thinking?"I asked as I sat beside him.

"Nothing" he sighed and continued"I was just thinking that tomorrow onwards I'm gonna live the same Zyon Rosington's life and say a goodbye to Stefan's life which I enjoyed " he smiled.

"I have a question?"

"Go on "

"Why didn't you choose a good place like Norway, Switzerland, Spain ,why Florida?"I asked

"Because I've been to those places" he shrugged

My eyes grew big and I gasped" you've been to those countries"

"Not only those I've been to Canada, New Zealand, Morocco, France....." He listed some more other countries and my eyes grew big .

"OMG! You've almost visited most of the countries"

He nodded

"How rich are you ?" I asked, astonished.

"For God sake I'm a billionaire"

I scoffed " stop boosting yourself"

"I'm not boosting, it's the reality" he said as a matter of fact.

"Whatever" I rolled my eyes. " You lied in the hospital because you found me attractive , right" I joked.

"No, not at all , I lied because I wanted to teach you a lesson for hitting me with a car" he said.

"And what lesson you taught me" I raised a brow.

"I made you spend most of your savings on me , and I know your savings are your priority and in that way I taught you a lesson ' not to hit a person with a car' "

"However I'm gonna get my money back and that's the reason I'm coming with you" I stuck my tongue out.

And then there was a deep silence. After sitting for a while I got up and Zyon looked up at me,

"Today I'm gonna sleep in my room and your gonna sleep on that couch" I said pointing to the couch

"Fine, however it's gonna be your last time sleeping in your bed " he said smirking.

'Did he just smirk?'

"What?" I asked confused .

"Oh nothing, goodnight"

Chapter 12

My alarm atlast buzzed at 6, I've been waiting for it to buzz, I already woken up at 5. Last night I couldn't sleep properly due to the excitement, which was brimming in me. I got up from the bed and went to the bathroom and brushed my teeth followed by a nice bath.

I wore a pair of jeans and a white chiffon shirt and looked at the time, it was 7:25. I sauntered outside my room and was about to go the kitchen, when my eyes wandered around living room and my sight fell on the guy who was sleeping on the couch.

I don't know what came over, I moved towards him and kneeled down, taking in his appearance. His black sleek hair fully messed, his prominent jaw, everything in him screams perfection. But my time didn't long-last as his phone suddenly started buzzing and I fell on my butt groaning and he opened his eyes and saw me. "What were you doing?" He asked narrowing his eyes.

"No.. nothing" I stuttered and blushed

"Were you eye fucking me" he blurted out still with those narrow eyes.

"Oh my god!" I gasped and blushed profusely keeping my right hand on my mouth " Why would I do that?"

"Then why are you blushing? "

"As I said you earlier my cheeks are naturally pink so I'm not blushing"

"Okay whatever" he smiled.

He got up from the couch and went to the room, maybe going to the bathroom. I made my way to the kitchen and started preparing breakfast.

' He has changed alot within a night'

....

It was almost 9:30 when we both finished our breakfast and I was waiting for the doorbell to ring and when it rang I ran to the door and threw it open expecting to see Gregor. But unfortunately it was Steve, Chase and Clara standing there with a big wide ear to ear smile.

"Oh Ashley! I'm so happy for you, I knew it was always your dream to go to the sleepless New York and it is coming true and that to for free" Clara sqeuled.

' couldn't she say that free word with a low volume'

I gave them a tight smile and moved aside so that they so could come in.

The four of them were talking and smiling while I was pacing back and forth waiting impatiently to see how Gregor looks like.

"What is wrong with you?" Steve asked raising a brow.

"Nothing"I answered still walking.

"Do you wanna poop?" Steve asked chuckling while Stef- I mean Zyon was biting his lips to stifle his laughter. I was deeply embarrassed.

"Shut up Steve" I yelled.

"Then why are you walking like, as if your are controlling your poop"

' Bastard, Why does he always embarasses me?'

"I. Said. Shut. Up" I yelled.

They all started laughing at my face and I was about to fireback , when the doorbell rang. I opened the door and saw a man in his late forties with some wrinkles on his face and slightly bald with his tummy out. He was wearing a suit and had poker face.

"How can I help you?" I asked giving him a small smile.

"I'm here to meet Mr Rosington "

"Mr Rosington?" I was confused and then realised Mr Rosington as in Zyon.

I called out for Zyon and he came towards the main door and saw the man.

"Oh, hey Gregor did you bring, what I asked for?" He asked Gregor.

My eyes widened,

' Is he Gregor?'

I thought Gregor would be handsome ,late twenties guy but he turned out to be an old man 'Oh god'

"Yes, Mr Rosington" Gregor replied.

Gregor handed him a bag and he took it and went to my room.

' what's in that bag?'

After a few minutes later Zyon returned wearing a three piece black suit and looked, oh my my , he was looking professional along with hot, gorgeous and handsome.

" So now we can leave" Zyon said pulling me out of my trance.

I cleared my throat "Yeah, sure"

Then two men in black suit came and took my suitcase. I only took one suitcase, I didn't bother to bring a lot of dress just some pair of jeans and tops along with some sundresses. While Zyon didn't have any luggage.

I bid good byes to my friends and Chase even said that if Zyon hurts me, I should not hesitate to call him so that he could call 911.

' Chase I can call 911' I wanted to say but kept quiet as he was just being a caring friend.

I left a message to my mom saying that I'm leaving to New York for a week because of a business work.

Yes I lied, I can't say that I'm going to New York with a stranger who owes me, right. So I lied.

Outside my apartment, was three black expensive cars parked and I was in too awe. I couldn't even imagine of sitting inside those cars. They were too expensive.

I ran towards the first car and was about to open the back seat door when Zyon called me. " Ashley, your not going in that car" I frowned.

"Why not?"

" Because your coming with me in that middle car" he said pointing to the middle car.

"Why in the middle car? You can sit in that car also. All three are same " I shrugged.

"You know I'm the boss for all these men " he said pointing to all the men standing there.

They were total of eight men here to escort him.

"And my safety is their priority, so for them to keep me safe, we are going in the middle car" Zyon said

"They want to keep you safe not me, so you go in that middle car and I'll come in this car "

And instead of replying he strolled towards me and grabbed my hand, started dragging me to the middle car.

Before I could protest he said, "We are running out of time, we don't have time for any argument"

He opened the car door for me and I got inside the car and he got in with the other door and sat beside me in the back seat.

And as the chauffeur started the engine my excitement skyrocketed.

Chapter 13

I was sitting inside a private jet with a wide smile on my face, I've never even saw a private jet before for real.

My head was snapping right and left looking around the interior. I pinched myself to check whether it's true or not.

" It's for real, Ashley" Zyon said and chuckled.

"I can't believe I'm sitting in such a beautiful private jet" I squealed.

"There are a lot of things you won't believe, Ashley" he smirked.

"What?" I asked in confusion.

He shook his head and smiled. " Wanna take a nap?"

"Nah, I only have two hours to explore the jet and sky, so not taking any nap"

"Fine" he shrugged.

I was so excited..

....

After two hours of short flight we reached New York and now we were standing again infront of three black sleek expensive cars.

We took the middle car and sat inside it, as chauffeur started the engine.

After a while, the car came to a stop and I looked up to see a massive skyscrapers building with a 'Madison square' imprinted on it. We both got out of the car and sauntered inside the building.

" I thought you live in a big house but it turns out that you live in an apartment"

"Not actually an apartment but I live in a penthouse"

"Oh"

We both got inside the elevator and he pressed the button to the top floor, as soon as it dinged we got out and reached for his door.

As soon as he opened the door with his card I saw a tall girl with hourglass body and a strawberry blonde hair sitting in the couch, and as she saw Zyon, her face lit up and she came running towards Zyon with her five inch heels and hugged him.

As I saw her closely, I saw she was flawless with a beauty of a goddess and also caked up with make up.

Her round plump lips were covered with full of red matt lipstick and her grey eyes were gorgeous.

'I've seen her somewhere. Isn't she the famous supermodel , what's her name, Caroline , Cara. Ugh what's her name.'

She hugged him but he didn't hug her back , an expression of irritation laced over his face.

She pulled back and was about to peck him on the lips when he turned his head to the right side and her lips landed to his left cheek.

'Is that his habit to snap his head to the other side when someone kisses him on the lips.'

"Why do you always turn around when I kiss you, baby?" The strawberry blonde hair girl asked him.

'Baby?'

He just gave her a tight smile without saying anything.

Her eyes landed on me and she gave me a warm smile and I smiled back.

"Who is she?" She asked Zyon while eyeing me up and down.

"What are you doing here Carol?" He ignored her question.

'Yeah, Carol Hobson, the famous supermodel.'

"Gregor said that today your coming back from your vacations, so I thought of visiting you" she said tracing her index finger across his jaw.

He was annoyed I can say that by his expression.

He grabbed her hand and pulled it down.

"Carol please, can you visit me tomorrow at my office, I'm tired, I just returned from my vacations " he stated

"Okay, but who is she?" Carol asked looking at me and as I was about to answer her ,Zyon snapped.

"I said TOMORROW" he said a bit louder.

She huffed and stomped out the door.

"Make yourself comfortable" He said softly to me.

And I nodded.

My mouth was itching to ask who was she to him but refrained myself as it was none of my business.

' she might be his girlfriend'

I shook the thought of and eyed his humble house.

It was luxurious penthouse, obviously he's a billionaire. Everything in here screams rich and powerful,there were golden flower shaped chandeliers attached to the ceiling, white walls, a comfortable sofa set and large TV across the sofa and a large glass windows in which the view of the city at night would be wonderful.

"I guess your tired, come let me show you your room " he said and I nodded silently.

We both climbed up the stairs and there were four door. He opened the door to the right, " My lady this is your room" he winked.

This is the rare side of him which I'm seeing now, back in Florida, he was all gentleman.

I nodded and walked inside my luxurious room which had white curtains and king size bed in the middle of the room draped with white silk sheets across the bed was a big TV and at the corner was a study table and at the other corner was a dressing table. I saw my suitcase near the threshold and I pulled it inside my room.

"If you need anything, my room is just beside your room" he said pointing to the door beside my room.

I nodded.

" Why are you nodding all the time?" he asked , annoyed.

"Uh..?" I didn't know why I was nodding nor I knew the answer for his question.

"It's okay I'll see you later" he said and walked off.

Chapter 14

It's been total of three days, I mean three freaking days and I hadn't yet roamed around the city nor gotten my ass into time square. Since we came here, Zyon got totally busy and he has already apologized. He wakes up early in the morning and leaves for his office , returns late in night and he has reasoned out, it's because of his one week vacations in Florida and now he has tons of works to do.

And now here I am relaxing in his luxurious penthouse watching 'the vampire diaries' , season 5 where Silas pushes my baby Stefan into a safe and locks it and throws that safe into the vast lake and I'm already sniffling seeing my dear Stefan's condition.

There was a slight knock on my door and I said a small come in , when the door opened Zyon came into view and I sniffled again,

"Are you crying?" He raised one of his brow.

But I ignored his question and asked, "How come your early today?"

"Actually it's already 10:30 PM"

"What?" My eyes widened.

"Yeah" he rolled his eyes "and now, why are you crying?"

"Because Stefan got drowned" I sniffled and dramatically wiped my tears.

"What?" He points a finger to himself " but I'm standing here all fit and fine" he said with a grin.

"First of all your not Stefan, your name is Zyon Rose.. something"

"It's Zyon Rosington"

"Yeah whatever and secondly I'm talking about Stefan Salvatore, Damon Salvatore's little brother"

"Who's Damon and Stefan Salvatore?"

"Oh my god!" I gasped " you don't know them "

He shook his head.

"See" I pointed towards the TV screen " it's Stefan" I said as I saw Stefan literally suffocating inside that safe.

"You named me after him?" He asked with a frown.

"What? He's handsome"

As he was about to reply I asked, "Wanna watch next episode with me?" He nodded and I played the next episode.

And in the next episode it was hot make out session of Elena and Damon smooching each other's faces and I slowly glanced at him to see, he was blushing profusely.

'Didn't he see somebody making out before or is he imagining himself as Damon, huh'

I cleared my throat and turned the TV off, "Enough of watching TV" he looked at me and I saw he was still blushing. " Are you blushing?"

"What... No no" he stuttered and continued" actually my cheeks are always red"

'My dialogue to me only, huh?'

"Your blushing " I stated firmly.

"No I'm not"

"Yes you are"

"No"

"Yes"

"Whatever, I came here to say that tomorrow I'll be coming home in the evening as I don't have a lot of meetings , so we can roam around the city" he said with stoic face.

"Sure" I gave him a huge grin.

"So goodnight" he smiled.

"Night"

....

The very next morning I woke up and freshened up and was about to go downstairs when my phone beeped. I checked the caller ID and it was Steve.

" Hello"

"How is our virgin girl" I rolled my eyes

"Fine, is there Chase around" I asked.

" Yeah the phone is on speaker"

"So how is chief with my excuse for a leave"

Actually I can't say that I'm going on a vacation so instead I said that my dad is very ill and he needs me near him and took a leave for a week. And my chief happily granted me.

"She's going pretty good on your lie" Chase said and I felt a bit proud of myself for decieving that witch.

'Duh, she's a pain in ass kind of chief'

"How are things going there in new York" Chase asked.

"Things are going pretty well in New York because I suggested her to tag along with Stef- I mean Zyon" Steve said and I could also picture a smirk on his lips.

"But still I don't have a good feeling about it " Chase said.

"Why?" I asked.

"Don't know but if anything happens always remember we are there for you" Chase said as my eyes welled up.

"Yeah" Steve agreed.

"Gotta go, Ashley call you back later" they both said and declined the call.

Since three days they've been calling and kept checking on me if I'm okay and for once I'm very grateful to have them as my friends.

I sauntered downstairs and saw Zyon already sitting at the dining table looking hot in his three piece black suit and eating his breakfast.

I pulled a chair for myself and sat on it and looked at my breakfast which was already placed on the table.

"Get ready sharp at 5" he said digging in his food.

I nodded.

"And before I forget I need your ID ." He said.

"Why ?" I asked.

"Last month some thief broke in, in one of the apartment since then the security in here is tight and needs all the details of a visitor or a guests, so that's the reason, they've been asking me about your any detail documents, since your ID is the only thing you have for your identification".

I was still not sure about it but however I trust him and what he's gonna do with my ID.

"It's just their protocol, after finishing all their works they'll give you your ID back" he stated.

" No problem" I stood and ran upstairs and brought my ID with me and handed it over to him.

After a while he left for his office and again I was all alone.

Chapter 15

"Are you ready?" Zyon asked as he started his engine.

"Yeah" I squealed.

As he said, he returned from his office exactly at 5 and thank goodness that I was ready.

And now we are sitting in one of his expensive cars, ready to go.

I leaned on my seat enjoying the view of the city and then slowly closed my eyes feeling ecstatic.

But suddenly the car came to a stop and I snapped my eyes open and saw, it was the traffic which stopped the car.

This is the one thing I hate about New York, traffic.

However we passed the traffic and Zyon manoeuvred his car around the Mall's parking lot and we both got out of the car.

"OMG!!" I gasped

"What happened ?" Zyon asked looking concerned.

"I just forgot my card at your house"

Zyon chuckled "don't worry I'll pay for your stuff's"

"I'm very capable to pay for my stuff's"

"Even you bought me some clothes and stuff's back in Florida, remember, so I owe you" he said "So let me pay for your stuff's "

I nodded.

We entered the mall and directly went to the clothes store.

....

It was nearly an hour,me still shopping in the cloth Store and I thought Zyon would irritate me by asking 'done done and done' but instead he didn't even utter a word he was tolerating my shopaholic habit and was even giving me suggestions on some clothes which I selected.

After 3 hours of shopping we finally got out of the mall and got into his car as he started the engine.

"Hungry?" He asked.

"Hmm" I hummed and our next stop was a grand restaurant named ' lebanardin ' .

After entering the restaurant and taking a good veiw of it, it was heaven and I am damn sure the food here will also taste like heaven.

After taking our seats near the window at the top floor, giving a nice veiw of the city.

I took the menu book and as I opened it my eyes popped out of their socket. This restaurant is damn expensive and food in here costs like hell.

After ordering our respective dishes there was pin drop of silence.

"Okay let's play 20 questions as you know who you are" I said as I glared at him.

"Okay" he gulped.

"I'll go first" I said "why don't you have any maids in your penthouse" I was curious, why he doesn't have a maid in his house, I mean he a freaking billionaire.

"Because I don't like people barging into my house"

"And what about me?" I asked.

"Your different, I owe you" he said "my turn ,why you don't have a boyfriend?"

"Because I have my dreams to fulfill and I just can't waste my money by going on dates" I continued "who is Carol to you?" I asked

I stared at him as his jaw clenched but he didn't utter a word. So I asked again, "Is she your girlfriend?"

"She's nothing to me, she's not my girlfriend" he snapped. He was pissed off by that question so I didn't asked him any further questions about Carol.

"O.. okay"

He took a sharp intake of breath to calm himself and continued, "My turn" he said and I was eagerly waiting for his question and when that question left his mouth, my body was shaking with rage. And the question was, "Why are you a virgin?"

" What kind of a question is that" I snapped.

"It's a question which you have to answer" he said with a smirk.

"Okay" I huffed " I have my insecurities and now my turn" Steve was enough to annoy me with that virgin topic and now even he has started and now I want him to feel the same rage that am feeling now, "How was your first time, I mean sex with Carol" I noticed that mere name of Carol pissed him as now again his lips twitched downwards on distaste.

As I was eagerly waiting for him to answer and he was seething.

As he was about to open his mouth ,the waiter came and placed our dishes and greeted Zyon.

"What a pleasure to have you here Mr Rosington"the waiter said and I had the urge to scoff plus roll my eyes.

And again another waiter came and placed an orange juice to his side of table and at my side an expensive red wine.

I raised a brow at him as the waiter left.

"What?" He asked.

"Why they gave you an orange juice instead of red wine"

"Because that red wine has 12% of alcohol in it" he stated.

"So?"

"So what?, I don't consume alcohol " he said and I was amused.

"Why?" I was stunned like most of them drink red wine which has just 12% of alcohol.

He sighed " I have a bad effect on alcohol either I doze off or I'll have a very wild behavior "

"Oh!" Was all I could say.

I remembered the day in my apartment, when I offered him a red wine and he didn't even take a sip and instead I drank his red wine unconsciously.

We started digging in our foods and OMG! The steak tasted heavenly.

After having dinner we roamed around the city for a while and again went back to his penthouse.

Chapter 16

I was pacing back and forth towards my closet and my suitcase which was placed on top of my bed. Yes, I was packing my bag as tomorrow morning I'm leaving , back to Florida.

It has almost been a week since I'm staying here and however my leave excuse was only for a week and if I stay here any longer by taking some more leaves from my office, my chief is gonna bite my head off of my body, so no risk.

There was a slight knock on my door and it was Zyon, as it was Saturday, so he has no work to do today.

" Your packing?" he asked

"As you can see" I said as I was folding my jeans.

"When are you leaving?" He asked.

"Tomorrow morning and yeah, before I forget, I need my ID to get a seat in the flight, from New York to Florida" without my ID I cannot just go back to Florida and he has not yet returned it.

"But why are you leaving so soon, you still haven't seen New York completely"

" I've seen time square aand that's enough for me, and my work, my life and my dreams are in Florida, so I have to get back there as soon as possible" I smiled. "And please don't forget this time, my ID"

He nodded. " Come I want to atleast show you my penthouse properly"

Well I've not seen his penthouse yet, so I nodded.

We both went around his penthouse and he showed me each and every corner of his house except for his bedroom, he hasn't shown me his bedroom.

After moving around we both sat on the couch in the living room.

"I..uh.." he started

"What?" I asked.

"I want to ask you something" I nodded, is he gonna propose me, why is he flushing so bad.

"Actually.." he began " tonight I have a family dinner with my family in my parents house..."

"So?" I interrupted.

"So I want you to accompany me "

"WHY ?" I screeched.

"Because I want to show my parents that even I can make friends"

"What? You mean you don't have friends and who said that I'm your friend"

"Yes we are friends, I stayed with you for a week and you stayed with me for a week"

"Whatever" I rolled my eyes" so you mean you don't have friends except me"

"I have one but he's my mother's best friends son, so in order we are also friends"

Okay he has a friend and I think he's good looking, I can try my chance with him.

"What's his name?"I asked

"Who's?"

"Your friend's"

"Oh! His name his Liam Roberts" he said and raised a brow "why?"

"Is he good looking and does he have a girlfriend?" I ignored his question.

"Again why?" He asked.

"Because I wanna try my chance with him "

"You WHAT?"

"You heard me " I said

"Nah, he's not your type "

"Is he coming tonight?"

"Yes ,. But. He's. Not. Your. Type" he said emphasizing each word.

"Wait ,does he have a girlfriend"

"Yes and no, find it by yourself"

'Is he jealous?'

"Are you jealous?" He didn't say anything. " Okay I'm coming" I stated

"Be ready at six" he said with a stoic face and walked off.

'What's wrong with him'

....

I was wearing a knee length pink dress with some laces around my hands and neck and it was really beautiful and Zyon bought me this dress when we went for a shopping two days ago.

Wearing a matching heels and carrying a small handbag I was waiting for him in his living room.

He came downstairs wearing a black two piece suit and his hair cleanly combed and was looking incredibly gorgeous.

"Ready?" He asked and I nodded.

....

We were both sitting in his car and he started his engine ,

"It's a one hour drive, you can sleep if you want"

"Nah, I don't have a habit of sleeping in the car and what if you kidnap me while I'm sleeping" I gave him a pointed look.

He just rolled his eyes.

' did he just roll his eyes at me'

"Tell me something about you " I said because I like to talk whenever we are in the car.

"Like what?"

"Like introduction"

"You can google me, you can find everything about me there"

"Really?" He nodded and I took my phone out of my purse and opened Google and typed Zyon Rosington..

"Read aloud" he said smirking.

So I read loudly so that he could hear me clearly,. " Zyon Rosington, the current CEO of CTC, the wealthiest company in New York. He has achieved a lot of awards like the best buisness man award , ..." They were a lot of awards which he won and I was least intrested in them ,so I scrolled down and something piqued my interest and I tapped that " The current love life of Zyon Rosington" I read aloud and suddenly Zyon stiffened as I continued. " USA'S most wanted bachelorZyon Rosington is now engaged to a supermodel Carol Hobson , daughter of the famous billionaire Louis Hobson and Elena Hobson, the owner of the Fashion minds." There was a sexy pic of Carol just in lingerie. And I scrolled further more down to see a picture of Zyon and Carol standing beside each other with a maximum distance between them.

"Zyon " I called and showed him the picture " why is there so much of distance between you two, I mean she's your fiancè and you said she's nothing to you"

Suddenly his jaw clenched and he clutched the staring wheel so hard that his knuckles turned white. And again suddenly he snatched my phone from my hand and pressed the home button and tossed the phone to me and I quickly tossed it inside my handbag,scared

' what if he breaks my phone into pieces or even worse throw it out of the window'

I didn't even dare to utter a word seeing his state, seething with rage.

And again I thought

' what is wrong with him...'

Chapter 17

I got out of Zyon's car and in front of me stood a large mansion in between the woods. Ahead of me was a cobblestone pathway which led me to a large mahogany doors accompanied by the bushes. It was night and the lamppost stood beside the bushes were glistening with the yellow light.

Everything here was luxurious and screams about richness and power.

Suddenly Zyon placed his hand on my waist, " Let's get in" he said and I didn't say anything. I was stunned due to his coziness. He never touched me before like this, like........ possessively.

We strode towards the large mahogany door and Zyon rang the doorbell. In an instant the door flew open by a maid and we both sauntered in. Everything inside the house screams rich and expensive ,with expensive furnitures and expensive portrays hanging on the walls and the big windows which were covered with white curtains.

Suddenly a handsome guy came and stood infront of us as he patted Zyon's shoulder and grinned widely at him. "Hey bro, how are you and how was your vacations" he asked.

Zyon smiled "I'm fine Liam and my vacations were awesome"

OMG! This gorgeous man is Liam. Liam's gaze fell down on me and he smirked. " And who is this beautiful?"

He extended his hand out for me to shake and I gladly took it. He raised my hand towards his mouth and was about to kiss my knuckle but within a second my hand was pulled out from his grasp and it was pulled by Zyon.

" She's Ashley Grayson " Zyon said with a irritated expression on his face.

"Ashley, nice name" Liam said.

"Thanks" I blushed.

"Wanna have a drink with me" Liam asked and I was about to say yes but Zyon beated me in that.

"No actually she wants to meet Rebecca, so I'll just take her to Rebecca"

' who is Rebecca?'

Before I could ask him who is she, he pulled me out of Liam's sight.

He stopped near the bar counter and I pulled my hands out from his grasp.

"What is wrong with you? I wanted to talk to Liam" I whined.

"Stay away from him" he glared " he's a womanizer"

"You said that he's your friend?"

"He is , and that is the thing I hate about him" he gritted.

I sighed " who is Rebecca?"

When he opened his mouth two women came and stood infront of us.

"Hi baby" Carol came and traced his jaw

And I wanted to roll my eyes at her for showing off her romance.

As usual Zyon pushed her hand from his jaw and she huffed.

Well Carol was looking gorgeous in her off shoulder red knee length mermaid dress with her waist length hair pushed to the right side of her shoulder.

There was another girl with her who was wearing a knee length black dress, she gave a warm smile and I smiled back .she had those piercing green eyes like Zyon and had a petite figure with a black hair. She was around 20 years according to me by her appearance.

"Who is she?" The girl asked Zyon with a smile.

"She's Zyon's friend " Carol answered instead of Zyon with a smile.

Actually I like her.

"Oh" the girl said. She extended her hand to me for a shake and I gladly took.

"I'm Rebecca Rosington, Zyon's sister"

"Ashley Grayson"

"Enjoy yourself Ashley" she said with a small smile and walked off.

"Rebecca!" Zyon called and followed her.

So now I was stuck with Carol who was giving me a small smile and in return I also smiled.

I saw Zyon's retreating figure disappear along with his sister.

Carol snapped her fingers infront of my eyes and I blinked before looking at her.

"You just zones out " she said, did I ? " how is Zyon with you , he doesn't disturb you right "Carol piercing grey eyes looked at me.

"No not at all he's a gentleman and your very lucky to have a fiancee like him" I said and she blushed.

She wasn't a bitch like other billionaire's fiance, which I read in billionaire novels

She was about to open her mouth when Zyon returned and she gave me a smile and slightly patted my shoulder and said "Take care, Ashley." She walked off after blowing a flying kiss to Zyon to which Zyon just scowled.

....

After an hour of chatting with everyone and claiming myself as Zyon's friend.,all the members who attended this family dinner gathered at the dining area and the dining area was like ' my gosh' with a big mahogany table and 14 seats and it looked pretty expensive.

At the head of table sat a man in his fifties with a grey plus black hair and pretty much fit in this age also and the man I guess is Zyon's father, Thomas Rosington. And beside him sat Lily Rosington , Zyon's mother and beside her Rebecca and beside Rebecca sat Zyon and beside him I sat and across Zyon sat Carol and beside her sat Liam and at the remaining seats sat some of the Rosington's other relatives.

The maids started bringing all the mouth watering dishes like lasagna, meat balls, mashed potatoes, steaks, chicken gravy, cheese balls, spaghetti and different continental dishes .

' gosh! I am very hungry '

The maids started serving and I had my plate full with all the dishes and one of the maids placed red wine for everyone except for Zyon and Rebecca they both had their orange juices.

Everybody started eating and even I digged in my food. Everything was so so so delicious I wanted to moan loudly.

After having the delicious dinner, everybody along with me sat on the huge living room and was served with deserts like apple pie, ice cream etc.

I took a piece of apple pie and sat at the corner and Zyon also came and sat beside me.

'Can't he go and sit with Carol, his fiancè'

I looked in Carol's direction and she had sadness in those grey eyes and I felt guilty.

Before I could say anything about this, Zyon grabbed everyone's attention.

"Attention please, people" he started and everybody looked in our direction. "I have an important announcement to do" with that everybody's interest piqued.

" I can't marry Carol Hobson"

Chapter 18

"WHAT? WHY!?" Thomas, Zyon's father was the first one to snap.

' What has my life turned into!!'

The room was dead silent. No-one dared to talk.

Zyon just glared at his father.

"Zyon dear, why can't you marry Carol, you know that your relationship with Carol is all over the media and they have even posted that your marrying her very soon" Zyon's mom, Lily spoke calmly.

"I can't marry her because I don't love her" Zyon glared at Carol.

"You don't love her? You'll learn to love her after your wedding, you just can't call it off, you have to marry her Zyon " Zyon's dad demanded " and you were the one who wanted to marry her to crack a deal."

Okay I love entertainment and gossip, I took a small peice of apple pie and ate it quietly enjoying the scenerio.

Meanwhile Carol stood up and walked towards Zyon and knelt down infront of him and touched his thighs softly, tears brimming from her eyes.

' I'm feeling bad for her'

"Baby, you can't do this to me and why can't you marry me, I love you" Carol said sniffling.

' Poor lady'

Zyon harshly swatted her arms away from his thighs, "Don't touch me" he hissed " I can't marry you because I have a girlfriend and I love her" he shouted.

"ZYON!!" Both his mom and dad shouted at the same time.

"You can't treat her like a trash" Zyon's mom yelled followed by his dad.

" You can't have a girlfriend Zyon, your marriage is an arrangement and you have to marry Carol" his dad screeched.

'Entertainment!'

I took another piece of pie and again slowly ate it enjoying the scenerio.

"Okay, I can't have a girlfriend, I can't love her, fine but what if she's pregnant with my child?" Zyon's voice boomed in the living room.

' New twist in the show'

Everybody in the room stood up, shocked. Even I was shocked.

'Who can possibly be his girlfriend and even pregnant?'

"WHAT!!??" Zyon's dad's eyes were wide with a hanging mouth.

" Yeah she's pregnant with my child , the next heir of our company, I can't just leave her like that, in this state" Zyon's chest was heaving up and down, breathing profusely.

' Right, he just can't leave her like that , good boy Zyon'

"Who is she? Your girlfriend" Zyon's mom,Lily asked.

' who is she Zyon? Even am curious '

He stared at his mom for a while and then slowly tilted his head to my direction.

' Why is he looking at me, am not his girlfriend nor I'm pregnant '

He slowly took my hand in his and kissed the back of my hand.

' WHAT IS HE DOING??'

"Ashley is my girlfriend and .." he kept his other hand in my lower stomach " the mother of my child"

WHAT ???

The plate of pie fell from my hand breaking into pieces and shattering around.

I . Was. Shocked was an understatement because I'm gonna have a heart attack now.

"Ashley and I met in Florida a few months ago, we fell in love and want to spend the rest of our lives with each other." Zyon stated. "And the baby.." he gently rubbed my stomach " ..is the proof of our unconditional love fo each other"

His lie was like a hard slap to my face.

A few minutes ago it was like entertaining show and now it's like a freaking nightmare to me with everybody staring at me.

'Now am the centre of attention, ugh'

He slowly pulled me in his embrace and softly pecked my forehead and I tried to push him away but his grip on me tightened keeping me steady.

He pulled away and when I was about to open my mouth to protest, somebody harshly turned me around and it was Carol, seething.

And now I was facing this infuriating Carol.

She started shaking me, " How could you do this to me you bitch, you knew I was his fiancè and yet you seduced him and now carrying his baby, you slutty whore" she raised her hand to slap me and I closed my eyes waiting for the impending pain to come but it never came.

I slowly opened my eyes to see Zyon shielding me by gripping her raised hand harshly. "Do not ever call her names and do not ever touch her with your filthy hands" he hissed menacingly and pushed her hand out of his grip.

He placed his hand on my waist and guided me to the door. " We are leaving" he stated and walked along with me.

"So now my hands are filthy for you, huh? " Carol shouted behind us " and you bitchy whore, you can't get away from me, I'll come for you" but Zyon just ignored her.

'OMG! Carol's bitchy face is scary and horrible'

' I understand her pain , how could Zyon do this to her'

As we reached the door I heard Liam's voice, " Atlast my baby Zyon lost his virtue "

We exited the House and sauntered towards his car and now I opened my mouth,

"It's not for real right, everything was just a prank right" I asked

"No everything was for real" he opened the car door for me and I subconsciously sat inside , again shocked.

Chapter 19

After coming out of my trance I snapped my head towards him to see, he was driving his car with no emotions on his face.

"Why did you do that?" I snapped.

"I did what?" He asked back.

" STOP PLAYING DUMB " I shouted. "Why did you lie to them?"

" Oh! about that "

" Yeah about that "

"I'll tell you everything about that tomorrow ,am too exhausted to even talk" he said yawning.

It was dark and cold outside but inside the car it was too hot because I was hot as fire, infuriating.

"How could you do this to me and Carol, I trusted you and in return you decieved me, how could you?" He ignored me but I kept going. " Till girlfriend it was okay but me pregnant with your child, that's ridiculous, eww" I shouted but still he was unfazed.

' he's getting into my nerves'

" Stop the car " I said getting irritated of his abnormal behaviour.

"What? Why !?" He said turning to me.

' good, got his attention '

"I said stop the car " I repeated myself again and he stopped his car and parked his car at the side.

"So now answ-" before I could finish my sentence, in an instant his soft pink luscious lips came smashing down to mine.

He kissed me, his perfect lips moving swiftly against mine with a passion and then suddenly he nibbled my lower lip pulling me out of my own trance.

My eyes widened and I pushed him away and that bloody bastard smirked. My blood was now boiling.

" How dare you ? you sick bastard you kissed me, ew.." I wiped my lips with the back of my hand " ..and now I have to sanitize my mouth"

' you always wanted his kiss, Ashley '

Shut up.

"Ahh" he groaned " you ruined my first kiss"

First kiss , that piqued my interest I know this bastard is trying to distract me from the main topic but now I want to clear this kiss topic and then again I'll go to the main topic.

"First kiss?" I asked with furrowed brows.

"Yes, your my first kiss " he said with a ear to ear grin.

I know he thought he won in distracting me , but don't worry I'll come back with the main topic and you have to answer me.

' So Liam was right, he is a virgin and he has never even kissed before'

But I just pretended that I didn't hear Liam saying that and used my acting skills.

"Then what about Carol?" I thought he would glare at me for mentioning her name but instead he smiled.

" She always tried to kiss me but I kept on turning my head to the other side and never I allowed her dirty lips to touch mine" he said while again starting the engine. "Who is your first kiss?" He asked and I shrugged.

" Don't know, kissed a lot of men " hurt crossed through his eyes but he covered it with a smile.

"Wait" I faked a gasp and widened my eyes as I started my acting skills "...that means your a virgin"

He just nodded.

"So who was your first girlfriend?" I asked

"I never had a girlfriend before but now your my girlfriend"

" Ugh! Am not your girlfriend" I gritted and continued "So it was only Carol" I asked, my whole body turned towards him.

"Carol was never my girlfriend" he gritted his teeth.

"Then who is she ?"

"She's the girl, whom my parents and I thought would be a perfect wife for me, she was nothing but an arranged bride chosen by my parents for me "

"Then why do you hate her so much"

" Can't you just drop the topic" irritation coursing his face.

" No "

"Well, I'm not answering that question until tomorrow"

" Why tomorrow, can't you just tell me now, why did you tell your family that I'm your girlfriend and mother of your unborn child "

He ignored me.

Fine, I pinched him hard on his arm ,

" Ouch " he winced and I pulled my hand away. "Why did you pinch me?" He narrowed his eyes at me.

"Same pinch" I squealed "you and I both are virgins" I grinned. " So I pinched you because we both are same and devil's maybe jealous of us for being the same and try to harm us so instead I harmed you, simple" I gave him a lamest reason for pinching him.

He wrinkled his nose " what nonsense is that"

"It's an old myth, you don't know"

He just gave me a look which said ' are you crazy'

And I just smiled like a maniac and again this evil bastard gave me an evil smirk.

"I understand all these hormonal issues.." I frowned , not understanding " and all these tantrums, in pregnancy it happens , don't worry" he chuckled and I gave him a death glare and smacked his arm.

"Ouch , your so violent" he laughed like a maniac while I was seething.

However this stubborn crazy asshole wasn't answering any of my questions so I slowly yawned and sleep took over me.

Chapter 20

I slowly opened my eyes and saw a white ceiling of my room , last night I remember that I slept in his car but I guess Zyon carried me to my room.

I got out of the bed and now the first thing am gonna do is, go to security lair and get my ID from them and leave New York as soon as possible.

I brushed my teeth and without bathing I pulled a jeans and a white t-shirt. And tip toed slowly out the door and made my way to the security room at the lobby.

"Hello, excuse me " I said to the man who was wearing a security clothes.

"Yes ma'am how can I help you" he asked politely.

"Actually I'm Ashley Grayson and I need my ID which was given here about 4 days ago".

"Actually, ma'am why would you give us your ID " I was dumbstruck .

"At one of the apartment there was a theft a month ago and it was a protocol in this building to get visitors identity checked ..." I faltered.

But he just gave me weird look, " We never had any theft in Maddison square " he said and smiled.

"What??"

"It's true ma'am" he said and I turned around to leave the lobby.

' That sick bastard lied to me again, ugh , how dare he?'

He took my ID from me so that I couldn't return back to Florida .

' Ugh, I should have never trusted that asshole'

I stepped inside the elevator and pressed the button to his floor and got out of the elevator and pressed his doorcode and opened the door and sauntered in and saw that he was sitting at the couch, chilling.

I strode towards him and grabbed his collar, pulling it and yelled.

" Your deadline has come Mr Rosington, you said you'll tell me today and now will you enlighten me "

He pulled my hands gently away from his collar, "Ookay" he smirked. "Will you have a seat, my lady" he said pointing to the couch.

I exhaled deeply and sat on the couch beside him.

He cleared his throat, "Carol Hobson is a certified slut. " He began.

"And your a certified asshole" I snapped.

He chuckled, "Please let me finish first"

"Okay"

"I was the one who asked Carol's hand for marriage to crack a deal with the Hobson's, but later on I recognised that Carol is a slut who sleeps around with different men even after our engagement, can you believe she even slept with Liam after our engagement" I gasped.

' calling me a slutty whore and she herself is a slutty whore'

I remembered her calling me names yesterday and I thought she was sad and angry, so she called me a whore.

" I thought Carol really liked me, everybody including my own sister said that she had a huge crush on me, so I thought of giving her a chance by making her my fiancè but she was nothing but a slut and marriage is a holy ritual which bounds two persons and I surely know that Carol is gonna cheat on me after our wedding and I just can't risk it "

"So..." I faltered.

"So I needed you, to call off the engagement" he scratched his forehead.

"Okay, you could have just called me your girlfriend but why did you say that am pregnant with your child" I asked wrinkling my nose.

"Because I have signed a contract paper saying that I will marry Carol Hobson and to come out of that contract problem I need my dad's help and dad wouldn't just help me if I just say that I have a girlfriend and for a solid reason I had to add that your pregnant with my child so that dad would think about the child and help me come out of this problem" he stated and everything here made sense.

"And why should I help you, you even stole my ID and your not even returning it " I was furious now " give me my ID back " I asked.

And he didn't replied, he just ignored me like a shit.

"Okay, fine don't give me my ID, I'll just go around the city and beg for my living " I bursted.

I got up from the couch and was about to move away from him to the door, when he grabbed my wrist and said. "Okay, let's make a deal"

"What deal?"

"I'll give you your ID back .." okay progress "... if I ever shout at you or get angry at you or even glare at you" I scowled

"Or even worse if you slap or hit me" I said.

"I would never do that"

" So your telling me that if you ever yell or even glare at me , your gonna give my ID back" he nodded " What a lame deal" I muttered.

"So deal?" He asked.

"Are you crazy and what about my job, if I stay here any longer my chief is surely gonna fire me and then what about my status , jobless." I emphasized on the last word.

"That's not a problem"

"And how is that not a problem?" I asked.

"If I ever get angry at you, which is never gonna happen and if I give your ID back, which is also never gonna happen, and if your boss fires you am gonna talk to the SDC company's boss which also happens to be my friend and I'll ask them to give you a job there in a better position and I can assure you that they'll pay you double the salary of your previous company"

SDC Florida's number one company getting a job there is like a dream come true, only more qualified and perfect people get job there and if I get a job there, I can easily accomplish my dream.

"The deal is fine with me" I flipped my hair in pride "and I'm gonna make your heaven life a living hell" I gave him a challenging brow.

I raised my two fingers index and middle finger at him " just two days you yourself will throw my ID at my face and drag me and throw me out of your so called penthouse"

"Are you challenging me because it's never gonna happen" he gave me a equally challenging smirk.

"And how are you so sure about that you will never get angry at me?"

"Because which face lightens my bad mood and brings a smile to my face, how can I ever get angry at that face " he said stroking my cheeks.

I swatted his hands away, " Firstly, don't touch me and secondly, stop with those pick up lines can't you see am cringing so hard" and that bastard just chuckled. " I have another question to ask "

"Go on " he said staring at me intently.

"Why is it me whose helping you , I mean you could have chosen someone else "

"As I said I didn't have any girlfriends before so I don't know about females around me and as for you, I know you as I stayed with you for almost two weeks and I can trust you"

"You could have paid someone to pretend to be your girlfriend for a month or two and which fool of asshole said that you can trust me!??"

"I can't pay someone to be my fake girlfriend as now I have a real girlfriend" he said and grinned.

" Who is she? Your real girlfriend"

"You, your my real girlfriend"

"I'm gonna go crazy if I sit here any longer, so bye " I stood up from the couch, frustrated and made my way to the stairs.

'Come on Ashley ,you can piss him off and free yourself'

Chapter 21

"AHHHHHHH !!!!!! " I cried facing my phone as I was in the facetime with Steve and Chase , inside my room.

"What happened, Ashley ?" Both of their voices were alarmed.

"He decieved and lied to me thrice " I said pointing three of my fingers at the mobile screen.

"What did he do again?" Chase asked and I told them everything about how he took my ID from me by lying and left no way for me to escape from New York. And then about how he took me to his parents mansion and told his family members that I'm his girlfriend and I'm pregnant with his child.

And I even told them that he's a virgin and that I was his first kiss and also told them about his alliance with Carol Hobson, the supermodel. And why he broke his alliance with her.

"Which idiot would leave a supermodel for a simple girl like Ashley " Steve spoke insulting me but a huge part of me knew that he was right.

"Yeahhh, she is an exquisite goddess " Chase said agreeing with Steve.

"And Zyon said that she is a certified slut" I snapped annoyed by their continuous praises about her beauty .

"Yeah but also-" Steve was cut off by me.

"Okay enough about her beauty, and now help me get out of this" I said and continued " he has placed a deal for me, that if he ever gets angry at me or shouts at me or even glare at me, he's gonna give me my ID back to me"

"WHAT!!??" they both asked in unison.

"I know it's lame "

"No it's not lame, it's an easy task to piss a man" Steve said

"And how is that? " I asked.

"Go and give that Zyon a hard kick on the place where sun doesn't shine and he'll automatically shout at you giving you a deathly glare" it was Steve's plan but I did not agree with him.

"No, I don't want any violence " I stated dryly.

"Am I dreaming Chase, pinch me please, is this our Ashley, how come she don't want any violence " Steve said dramatically.

"Shut up Steve I want to act civil with him"

"Yeah, we should act civil and get her out of this mess" Chase said to Steve. Thanks to God that I have Chase because of whom I'm still sane.

I opened one of the drawers in my study table and took a pen and a notebook out.

"Okay guys give me some plans on how to piss this Mr perfect Rosington"

"Okay plan A " Chase started "does he have a office in his penthouse? " he asked.

"Yes" I nodded As I remembered him showing me his home office.

"Good, take the scissors with you and go to his office and tear all his business papers into tiny pieces and I'm 101% sure that he will atleast glare at you " Chase completed.

"And that's our plan A" Steve said.

"Noted" I wrote the plan in my book. "Now plan B "

"And if plan A didn't work, you're going to run into his room with scissors and tear all his clothes and destroy his luxurious room and that's our plan B" Steve said.

"And what if plan B didn't work, we need a plan C "I said.

"And plan C is, go to the kitchen and break all the expensive plates, glasses and whatever you find there" Chase said and I wrote all the plans.

"Ah, there's so much of money waste in these plans" I muttered which was inaudible to them.

"And after these plans he still didn't glare or yell at you, beat the shit out of him and that's plan D " Steve ordered.

" Steeeve ! I wanna be civil. "

"Hmm" he hummed. "You should have never gone there" he said with a pout.

"It was all because of you" I snarled " you told me to accompany him to New York "

"So now it's all my fault and who wanted to fulfill dreams without any expenses " he shouted.

"You-" I was cut off by Chase

" chill Ashley, he's just missing you alot " he said and instantly my eyes moistured.

"Aww, I miss you both also alot" I sniffled.

"We don't miss you, I'm glad that your stuck there" Steve said with a stoic face.

"Who is we, I do miss Ashley alot" Chase said and continued "Ashley another important notice"

"Yes"

"Chief said that, if you don't return within this week , she's gonna take a strict action against you" he said and I smirked.

"I forgot to tell you'll an important thing " I gave them a ear to ear grin.

"And what is that? " Steve asked.

"If I succeed to piss him off, he's not only gonna give me my ID back but also a job offer in SDC "

" SDC " they both screamed " Oh my God Ashley, if you succeed in pissing him, your gonna be the luckiest woman present in the world "Steve said grinning and Chase was equally happy for.

"Yes, you have to succeed and all the best " Chase said clapping.

"Sure and thanks" I said and bid our goodbyes and declined the call.

' Time to put our plans on action. '

Chapter 22

I slowly tiptoed and made my way out the door of my room. With each gentle footsteps I sauntered slowly downstairs and saw him in the kitchen making dinner for us, it was around 7 in the evening. Again I slowly made my way to his home office which was downstairs ,at the end of the lounge.

I reached the door and turned the knob slowly but the door didn't open, it was freaking locked. I tried again and again and to my disappointment it was really locked.

' He never kept his office locked!'

"I knew this would be one of your plan, to destroy my office work" he said and I turned around nervously.

He had some bunch of keys in his hand which he was shaking and smirking down at me.

Bastard....

I raised my chin and flipped my hair in pride,

"What do you think, I have only plan A, huh?" I smirked.

'Time for plan B'

I pushed past him and ran towards his room.

"Where are you goi...." His voice was cut off.

I reached his room and opened it and it was my first time entering his room and his room was beautiful. I thought it would be black and grey colour combination but it was nothing like that , it was same as my room but larger than mine, white walls with a king-size bed in the middle with white silk sheets draped on it. And at the side there was a glass window in which the view of New York was exquisite.

' You don't have time to praise his room'

Yeah, right.

I made my way to his walk in closet and opened his huge wardrobe.

"If your searching for your ID it's not here" Zyon said from behind.

I opened his large wardrobe and...

'Oh my god! '

There were so many suits, shirts pants, ties and a dozens of leather shoes.

' How am I gonna tear all of this?'

So I opened a drawer and found boxers in them.

' let me start with the smaller ones'

I took one of his boxers,

"Ew, are they even clean" I scrunched my nose holding his boxers in the tip of my index and thumb fingers.

"They are very clean you can touch them properly and even smell them " he smirked.

"Ew!!" I threw the boxer on his face and took one of his shirt ,which was branded and expensive, to tear it into pieces.

I held the scissors to tear his shirt when he said, " it atleast costs around $500, I guess"

"WHAT!!" I held the shirt tightly scrutinizing it and found out that it was a branded shirt.

What is there in this shirt for him to pay $500.

"Go on, tear it" he challenged.

I exhaled deeply , so now I'm gonna waste $500.

I held the scissors tightly,

'Are you sure ,your gonna waste $500 '

I would have bought so many clothes for myself in $500.

'So plan A and B failed'

I let go of his shirt and made my way to his kitchen.

"So now , plan C " he said and I ignored him.

And before he could come to the kitchen and tell me the cost of all these plates and glasses, I broke them .

I took one of the plate which had blue colour leaves printed on them and it looked quite expensive and I broke that plate also.

I kept breaking glasses and plates until he came and saw me and ... Smiled.

"Go on" he challenged.

"ENOUGH!" I yelled

'now for plan D'

I know I said I'll be civil with him but enough and now plan D, according to Steve ' beat the shit out of him'

I made my way to him and grabbed his collar and was about to punch his beautiful nose, hard. When he caught my fisted ball and pulled me towards him until my head hit his chest.

He suddenly leaned in, until we were inches apart and his breath was tickling my face. He leaned to my ear and said " no violence, sweetheart " he said huskily and grazed my earlobe.

A shiver ran down my spine and I felt something in my stomach.

' Am I having butterflies in my tummy? '

He pulled away with a stupid smirk plastered on his face and my eyes widened.

"You filthy peice of shitty bastard " I bursted and he had an amused smirk curling up on his lips " who are you? Back in Florida, you were all saint type of guy and now what happened to that saint guy?"

"Oh I left that guy in Florida and this is my new me who happens to live in New York" He said still with that sexy smirk of his.

He suddenly pulled me towards him and kissed my cheeks and said, "You look hot when your angry"

I pushed him , "You'll look too hot if you get angry" I retorted.

He took a step towards me and before he could pull me towards him and lick my earlobe. I quickly pushed past him and ran to my room , my heart beating rapidly. As I reached my room, I locked it and try to calm my crazy heart

' I failed to accomplish all the plans. Plan A ,B ,C and D' facepalmed.

Chapter 23

Zyon's Pov:-

I was tapping my foot impatiently on the floor waiting for Gregor to bring my remaining files.

The door opened and Gregor along with Liam entered.

" Sir, your remaining files " Gregor said placing the files on the table.

"This is my only remaining work for today, right " I asked taking one of the file .

"Yes sir" Gregor said.

"After this I'm free, right?" I asked impatiently as I was signing the paper after reading them.

" Yes sir "

"Okay, you can leave" I raised a dismissive hand and he nodded and walked off.

"Hey bro! What's up" I forgot that even Liam was present along with Gregor.

"Nothing's up, Liam" I said in a bored tone without even glancing at him and my attention focused solely on the files on my table.

I have to finish them as soon as possible.

" And how's your hot girlfriend and your baby in her womb " Liam asked and I couldn't help but smile thinking about Ashley and her ways to piss me off.

"She and my baby, both are fine and please don't disturb me Liam, I have to finish my work as soon as possible"

"Okay" he shrugged " I've heard that your father has cancelled the deal with the Hobson's and even the contract that Hobson's has made for you"

"Yeah, you heard right" I said while signing another file.

That contract made by the Hobson's was a pain in ass contract. And without my dad's help I couldn't get out of that.

"You know your ex- fiancè is a crying mess "

"So what should I do? She deserves that" I gritted " and if your here to talk about her ,then you can just leave "

"Woah ! Sorry bro " he said in a dramatic way. " Okay let's talk about your girlfriend and your baby" he said when I finished signing my last file.

"Sorry Liam ,I have to go "

"What? Where? it's just 5 in the evening" he said with wide eyes " you used to leave your office around 10 at night" he was astonished.

Well that's true, but now I have a reason to leave soon

Ashley..

" My girlfriend is waiting for me and I also have to take her for a long drive, so sorry" I said as I got up from my chair.

"You've been with her for few months and why didn't you tell us about her and her pregnancy?" He questioned and that stopped me.

I turned around and faced him, "Because she wanted privacy, she didn't want everybody to know about her pregnancy"

"How old is your baby?"

Why is he questioning me like this.

"It's been a month since she's been pregnant" I blurted out and he nodded. " So, now can I leave"

"Yeah " he raised his hands up in air and I left.

Well I'm a good liar..

....

As soon as I reached my penthouse, I slowly opened the door and tiptoed inside and saw Ashley sitting in the couch with a glass of chocolate mousse. She dipped her index finger inside the mousse and then pulled out and slowly sucked her index finger.

It was quite a sexy scene.

I cleared my throat and she jolted up and turned around to face me with a scowl plastered on her face. "What are you doing here?" She asked

"It's my house" I answered and when she was about to open her mouth , I interrupted, " Correction it's our house" I said.

"It's not my house" she gritted "and how are you so early today"

"Today we're going for a long drive an-" I was interrupted

" I'm not going anywhere with you because I can't trust you, you deciever" she stated.

"Oh! How sad I thought I would be sitting in the passenger seat and you would drive the car" I pouted.

Back in Florida ,on Chase's anniversary party she was a drunken mess, after she blacked out I carried her to the car and while driving she stirred and opened her eyes and said a lot more secrets about her,

" hey Mr amnesia "she slurred. " I want to marry someone who has those green eyes like yours , so that my kids could get those eyes , shame I can't have them " she hiccuped.

" You know I love to drive cars especially expensive ones" she hiccuped again

" Ashley, sleep" I ordered

"Nooo" she slurred. " I want to talk" " You know back in high school and college , I had so many boyfriends " she sniffled " but they never loved me instead they always wanted to take my virginity and give me pain" she sniffled wiping her fake tears. " That was always the reason of our breakups and I hated it. so now I don't have any boyfriends and I'm single and very very happy" she smiled and closed her eyes.

Back to present..

"Okay , I'll come however I'm bored just sitting in here " she said

"Okay just give five minutes, I'll just go and take a quick shower" I said as I made my way upstairs to my room.

....

It was half past six now and I sprayed some cologne on white shirt and left my room to see Ashley sitting on the couch scrolling her phone.

"Let's get going" I said as I took my car keys and passed it to her.

"Let's go " she squealed holding the car keys tight in her hand.

We made our way to the parking lot and she unlocked the car and sat in the driving seat while I sat on the passenger seat.

" Ready? " anybody could say that she was excited, by her face.

" Yeah" I nodded.

She started the engine and I was smiling widely, feeling her presence beside me.

' I hope everyday would be like this'

Chapter 24

OH MY GOD!! I can't believe that I'm driving this luxurious expensive car, I was so happy. It has been an hour of me driving in a long peaceful silence along the wide forest stretched at the sides of the roads.

Everything was peaceful until Zyon opened his mouth ,

"I heard that you want to marry a guy with green eyes like mine, so that your kids could have green eyes." He smirked.

Did I ever mention that to him?

No.

How does he know about that?

I don't know.

"Who said that to you, it's a lie." I said .

"Oh come on, don't lie to me " he said still with that smirk of his.

"Unlike you, I don't lie to people and you lied to me thrice or god knows , even more than thrice." I said still staring at the screen.

And this time he had an amused smirk curling up. "I didn't lie to you thrice"

"Come on, now it's the fourth time your lying" I rotated the wheel and continued " first, you said you have amnesia and second , you said the security needs my ID for identification ,unlike it was you who wanted my ID and third, me being your girlfriend and mother of your unborn child, how lame"

"Okay okay " he sighed " I lied to you but there are reasons behind it "

"Oh yeah!!" I said ,my voice filled with sarcasm.

"Let's change the topic" he said and I was about to open my mouth, when he asked me the most stupidest question ever " what if you were really pregnant with my child, huh?"

I instantly snapped my head in his direction and scowled. "Where is that question coming from ?"

"Just wondering" he answered nonchalantly.

"Just for you to know, I would never ever be pregnant with your child" I snapped and that bastards smirk deepened.

"But you want your kids to have my green eyes so what if we make this fake pregnancy a real one ..." I cut him off

"SHUT UP" I shouted and my whole attention focused on him.

Before I could say anything...

"ASHLEY!!" Zyon screamed my name and in an instant I averted my gaze to the windscreen and there was a large van approaching, right in front of the car and I was paralyzed and Zyon's hand suddenly came over the wheel and he turned the steering wheel to the right and the car was hit to a tree trunk and a whitish grey smoke appeared from the hood of the car.

We both got out of the car abruptly to see the front section of the car was fully damaged.

'Thank god none of us were hurt'

"I'm sorry, I'm sorry, I'm sorry" I repeated myself with many sorrys to him.

'What am I gonna do , the car was too expensive and I just crashed it. Why does it always happens to me?'

A sole tear rolled down my cheek and I was too damn scared.

Suddenly a strong hands were wrapped around me and it was Zyon who embraced me in a warm hug.

I didn't push him away instead I hugged him back.

"I'm sorry , I'm really sorry" I whispered while hugging him.

He gently rubbed my back and placed a soft kiss on top of my head. "Shh, it wasn't your fault , the van driver was driving on the wrong lane"

"But I should have paid attention on the road instead of shouting at you" I whispered.

He slowly pulled back, " Then it was my fault, I was trying to get your attention " he smiled

"And what about the car?"

"Don't worry about the car I have lot more car in my garage , what if one is gone?"

"What are we gonna do in this middle of night and what's the time?" I asked and took my phone out to check it was quater past eight.

"Ugh!" Zyon groaned.

"What happened?"

"This area is out of network , I can't call Gregor nor Liam "

I again unlocked the phone to see that even my phone was out of network

"So now?" I asked

" We have to search a place to stay for tonight"

I nodded and started walking along with him.

"I swear I'll never ever drive a car again" I said while walking in the middle of nowhere.

"And why is that?"

" Because last time when I drove Steve's car I hit you and this time I just crashed your car "

"Don't blame yourself " he said softly with a smile.

....

After walking for some what an hour, I was panting vigorously.

"Stop, I can't walk futher" I panted.

"What? We walked only for 20 minutes"

"I can't walk " an evil smirk was curling up on his lips and I frowned.

"You should have a habit of going for a morning walk Ashley it's good for you and also for our baby"

"Shut up" I bent down " carry me I can't walk "

"What?"

"Carry me " I demanded and he came towards me and carried me in bridal style.

"I think our baby is growing fat inside your tummy "

"Shut up " I hissed and smacked his arm and he just chuckled.

After walking for another 10 minutes we saw a yellow light peeking through the woods and Zyon followed the light and while following some droplets were falling on us and when we saw up, it had already started raining slowly.

"Hurry up Zyon it's going to rain"

"Yeah, yeah" he couldn't run carrying me and it was also late, because now it was raining heavily and our clothes were drenched.

After following the yellow light we reached a small old stone cottage and Zyon made his way to the porch and slowly set me down on the floor.

"Does someone own this place? " I asked wrinkling my nose.

"The light is still on, that means somebody is in there" he panted and thumped his hand twice on the door.

We waited and suddenly the old wooden door opened with a creak .

And a old woman in her late fifties, was standing behind the door with a pair of thick glasses on her eyes and was scrutinizing us up and down.

Zyon cleared his throat and the old woman looked at him in the eye.

"How can I help you?" She asked with authority in her voice.

"Actually our car got crashed in the middle of the forest and our phones are out of network so we can't call for help and this is my girlfriend.."

'Did he Just had to mention that.'

"And she's....."

'No no no..'

"Pregnant" the old lady was staring at my belly.

"Is she really pregnant?"

"Yeah " Zyon answered " can we just stay here for a night"

She stared at us contemplating whether to allow us in or not.

"Wait a minute, let me ask my husband" she said and went inside and now I was shooting daggers at him.

"Why did you tell that I was pregnant" I whisper yelled.

"Because that lady would think about your pregnancy and allow us to stay here" he whispered back.

Before I could open my mouth the old lady came back with two towels in her hand.

"Here" she gave us the towel " come inside and make your-selves comfortable and before coming in, please do remove your shoes" she said pointing to our shoes.

We both nodded in return.

We entered the cottage,

"Your clothes are wet , let me get you some dry clothes or else you people would catch cold" she said and made her way to the small door.

I averted my gaze to the cottage. It had a small lounge with all the old rusty wooden furnitures . And across the lounge there was a staircase leading upstairs.

" Here your clothes" she said while giving us the clothes.

And when I saw my cloth, I let out a small gasp.

'How am I gonna wear this??'

Chapter 25

I stretched my hands infront of me holding the dress to get a better view of the dress. It was a red silk short night gown which would reach right below my butt and the strap of the gown was too thin. I stared at the dress in disbelief while Zyon's eyes were wide like saucers.

"Come, let me show you your room " the old lady made her way to the staircase and we followed suit.

We made our way upstairs to see only one door at the corner. The old lady took us to that one room and opened it and switched on the light.

I moved forward to have a good view of the room. It was a simple old bedroom with a single bed with a old dirty sheets draped on it and at the corner of the room there was a door maybe leading to the bathroom.

'Wait, are we gonna sleep in one room '

'No no no, I can't wear this sexy revealing night gown infront of him'

I cleared my throat, " Excuse me ma'am, can I get something more appropriate to wear" I said pointing to the nightgown.

"Oh honey, it's my daughter's nightgown and other than that I don't have any other clothes for you" she said and smiled " and however he's your boyfriend and he has already seen you naked ,as your pregnant" I choked on my own spit at her comment and I tilted my head towards Zyon whose cheeks were tinted pink at her comment .

' is he blushing at her comment'

" And one more thing" the old lady started "don't do any unholy stuffs in here or make any weird noises because my husband is not a heavy sleeper and if he wakes up he won't let me sleep" she started giggling and now I was red at her comment. " Okay good night and have a good sleep" she winked and walked off.

'What a weird old woman'

I stared at her back until she vanished away.

And again I saw my room. How am I gonna sleep here because there was only one single bed not even a queen size bed. And the roofs were damaged and due to the heavy rain there was a water leakage also.

Zyon made his way inside the room and sat on the bed, eyeing the room.

"What did she give you..?" He raised a brow questioningly " ..to wear "

"Oh me, she gave this " he said giving me his clothes.

The old lady gave him a very big shorts and a very small t-shirt, which I guess won't fit him.

"I'll change here, you can use the bathroom" he said and I nodded.

" Why were you blushing when she said ' naked' " I don't know what came over me to just blurter out something without even thinking.

And as expected, he smirked. " I just imagined you naked underneath me"

' Bastard, how dare he imagine such things'

And my once emotionless face turned into complete anger.

"Filthy bastard, you have such a dirty mind" I huffed angrily and stomped to the bathroom.

And again in the bathroom I had difficulty in removing my skinny jeans as it was wet ,it made it harder to remove.

I removed my shirt first and pushed that gown over my head and wore it. As I guessed it reached below my butt and I was looking ...... Sexy.

And now again with the skinny jeans, I groaned and groaned and groaned pulling this skinny jeans down but it wasn't coming down.

" Ashley are you doing some unholy stuffs in the bathroom because I can hear you moaning" Zyon said and I could picture a smirk on that beautiful face of his.

"I'm not moaning, you stupid" I snapped.

"Why aren't you coming out of the bathroom?"

"Because I'm having problem with my jeans"

"What?"

However I should go to the room and sit on the bed and remove this pant as the bathroom tiles were dirty.

' God ! I'm tired as hell'

"Zyon!?" I called.

"Yes" he answered instantly

"Can you do me a favor"

"Sure"

"Can you close your eyes and sit in the corner of the room"

"What? Why?"

"Please, pretty please"

"O.. okay"

Actually I could have just asked him to switch off the light but I am afraid of darkness and there's too much of water on the floor, what if I slip and fall flat on my butt or face.

I covered my upper body with the towel and opened the door and saw him sitting on the corner , his bare back facing me.

'Wait bare back! He's shirtless'

Now I don't have time to shout at him so I made my way to the bed and sat on it and started pulling my jeans.

I was a panting mess but this jeans was not coming down.

"Are you alright, Ashley"

"No I am not"

"What happened? do you need any help?"

'Can he help me in pulling my jeans'

Ofcourse he can. I covered my upper body properly with the towel and held it tightly against my chest.

"Yes I need your help" I said and he stood up and made his way to my direction.

This time he didn't cover himself with his hands and I could properly see all his abs and muscles,he has a nice body and as my gaze went further more down I saw how that shorts was hanging dangerously low showing his boxers brand.

"Why is your upper body naked?" I asked

"Because that shirt is too small for me and also suffocating"

"And why is that hanging so low?" I asked gesturing his shorts.

"Don't tell me that you even want my lower body naked" he gasped

"What! No, ew, shut up" I gagged.

He chuckled as he pulled his shorts upto his hips.

"This shorts is really very loose and it keeps slipping down" he reasoned " how can I help you?"

"I want you to help me pull my jeans out" I said pointing to the jeans and his eyes grew big,

"What!!?" He asked with wide eyes.

"God, you have such a dirty mind, I can't remove my jeans because it's wet and has sticken to my legs, so I need your help, to pull them out, nothing more that that" I said in a one go and exhaled deeply.

"Okay, are your pant buttons open" he blushed.

'Why is he blushing, I bet again he's thinking some unholy things'

"What?"

" Pant butto..ns, is that op..en , to pull your pa..nts " he stuttered.

"Ye..s" even I stuttered.

He kneeled down infront of me to pull the pants from the bottom hem and now even I had all the wild imagination running in my head.

'How will it feel when he will ...'

'Stop it Ashley, don't think such things'

He started pulling my pants and I tightened my grip around the towel.

And atlast with one last pull the pant came out and he stood up with my pants in his hand and I don't know what happened but after he stood up, he lost his balance and landed on top of me.

"Ahhh!" I screamed and Zyon kept his hand on my mouth, covering it.

"Shh, don't scream, the old lady said not to make any noise"

My back was on the mattress and he on top of me, our chest pressed and my towel was not covering me anymore, my cleavage was exposed to him.

He got a glimpse of my cleavage and again he blushed.

' I swear, I'm gonna kill him if he gets any dirty imagination'

He stood up and I pulled that stupid nightgown upward to cover my cleavage and wrapped the towel around me.

I cleared my throat, " You can take this sheet and sleep on the floor"

"Whose sleeping on the floor?"

"Obviously you"

"It's cold I am not gonna sleep on the floor"

I smirked, "You know" I rubbed my stomach " I'm pregnant and me and my baby needs a comfortable sleep "

And he gave me an equally challenging smirk, "Even I wanna sleep with my baby "

"Then where am I suppose to sleep, if you sleep on the bed"

"With me, on the bed" he shrugged.

I looked at the single bed and at the floor, floor was a complete mess with waters all around.

'How are we both gonna sleep in that small bed'

I sighed, "Fine, but don't touch me"

"Fine" he smirked

I got inside the bed and he switched off the light and got in the bed beside me.

A very small distance was avoiding us from touching.

I turned around to the other side not facing him instead facing the cracked windows.

Suddenly the streaks of lightning illuminated following by loud roar of thunder. I jumped and turned around facing Zyon , who was already facing me.

I grabbed his one arm and held it tightly.

"What happened about no touching "

"Just forget about it and stay still , it's cold" I said still holding his arm.

He wrapped one of his arm around me and pulled me closer until my hands touched his bare chest and I could feel the warmth of his body.

" Wh..at ar..e y..ou doi..ng" I stuttered

"It's cold" " Good night Ashley" he gently rubbed my stomach" and good night baby" I sighed accepting my defeat.

I don't have any energy left to argue back so I just closed my eyes as the sleep took over me.

Chapter 26

The sunlight beamed through the cracked windows directly to my face and I stirred and snuggled closer to something warm and slowly opened my eyes to see Zyon peacefully sleeping beside me and I slowly raised my head up from his one arm to see that his arm was wet.

' did I just drool over him' I facepalmed.

I looked at myself, the straps of the dress was fallen off my shoulders and the neckline of my dress was hanging low ,exposing my cleavage.

I groaned and pulled the straps and neckline up. And then got up from the bed and took the t-shirt ,which the old lady gave to Zyon and ran to the bathroom and wetted the hem of the t-shirt and came out and sat on the bed and started wiping the drool off of his arm.

Zyon groaned and opened his eyes, while I was wiping his arm

What a unlucky day!.

"What are you doing ?" He slowly rubbed his eyes .

"I wasn't eye-fucking you, okay " I said before he could comment something nonsense.

"Were you licking my arm?" He asked as he touched his arm " why is my arm wet"

"What nonsense are you uttering, why would I lick your arm" I snapped " for your information I wasn't licking your arm ,I was just wiping your arm with this wet t-shirt " I showed him the t-shirt which was in my hand.

"And why would you do that?"

"Because " I paused searching for a reason " there were some dust particles on your arm "

"And why would you be too nice to me to rub the dust from my arm"

"Because I am a nice person and I know I hate you but I don't do enemies " I said.

"But-" he stopped as I got up from the bed and as I got up the strap of my right shoulder fell off again

Ugh! This dress.

I pulled the strap back to my shoulder and saw Zyon's eyes raking my body.

Suddenly I felt self conscious and I cleared my throat.

He looked away and I took the towel from the bed and covered myself and made my way to the bathroom.

I wore my shirt and jeans which was a little wet, I combed my hair with my fingers and left the bathroom.

As I came out I saw Zyon dressed in his shirt and pants and his hair was a mess like mine.

"So let's go" Zyon asked and I nodded.

We made our way downstairs and saw that old lady in the kitchen was with an old man, giggling.

As the old lady saw us, she straightened up . "Good morning kids" she greeted and we also greeted her back.

"Evan these are the kids ,yesterday I told you about... " she faltered and the old man whose name was Evan nodded.

The old man scrutinized Zyon with narrowed eyes and then asked. " aren't you the CEO of the CTC company and also that supermodel Carol Hobsons fiancé "

Before Zyon could answer him the old lady interrupted. " He can't be Carol Hobson fiancé, he has a girlfriend who is pregnant " she said to the man.

"No it's actually me, we just broke our alliance because our relationship wasn't compatible " Zyon said with a small smile " and however I am happy with my love " His eyes bore into mine with adoration and he kept his hand on my lower stomach " and the newcomer " he smiled

'What a good liar!'

The old man and woman smiled,

"However I am Evan Vincent and this is my wife Gloria Vincent " the man introduced.

"And I'm .."Zyon said but was cut off by the old man.

"Zyon Rosington " Zyon nodded "And what is your name beautiful "

"Ashley Grayson "

"And the future Rosington " the old lady said and giggled.

"How do you'll know Carol Hobson? " I asked

"Our daughter is the biggest fan of Carol Hobson, she keeps showing us her new pictures in the social media ,so that's how we know her" Gloria said.

"Ohh!" Was all I could say.

However ,Carol was a famous supermodel and whole New York knew her.

"I think we should leave, my secretary is on his way to escort us" Zyon said as Gloria passed us two steamy cups of hot coffee.

'When did he call Gregor'

The door bell rang and Gloria made her way to open the door.

She called Zyon and he also sauntered towards the door and then came Gregor with his stoic face.

He handed Zyon a paper and Zyon signed that piece of paper and handed it over to Evan.I slowly peeked and got a glimpse of that paper and I let out a small gasp.

It was a cheque of $50,000.

" Thanks for helping us out, Evan" Zyon said and handed him the cheque.

Evan hesitated to take the cheque, "Sorry Zyon , but it's too much I can't except it"

Zyon smiled " You can use it for yourself or even for your daughter's bills" Evan's eyes widened for a brief moment,as Zyon added " I insist"

Evan hesitated but agreed and took the cheque and we left the house.

We were in back seat of the car and the chauffeur was driving us back to Zyon's penthouse.

"What were you saying to Evan about ' daughter's bills'? " I asked.

"Last night, I woke to fetch some water for me to drink while you were sleeping. I descended downstairs and saw Gloria and Evan talking in the kitchen about their daughter, that she has a diplegia and they are worried about her hospital bills. So I thought of helping him out"

'Wait, what is diplegia?'

Should I ask him.

' no dumbass don't ask him, he'll think what a dumb girlfriend he got'

Wait? What? I'm not his girlfriend but it's right I shouldn't ask him.

I slowly took my phone out and tapped Google before typing, ' what is diplegia?'

As we were now in city so there was no network issues.

And google instantly answered my question, ' diplegia is a form of paralysis that affects similar body parts on both the sides of the body such as both legs or both arms.'

I gasped knowing that Evan Vincent's daughter has a diplegia.

" What happened?" Zyon inquired.

What should I say, what should I say????

" Um.. nothing , just a brutal accident case popped up in my phone." I lied smoothly and he nodded.

' Well even I'm becoming a good liar'

Chapter 27

"So are you falling for him?" Steve asked with his signature smirk.

"No! " I snorted and gave him a deathly glare.

I was on facetime with Steve and Chase as usual, I told them everything about how I damaged Zyon's car and then our stay at that stone cottage and everything except the night gown thing.

"So all our plans failed and he has not even glared at you" Chase asked and I sighed defeatedly before nodding.

"Our chief is on the verge of firing you and you have not yet returned" Chase sighed. " I said you not believe him and follow him to New York" Chase said and I felt guilty for not listening to him.

After a brief moment of silence at both the sides, I said, "I have some work, I'll call you'll later" I cut the call and tossed my phone on the bed.

As I was sitting and wondering about 'how to get out of this mess', there was a knock on my door and I made my way to the door and opened it ,to be greeted by a grinning Zyon.

"Hi " I said dryly.

"Hi " he replied enthusiastically. " I have an invitation for you"

"And what is that?" I asked in a bored tone.

"Come on, cheer up a little"

'Cheer up, my ass'

"Mom has invited us over for dinner, tonight" he said and I scowled, not liking the idea of going back to his parents mansion.

' wait, think Ashley, you can go there and tell Zyon's dad everything about how he lied to everyone'

A smile formed on my lips about thinking my plan and on the other hand Zyon gave me an evil smirk.

"I know what's going on,in that big brains of yours" Zyon said.

"And what's going on?" I asked in a challenging tone.

" Don't even think about telling my parents about my lies" he said and my smile instantly vanished.

' how he always gets to know about my plans'

"Or what are you gonna do if I tell them the truth" I narrowed my eyes and challenged him.

He just smiled and said, " Then you have to say bye-bye to SDC job offer and hello to status- jobless" I paled at the word jobless.

I huffed angrily and glared at him, " so now are you threatening me, huh?"

"No honey, I'm not threatening you, I am just warning you before you pull any unwanted stunt"

'It's a valid threat Ashley, just do as he says and don't mess up with him'

I exhaled deeply, " Fine ,I promise I won't tell them your secret".

"Good" " Before I forget,give me your phone"

"Why?" I asked and he raised a brow "Fine" I unlocked my phone and tossed it to him.

He tapped several buttons and suddenly his phone started ringing. He took out his phone and again tapped something on his phone and gave me my phone back.

" Here this is my number, for any emergency"

I saw he has saved his number with his name and either side of his name was the red hearts.

I looked at him and in return he winked at me and I just rolled my eyes at his behaviour.

....

We were in the car with Zyon driving and me on the passenger seat.

If anybody asks, ' how many months pregnant are you?' " Zyon asked.

"One month" I sighed frustratedly.

Zyon convinced me to play along with him with his lies and if his parents pester me with any question, I should answer the way he has told me.

"When did you meet Zyon?" He asked again.

"Why should I even help you with your lies" I snapped.

" SDC.." he dragged and grinned at my defeat.

"Jerk!" I muttered under my breath, " 5 months ago" I answered

"Good, so are you ready?" he said and got out of the car and opened the door for me.

We were again standing infront of the large mahogany doors and Zyon rang the bell after which a maid came and opened the door for us.

As we entered in,we were greeted by someone playing violin very smoothly with a perfect tune.

I made my way towards the music and saw that Rebecca was playing violin.

She was swiftly moving the bow against the violin strings in a professional manner.

I was awestruck at the music she was playing . As she finished her music, she lifted her head to see us.

" Hi " she greeted.

"Hello" I greeted back. " Who taught you that music , I've never heard that before" I stated truthfully because it was a indeed new piece of art.

"The music played by me now was created by an old friend of mine" she said with a small smile.

" Ashley, right" it was Lily, Zyon's mom, who gave me a huge smile and took me in for a hug.

I hugged her back and after a few seconds she pulled back. " Dinners ready, I'm sure your hungry as you have another one life inside you to feed" she giggled.

We all were seated in the dining area and the dinner was being served by the maids.

As I stabbed the fried broccoli using my fork, Thomas Rosington's voice reached my ears and I looked at him.

"Ashley, do your parents know about your relationship with Zyon" I coughed at his question and Rebecca passed passed me the glass of water.

'Think think think Ashley, what to say'

I looked at Zyon, then back at Thomas and slowly bobbed my head up and down.

"So where did you'll meet ?" Lily asked.

"Restaurant" " beach " Zyon and I answered differently in unison.

Zyon coughed for a brief moment and I can sense that he's trying to search a lie to cover his lies again.

"Actually Ashley and I met in beach first, then we went to a nearby restaurant and had our lunch together, right Ashley"

I nodded.

What a smooth liar.

And they asked a few more questions about my career and pregnancy to which even I lied smoothly.

After sometime we left the mansion and now we were sitting in his car going back to his penthouse.

I had a devious plan going on in my head and it will also be a punishment to him for threatening me.

As we entered the city I noticed a liquor store ,

"Stop the car at that liquor store" I pointed to the store.

"Why?"

"Because I need a bottle of wine to pull my life out of misery just for a couple of hours" I snapped.

"O..okay , but there's a 'no parking' board infront of the store" he informed and stopped the car infront of the store " you go to the store and buy a bottle, I'll just go there and park the car"

I nodded and got out before making my way to the store. After reaching the store I bought a nice bottle of wine and got out of the store.

As I was walking on the footpath towards Zyon's car, I heard someone calling my name from a distance. I turned around and my eyes widened and for a brief moment I was paralyzed because a van was coming towards me with a full speed and a metallic bat was stuck out of the van's window, aiming to hit my head with full force.

As the van neared me, suddenly someone pushed me down, so now my back was on the cement footpath and on top of me was Zyon, whose jaw was clenched.

Zyon got up and stretched his hand out for me to grab and I took it after which he pulled me to a standing position.

My wine bottle was safe in my hands as I saw the van going farther and farther and then vanishing away. I averted my gaze to Zyon who was staring at the vanished van with clenched jaw.

It was like , someone purposely wanted to kill me but who could it be. I don't have anyone in New York, relatives, friends nor even enemies.

' who could it possibly be?'

Chapter 28

After the incident yesterday Zyon was hyperventilating or can also say freaking out but here I am least bothered with the incident because Zyon was there to worry for me and I was solely focused on my next plan.

Well the plan is simple, just spiking his favourite orange juice with some alcohol as I remembered him saying me that he has bad effect on alcohol and then I'm gonna ask him about my ID and in his vulnerable state he's gonna return my ID back and I am gonna return back to Florida.

I grinned,

What a perfect plan I've got.

And it's also a punishment to him for threatening me yesterday.

However ,morning Zyon informed me that he would return by nine and to take care of myself. I averted my gaze to the clock to see, it was half past eight and again my wicked brain thought of a plan.

I made my way to the kitchen and turned the stove off and then transferred the spaghetti into a dish and then took my phone from the kitchen counter and dialled Zyon's number, on the second ring he received,

"Ashley wh-"

"Zyon- " I called breathlessly

"What happened?" His voice was alarmed.

"I.. I.. Zyon-" I pretended to sob " please help me " I cried breathlessly.

"Ashley jus-"

" AHHHHHHH" I screamed and then disconnected the call.

I laughed wickedly knowing that Zyon would be worriedly sick about me.

I turned my head to see the time and it was still quater to nine.

If Zyon really cares for me, he's gonna reach here within 10 minutes and if not, he doesn't care.

I was setting the table when I heard the turning of the door knob and I jerked my head towards the door and then to the clock.

My eyes widened, he just returned from his office within 5 minutes.

' He do cares for you, Ashley'

He opened the door, saw me and sighed in relief.

I took in his appearance, hair a mess, tie loose , creased shirt, the coat off and a horrified expression on his face.

He made his way towards me and hugged me.

"Thank god, your safe" he mumbled and kissed the top of my head and pulled back, his hands still resting on my shoulders. " Why did you lie to me, you know how worried I was?" He asked softly.

" It's an impact of staying with a liar" I smiled sheepishly.

His gaze averted to the table and he raised one of his eye brows.

"You cooked?"

I nodded " come let's have dinner together" I grabbed his hand moved towards the table.

As we reached the table, he stopped " Let me fresh up"

"Later, you can fresh up" I said and he narrowed his eyes doubtfully.

I was too eager to put my plan on action.

'Control, Ashley'

"Why are you being too sweet to me?" He raised a brow.

"I.."

'Think, think, think Ashley'

"I'm always sweet to you and besides I felt guilty for lying to you" I said with a straight face.

I pulled out a chair for him and he sat down on the chair, then I served him some spaghetti before making my way back to the kitchen, towards the fridge, opening it and pulling out the glass of spiked orange juice.

As I reached back to the dining table, I placed the orange juice on his side of table and sat across him, serving myself some spaghetti.

"It's nice" he complimented pointing to the spaghetti.

I smiled.

' Come on! Chug the juice in '

As he finished the last noodle from his plate, I was desperately waiting for him to chug the juice down his throat.

Atlast, he held the glass with his long fingers and brought it close to his mouth, then took a sip, "The orange juice tastes different" he pointed out.

"Because I made it with my delicious hands" I swayed my fingers and grinned.

He smiled and drank the whole juice in one go.

The wine I bought yesterday has a large amount of alcohol in it. So, if he has a very low tolerance level on alcohol then he would react really soon.

So I waited.

Chapter 29

"Thanks for the din.." he paused " ner,
d i n -
ner"

He stood up from his chair and blinked several times. I guess, his vision got blurry.

"I need some rest, I'll just be in my room" he tried to take a step but stopped and gripped the top of the chair before clenching his eyes shut for a brief moment, then he opened his eyes slowly and started taking baby steps.

' either I doze off or have a wild behaviour ' his voice came ringing into my ears.

' please god don't doze him off' I chanted mentally and as if God really listened to my prayers, Zyon made his way towards the lounge near the music box and turned on the music.

The high music made its way to my ears and I watched Zyon as he removed his tie and tied it up on his forehead and started swaying his hips to the music.

' Alcohol is doing its work' I grinned.

He raised his hands up in the air and started moving them. Although Zyon wasn't a bad dancer nor even a good dancer, he was in the middle.

I made my towards him not to mention with a huge smile on my face. As I neared him, he still didn't recognise my existence as he was so engrossed in dancing.

I tapped his shoulders from behind and instantly he turned around and gazed at me with his hooded eyes. As I was about to open my mouth, to ask him about my ID. He grasped my hands in his and turned me around and then made me fall in his arms after which he kept on rotating me until my head was a spinning mess.

However with the great difficulty I freed myself from him and rushed towards the dining area and he was still in the lounge, dancing like a maniac.

If I go there again, I'm damn sure he's gonna make me dance with him again.

I was glued to my place when I heard him call me, "Ashle yyy.." he slurred " come baby, dance with me "

'Holy shit, he's really drunk'

Ofcourse he's drunk I made him drink alcohol, knowing that he has a bad effect on it.

"Ashley come soon" he called and made his way towards me.

As he reached me, I instantly asked, "Where's my ID?"

"ID?" He blinked.

"Yes, identification card"

"Leave all that nonsense, come let's dance" he took my hand in his.

"First, give me my ID and then I'll dance with you" I bargained.

He smirked and without any word he just threw me at his shoulder and again walked back to the lounge. He started jumping up and down with me still in his shoulder.

Ouch, it hurts..

" Put me down, Zyon " I yelled but still he was jumping like a crazy monkey. "You bastard, put me down or else I'm gonna kick you so hard in the balls tha-" my words got caught in my throat ,when he suddenly threw me on the couch and I yelped in pain.

Senseless bastard..

It's my turn to escape from this kingkong. So I ran towards the kitchen and hid myself in the storeroom. I took my phone out and thought.

'Should I call 911'

Obviously no, I was the one who spiked his orange juice and I'm on the blame.

I dialled Chase, but he didn't receive so next, I called Steve, he received my call on the third ring.

"Hello?" He said in bored tone.

"Hello!" I said, panic dripping from my voice.

"Baby just give me few minutes, I'll be back" he said and I got that, he was with one his one night stands.

"What happened, Ashley?" He asked.

"Steve........" I started and told him, how I spiked Zyon's orange and then his wild behaviour and so on. " How to get his ass back to sobriety ?"

"Don't be stupid Ashley, go and check it on Google"

" I can't type, my hands are trembling" I reasoned.

"Then use that microphone and ask google."

" Even my voice is trembling, google will not understand my voice" I cried and he sighed frustratedly.

" Fine, I have one solution, go fill a bathtub with cold water and dip his face until he is back to his sober state"

"Is it gonna work?"

" Hundred percent"

I cut the call after saying a small thank you and made my way towards his room. I let myself inside his bathroom and started filling the tub with cold water.

I descended downstairs and saw him still dancing like a maniac. I reached him and again tapped his shoulders and whispered in his ear a little seductively. " Let's go, dance in your room" he smiled and nodded.

And now we were in his room ,after a lot of tantrums he threw at me on the staircase and atlast I succeeded , I grabbed his arm and sauntered to the bathroom and as I reached I gasped. The water was overflowing, I rushed towards the tap and turned it off ,then turned around to see Zyon was vanished.

"Ugh, ZYON!!" I screamed.

I rushed downstairs and saw, he was nowhere in sight.

Suddenly two strong arms grabbed mine and pinned me to the wall and I shrieked.

Zyon was looking into my eyes with an indescribable emotion and then his gaze lingered on my lips. He licked his bottom lips and with a blink of an eye, he attached his lips with mine.

At first it was slow and passionate ,moulding perfectly against my lips, he nibbled my lower lip softly but I didn't open up because I was shocked. Suddenly his hands grabbed my ass and he lifted me up and my legs automatically wrapped around his waist. He again nibbled my lower lip but I still didn't open so he harshly squeezed my ass and I gasped, he took it as his chance and slipped his tounge inside my mouth, devouring every nook and corner of my mouth.

He slowly let me down on my feet and pulled apart, leaving both of us in a breathing mess.

I want more of your kisses, Zyon.

As if he heard my inner voice, Zyon kissed me not on lips but on the neck, his hands slowly reached the buttons of my shirt and he started unbuttoning it. As he finished unbuttoning my shirt ,he slowly pulled the collar of the shirt down and sucked the bare skin of my neck and shoulder joining junction. I moaned at the sensation he was building inside me and he trailed kisses from there to my bare shoulder pushing my strap down. Suddenly he carried me in his arms in bridal style and took a step forward.

' am I gonna loose my virginity today? '

'Should I stop him?'

'No I don't want him to stop'

As he was walking ,with me in his arms, he stopped in his tracks. Suddenly he started gagging and the next thing

I know is that, he again threw me on the couch and rushed towards the kitchen.

I got up from the couch, pulled my shirt up and started buttoning it after which I made my way towards the kitchen to see that ,Zyon has just vomited in the kitchen sink.

Even I gagged seeing those fluids coming out of his mouth, " I'm never gonna wash dishes in that sink again" I said.

After throwing his guts off to the sink, he turned around and I saw some of the fluids on his shirt and he was stinking.

"I think I should clean you up first" I said as I scratched my head in frustration.

We made our way back to his room upstairs,

' never in my life I'm gonna give him alcohol again' I promised myself.

"Remove your shirt" I ordered and he just shook his head in no.

I groaned and started unbuttoning his shirt and then pulled it out from his arms and tossed it on the laundry basket , revealing his muscular torso.

"Atleast unbuckle your pants" I pleaded and again he shook his head in no.

I unbuckled his pants and slowly pulled it down, leaving him in nothing but his boxer briefs.

His hands were dangerously wrapped around his boxers waist band, ready to pull it down.

I pulled his hands away from the waist band, " DON'T " I gave him one of my hard glare.

'He couldn't remove his shirt and pants but he's ready to remove his boxers, jerk'

He just smiled and nodded.

We went inside the bathroom and I took a cloth from his wardrobe and wetted it , I wiped his bare torso and arms .

We returned back to his room and I said him to lay down and again he shook his head in no.

"What's your problem, can't you just go to bed an-" I was cut mid-sentence when his arms encircled around my waist and he pulled me towards him.

There was no space between us, our faces inches apart, "I want you to sleep with me" he said huskily at which a shiver ran down my spine.

And without listening to me, he jumped into his bed, with me in his arms.

"Leave me" I protested.

"No "

I struggled in his arms at which his hold on me tightened.

I kept on struggling in his arms and I don't know when sleep enveloped me.

Chapter 30

An annoying source of sound was buzzing beside my bed but I just ignored it and snuggled closer to something warm, which was beneath me.

Something or someone..

I instantly shot my eyes open to see Zyon's bare chest. I tried to get up from him without waking him but in process I failed, he stirred in his sleep and slowly parted his eyes to reveal those beautiful piercing green eyes.

"Ah! My head" he groaned still in his sleeping position.

As soon as his eyes landed on me, he got up from the bed and stood tall infront of me. I tried my best,not to see below his neck.

"What did you mix in my orange juice?" He asked as is one hand rested on his forehead, massaging it.

"Nothing" I mumbled.

"What?" He asked with a raised brow.

"Alcohol" I muttered.

"What?" He asked incredulously with wide eyes.

"You heard me" I stated nonchalantly.

"You knew I have a bad effect on alcohol yet you made me drink it" he asked.

His almost naked body was distracting me so instead of answering him, I snapped, "First, cover yourself"

"Wha-" his words got stuck in his mouth as he lowered his gaze towards his body. "Oh my god!" He gasped and took the blanket which was neatly placed on his bed, unfolding it, he wrapped the blanket around him, covering himself.

"Why I'm naked? Where are my clothes?"

" Your clothes are on that laundry basket" I pointed to the basket which was kept in one of the corner of his room. "And the reason behind your nakedness is, you vomited on your clothes,so I had to undress you" if it wasn't for the deal, he would have shooted daggers at me with his eyes.

He opened his mouth to say something but closed, as his eyes fell on my neck.

"Is that a hickey?" He asked pointing to my neck.

In confusion I made my way towards the mirror which was placed at the corner of the room. I saw my reflection in the mirror and then I saw a hickey peeking out of my shirt.

All the memory of yesterday came crashing down to me, first, his kiss on my lips, then sucking my delicate skin, unbuttoning my shirt, carrying me in his arms and atlast throwing me on the couch.

And now I know I was crimson red by blushing profusely, I inhaled a sharp breath and turned around to face him but didn't reply to him.

"Did I..." there was a hint of hesitation in his voice " did I force myself on you ?" he asked with his voice dripping from guilt.

"No" I said without wasting a second.

"No?" His face brightened up.

"No you didn't force yourself on me, there was a weak moment where both of us couldn't stop.." I lifted my head to see that Zyon was smirking down at me. " why am I even telling you and wasting my precious time " I huffed and stomped out of his room.

"Ashley-" I heard him call me after me but I didn't bother to turn back because I was flushed red due to embarrassment.

....

To add to my misery, today was Saturday and Zyon was home. After the awkward encounter with him this morning, I didn't want to see his face.

What a bad luck I've got..

My stomach was growling so hard due to hunger but I didn't want to see his face.

After contemplating whether to go or not, I decided to go because I can't tolerate my empty stomach.

I slowly tiptoed downstairs and a sizzling aroma of french toast hit my nostrils and my mouth instantly watered.

I made my way towards the kitchen and the sight itself was delicious. Zyon was placing the french toast on two plates and beside the toast he placed some scrambled eggs.

Delicious..

"Good Morning " he greeted with a warm smile plastered on his face.

"Morning " I replied.

He balanced two plates in his hands and placed them on the dining table. I followed him and pulled out a chair for me and sat on it.

I saw the french toast infront of me and started digging in my plate. The french toast tasted delicious and I had the urge to moan but refrained myself from doing it.

The breakfast was silent. He didn't bring up the morning topic which I was glad of.

After breakfast we did talk about some little things after which he made his way to his home office and I sauntered upstairs to my room, to call Chase and Steve.

' after all it wasn't awkward to see his face again '

Chapter 31

It's been a whole month of me staying with Zyon. I've tried all my shitty-bitty plans but none worked on him, Zyon either chuckles or gives me a blank stare. Just to irk me, he keeps calling me his girlfriend and sometimes places his hand on my belly and cooes as if there's a real baby in my stomach.

Maniac..

One day while walking,we stopped by a cafeteria to buy us some coffee, and this jerk announced there that I am his girlfriend loudly to everyone. Thanks to God that he didn't announce that I'm pregnant. I was so pissed that I didn't talk to him. And when I was ignoring him, he arranged a beautiful candle light dinner at the top of the building. And from top, the the view of New York was breathtaking. I instantly forgave him for what he did.

But recently whenever he calls me girlfriend it doesn't annoy me anymore instead a faint smile appears on my face which I can't conceal.

I think because within one month I knew one thing that ,Zyon is a very good man whoever will be his future wife or girlfriend, she will be the most luckiest woman to have a man like him as her husband or boyfriend.

'Why not you?' My inner self asked me.

It can never be me because my life, my dreams and everything is in Florida and Zyon's is in New York. Me in a long distance relationship is not a chance, so Zyon and me will never be a thing.

Suddenly my phone rang which was beside me ,on my bed. It was Chase and Steve on FaceTime. I picked up my phone and answered.

"Hey Ashley, how are you? " Steve asked with a huge grin.

"Fine " I replied in a bored tone.

"What happened?" Chase asked.

Before I could respond, Steve butted in, " don't worry Ash, your soon going to piss him and get a job in SDC "

I nodded, my chief fired me from my previous job and now my status is jobless.

"Guys, it's been a freaking month of me staying with Zyon" I paused then continued "we need a solid plan guys, I can't just stay here and destroy my life and my dreams. I need to get out of here, think guys think" I pleaded.

"Ashley relax, you're gonna come back to Florida " Chase was trying to calm me down but it wasn't helping.

"But how?" I almost yelled.

"I think I've got a solid idea " Steve said with a raised index finger.

"What's the plan? " I asked raising one of my eyebrows.

"The plan is simple you have to kiss a stranger guy infront of zyon" Steve stated.

"What!?" Chase and I asked incredulously.

"Just kiss a guy infront of him, any boyfriend cannot tolerate the sight of his girlfriend kissing another guy instead of him" Steve said pointedly.

"But he's not my boyfriend " I said

"True, but for him your his girlfriend right "

I nodded as I remembered him always calling me his girlfriend. "Wouldn't it be like I'm cheating on him"

"Is he your boyfriend? "

"No" I said instantly.

"Then how are you cheating on him?"

"True " I agreed. " but Steve, I don't kiss strangers "

" for God sake Ashley, I'm not asking you to sleep with a stranger and loose your virginity, I'm just asking you to kiss him and it's not like your loosing your first kiss on a stranger " Steve completed.

"It's the best plan I could have ever thought of " Chase said " the sight of Clara kissing someone else would make my blood boil even thinking about it makes me angry "

"Ashley, if you want your old life back and want to return back to Florida, you have to try it out" Steve said .

"Ashley, now your main aim is to piss that freak Zyon and I'm hundred percent sure, that it's gonna work" Chase said.

I nodded, "I'll try" I agreed to their plan.

....

I've been sitting on the sofa inside the lounge, waiting desperately for Zyon and exactly at half past five in the evening Zyon returned back.

"Hey!" Zyon greeted.

"Hi" I greeted back with a toothy grin.

"Were you waiting for me? " He asked as he loosened his tie.

"Yeah, actually I'm bored, just sitting in the house and watching TV, I wanna go out " I responded

"Out? Where?"

"Club" I answered.

"Club?"

"Yeah, it's Friday night so club is the best option "

"But why club? We can go have a dinner in a nice restaurant " he winked.

"No, I wanna go to club, it's been a long time since I didn't do clubbing and besides I want to see a New York club too" I said lifting my hands up in air.

"Fine, we'll go to club tonight " he sighed.

After that he made his way towards his room and I kept staring at his retreating figure until it disappeared.

Do I really wanna piss him off, I mean he's such a good and a kind man.

'Focus Ashley Focus , your aim is to piss him off and return back to Florida and get a job in SDC, remember that ' My subconscious reminded me.

My dreams, my friends, my family everything is in Florida, I don't have anything in New York, I have to get back to Florida at any cost.

'I'm going to try out this plan and succeed in it at any cost'

Chapter 32

I was standing in front a grand club in New York, which was massive and sophisticated.

"Let's get in" Zyon who was standing beside me said.

I nodded and one last time checked my dress which Zyon selected and also bought me. I was wearing a red bodycon with a spaghetti straps and my hair was pulled up in a messy bun. I had my light make up on with a dark red lipstick painted on my lips.

As we sauntered in, a loud music greeted us , " ahh! It's too loud " Zyon groaned. He never liked coming to clubs even in the car drive he was trying to convince me to go nice luxurious restaurant for dinner or something else better than club. But I was stick with an answer which was no.

We made our way towards the bar, Zyon and I both sat on the bar stools.

"Want to drink something?" Zyon asked.

"No " I replied and started looking around the club for a hot man.

Zyon ordered himself a soft drink and started sipping it and here I was searching for a guy, whom I can kiss. I was still contemplating whether to kiss or not.

"Why are you looking here and there?" Zyon asked while sipping his drink.

I gave him a sheepish smile and said, "I'm just checking on some hot guys, whom I can kiss tonight."

Zyon spluttered with laughter and I glared at him "Okay I won't laugh, but you and your funny stupid jokes " he started laughing again.

Now I'm gonna definitely kiss someone.

" did you just call me stupid " I gave him my hard glare.

"No" he bit his lower lip to stifle his laughters " I just called your jokes stupid "

"FYI, it wasn't a joke " I said still shooting daggers at him through my eyes.

"Oh! So you are really gonna kiss a hot guy " he asked and I bobbed my head up and down arrogantly.

He pressed his lips together and then looked around, "There is no one as hot as me, so you can kiss me" he pouted.

A part of me really wanted to kiss the hell out of him but I refrained and composed myself before clearing my throat, " No thanks I don't want to smudge my lipstick"

"Okay let's dance" he stood up and extended his hand out for me.

My eyes switched between his hand and face after which I finally took his hand and moved towards the dance floor where some bodies were covered with sweat and some were dirty dancing.

We stood near the corner of dance floor where there were less people, we started dancing as his one hand encircled around my waist and the other one clasped my hand. I kept my other hand on his broad shoulder and I started moving along with him in a rhythm. Somebody from behind pushed me and I ended up bumping with his hard chest, I looked up at him and he was already looking down at me with his beautiful green eyes that was filled with adoration. We were inches apart and he slowly leaned in as my insides were in turmoil.

Should I kiss another guy infront of him??

Yes, I should kiss the guy, I want to get out of New York and I want a job in SDC.

I pulled back abruptly and made a safe distance between us. After dancing for a while and my eyes wandering around the dance floor insearch of a perfect candidate whom I can kiss. Zyon excused himself to go to the restroom and I made my way towards the bar.

Standing near the bar my eyes wandered around the club, where some people were making out, some were stripping, some were drinking tequila shots and lot of people were dancing. Suddenly the bartender passed me a drink and I gave him a confused glance.

Seeing my confusion he said, " It's from the man standing over there" he pointed towards a muscular tall buit man with dirty blonde hair who was smirking at me.

I knew better, not to accept a free drink. Leaving the drink behind I made my way towards the blonde man.

"Hi" I said seductively.

"Hiii" he slurred which means he's drunk. I don't have a habit of beating around the bush so I directly came to my point.

Question A.

"Do you have a girlfriend?" I asked and his smirk deepened.

"No" he said "I don't know " he slurred " No, I don't have one"

"What?" I asked as I wrinkled my nose.

"I don't have any girlfriend" he said.

Question A- check.

Now Question B,

"Can I kiss you?, just a kiss nothing more" I said

He grinned, " sure"

I looked around and saw Zyon exiting the restroom and with no more words exchanged I cupped the blonde guys face and attached my lips with his as his hands automatically encircled around my waist.

According to me it should have just been a peck on the lips but this guy wasn't leaving me and instead he squeezed the sides of my waist, to which my mouth partly opened and he slid his tongue inside me.

And oh my gosh! His breath stinks and his tongue tasted too too bad.

Did he just puke and kiss me.

NOTE : Sanitize my mouth as soon as I reach home.

I tried to push him away but he held me captive and tightened his hold around me.

Again I tried and failed as he was more stronger than.

'Doesn't he want oxygen to breathe?'

Once again I tried but this time somebody harshly pulled me from him and it was none other than Zyon who was shaking with fury and here I was a panting mess due to the loss of air.

Instead of directing his anger at me, his fist collided with that blonde guy's jaw, "You motherfucker, how dare you kiss my girlfriend " Zyon snarled.

My eyes widened as again Zyon punched that blonde man's nose and the blood came oozing out.

'This is your chance Ashley, go and push his buttons until he growls at you'

Should I go, what if he punches me too.

As Zyon punched him once more, coming out of my trance, I walked and stood between both the men.

"Ashley not now, how dare he kiss you" his green eyes screamed danger as he said in his authoritative tone.

It would be a lie if I say I wasn't scared, I was freaking terrified and just one more snarl from him,I'm gonna pee on my panty.

However, I took a deep breath and braced myself for my next words, "It wasn't him who kissed me instead it was me who kissed him"

And the next thing I know is a stinging pain on my right cheek as my head snaps to the other side.

'Did Zyon slap me?'

Chapter 33

'Don't be Zyon, please god ' I prayed as I slowly raised my head to see who slapped me.

Thanks to God ,it wasn't Zyon instead it was a short red-head with petite figure, glaring up at me.

"BITCH!!" her voice boomed " how dare you kiss my boyfriend "

"What?" I scrunched my nose in confusion.

"What, what? Huh " she snarled.

"Your boyfriend said that he doesn't have any girlfriend " I pointing to the blonde guy whose face was now covered with bruises.

'Poor guy, I should apologize to him later.'

"Peter, did you really say that to her or is she lying " she asked that blonde guy who was staring at the crowd around us oddly.

"Fine, my boyfriend said that he doesn't have any girlfriend but you have a boyfriend then why did you kiss my boyfriend, are you a certified whore?" The redhead snapped to which my tongue got tied.

"I...I.." I tried to explain but nothing came out.

"ENOUGH!!" Zyon's voice boomed and without any other word, he grasped my hand in his and took me out of the club.

We reached the parking lot near his car as he opened the passenger door for me and pushed me inside, after closing the door he seated himself on the driver seat and revved the engine.

The drive was silent and I didn't dare to utter a word. During the whole drive I observed him, his eyes bloodshot, jaws clenched and he was clutching the steering wheel so hard that his knuckles were turning white.

As soon as we reached our building, he parked his car on the parking lot and again without any word he got out of his car and I followed him until we reached the elevator. We got inside the elevator and he pressed the button to his floor and in the whole elevator ride he just ignored me without acknowledging my presence.

He soon opened the door to his penthouse and directly went to his room. I just stood there in the living room watching his retreating figure until it disappeared.

A huge part of me was guilty for kissing that blonde guy but the question was 'why?'

He is not my boyfriend or something, I can kiss whoever I want because I'm freaking single. I guess, I'm guilty because I just ruined his night, he doesn't like club but still he accompanied me because he just wanted to spend time with me and yet I ruined it for him.

Suddenly a loud sound of glass breaking reached my ears and my blood rushed south. A shiver ran down my spine out of fear as I quickly made my way towards Zyon's room.

'Did he...'

No no no, don't be a pessimist.

As soon as I reached his room, I threw the door open and I gasped, my hands covering my mouth.

There infront of me was Zyon, with a bruise on his knuckles and along with that there was a bad gash, from which the blood was streaming down. And on the corner of the floor were the shards of glasses and infront of him was a broken mirror.

'Thisman just punched the mirror. ' I charged forward and took his bruised hand in mine but he just pulled his hand out of my hold and said, " I'm fine, just go " he said it in a dangerously calm voice without looking at me.

"Don't be silly Zyon, there's blood coming out of your gash ,let me just check it" I said as goosebumps appeared on my skin seeing him this serious.

"I said just go, just get out of my room" he said a bit louder this time.

I took a step behind, " Why are you angry? " I asked as I folded my hands against my chest.

He snapped his head in my direction and charged forward until we were just inches apart from each other. "Are you seriously asking me?" He asked back as I stared directly into those beautiful green orbs which carried a mixture of hurt, anger and sadness.

Something in my chest tightened as I saw hurt in those green eyes and my heart was beating rapidly due to the proximity. Then my eyes landed on his lips which looked quite inviting but I tried to shook that thought off.

"Why are yo-" Zyon was cut off as I placed my lips on his, I don't know what came over me but I couldn't control myself anymore.

At first Zyon was shocked as his eyes widened but after a brief moment he gave in and started kissing me back. He cupped my thighs and lifted me as my legs automatically wrapped around his torso, he then pinned me to the wall as my hands moved towards his hair, messing them. I bit his lower lip as he opened his mouth, we both fought for dominance and atlast he gave up and I took the lead. After kissing the hell out of each other ,we pulled apart as we both rested our foreheads against each other, panting .

"Do you really want to leave me that desperately?" He asked as his lips moved down towards my neck.

Yes I do wanna leave him because my life is not in New York ,it's in Florida.

I wanted to tell him but I couldn't. A part of me didn't want to tell him because I didn't want to see him sad.

His lips did wonders to my skin as he slowly sucked my soft spot earning a moan from me. "Ashley, answer me" he demanded.

He kissed my cheeks one last time and slowly set me down on my feet. He gently cupped my chin, "Come on, answer me" he said looking into my eyes.

I couldn't answer him, so I just looked away as he sighed.

"I..I should go" I said not looking at him but before I could pass him he grabbed my wrist and pulled me towards him.

"Please sleep with me for tonight " he offered as my eyes bored into his. " please " He added as his eyes were pleading.

The offer itself was quite tempting and I, hundred percent sure couldn't resist it, so I just nodded.

"But first let me clean your wound " I said as he nodded. " where's the first aid kit?" I asked.

He pointed towards the bedside drawer and I marched towards the drawer and pulled the first aid kit out and made my way towards him.

He sat down on the bed and I seated myself beside him and started cleaning his wounds. I took a cotton dipped with antiseptic and dabbed it to his bruised knuckles to which a wince escaped his mouth. I mouthed a sorry and continued.

After cleaning his wounds I made my way towards my room to change myself in pajamas and went back to his room.

I saw him seated on his bed in his sweatpants and t-shirt,as his gaze fell on me, he patted the place beside him on the bed and I sauntered towards the bed and sat beside him.

"Am I permitted to sleep in this room only for tonight ?" I teased to which he smirked.

"Oh, you're always welcomed in this room and also in my arms, always" he opened his arms wide, I couldn't help but chuckle.

"Good night " I said as I laid down beside him.

"goodnight" he replied and kissed my forehead and tuned off the lights.

'Sorry Zyon, for hurting you '

Chapter 34

I was drying my wet hair with the hair dryer after which I combed my tangled hair neatly. I opened my closet and took a black jump suit,which Zyon bought me three days ago when we both went for shopping, actually me ,Zyon just accompanied me and helped me in selecting dresses. I removed my bathrobe and slid into the jump suit after which I did my light usual make-up.

After doing all the necessary things, I left my room and made my way towards the lounge.

It's been a week since I hurt Zyon by kissing that blonde. But things were going pretty well between us and I made a vow to myself that I would never in my life would listen to Steve.

I often slept with Zyon at night, cuddling with each other to sleep. Waking up in Zyon's arms is the best thing that has ever happened to me.

Am I falling for him?

No, it's just an attraction or infatuation.

And today Lily Rosington, Zyon's mom had asked me to come over to her mansion so that she could introduce me to some of her relatives. And I agreed.

"Are you sure, you wanna go there?" Zyon asked.

I nodded happily and to mention, this is the tenth time that Zyon is asking me. " Well I'm ashamed of myself for what I did in club. So I thought of dropping the deal and I don't consider that deal anymore.."

"Which deal?" He asked with furrowed brows.

" 'To piss you off' deal" I reminded him and continued "and you told me about the Hobson's contract, remember" he nodded " until your out of that contract, I'll help you by pretending to be your girlfriend"

"Actually..." He started.

"Yes?"

"Nothing"

"Is that Hobson's contract cancelled?" I asked with narrowed eyes.

"No...no, we are trying our best to cancel that contract" he said and I smiled.

"Okay, let's go" he nodded.

"And thanks" he said and I raised my brow " for helping me" he smiled.

"What are friends for" I winked.

"So we are back to friend zone" he asked and I just smiled.

....

I was sitting in the living room with Zyon's mom beside me and some other women who were their relatives.

" Which month is it, your pregnancy" the lady with blonde hair whom Zyon's mom introduced as Mrs Cole asked me with a smile.

I blinked for a while thinking, after which I said, "It's been two months since I became pregnant" I smiled.

My cheeks were hurting due to the continuous smile on my face.

"Oh come on Ashley, only two months, your so slim and you don't even have a baby bump" Mrs Cole said.

My body tensed up at her words but fortunately Lily, Zyon's mom came for the rescue, "Julia, she's just two months pregnant, some do get a slight baby bump but some don't" then she turned her attention to me and said " Ashley dear ,as I said earlier you're eating for two so do eat properly. Last time when I asked Zyon, he said you were good and getting fat but your too thin." I didn't say anything I just smiled and nodded.

"Sweetie" Mrs Cole started and I turned my attention to her " my daughter in law is also five months pregnant, she just stays a few blocks away from your building. She daily goes for a morning walk because it's very healthy for her and her baby" she smiled " but the problem is she's all alone ,my son stays in Texas due to his work and I was thinking.." suddenly her eyes were gleaming with hope as she continued" will you join her for the morning walk" she asked and I gulped.

I didn't know what to say so I just bobbed my head up and down.

"Thank you sweet Ashley, I'm so grateful. Can you please pass me your number, so that I can give it to Lucy and she can contact you in the morning and besides the morning walk is really good for your baby and you might soon get a baby bump" Mrs Cole rambled.

I gave her my number and she thanked me for that.

After a while, all the relatives left and now it was exactly six in the evening, when Zyon entered the house and greeted me.

"Hey sweetheart,how was your day" he asked and pecked my cheeks.

I acted like a lovey dovey girlfriend and replied, "Good" I smiled shyly as I pushed a loose strand of hair behind my ear.

"I think we should leave" Zyon announced.

"Have dinner and leave son" Lily said.

"No mom, actually Ashley wants to eat Italian food tonight,so we are going nice Italian restaurant"

When did I ask him to take me to a Italian restaurant,liar..

"Okay bye then, have fun" Lily waved her hand at us as we made our way outside.

As we were inside the car Zyon asked me about my day and I told him how I accepted Mrs Cole's offer and in reply he just chuckled.

After having dinner in one of the nicest restaurant, we were again off to his penthouse. As we reached home,the first thing I did was, going to my room,to have a nice bath. As I opened my closet, I gasped. " ZYON!! ZYON!!" I screamed at the top of my lungs.

Loud footsteps rushed towards my room, "What happened?" Zyon asked in panic.

"My clothes.. my clothes aren't here, they got robbed." I said as Zyon heaved a sigh of relief.

"I shifted your clothes to my room" he said

"What? Why?" I asked.

" You usually sleep in my room,so I thought.." he faltered.

"Okay okay,fine " I said and made my way towards his room.

I opened his closet and my clothes were neatly arranged. I opened the first drawer and saw my under wears also neatly arranged.

Wait,did he touch my under wears.?

" Who shifted my clothes to your room?" I asked.

"Actually I called a maid from my parents house,she shifted your clothes" he scratched the back of his neck and this time I sighed in relief.

I took one of my pajamas and made my way to his bathroom and washed all my day exhaustion away.

As I came out of the bathroom, I saw Zyon sitting on his bed typing something on his laptop and as his gaze fell on me ,he shut his laptop and I made my way towards his bed beside him as he switched off the lights and wrapped his one arm around me.

And slowly my eyelids felt heavy and soon sleep enveloped me.

Chapter 35

"Buzz! Buzz " I stirred and turned around in my sleep.

"Buzz! Buzz! " And that annoying sound rang again.

As I turned again, I felt someone beside me. "Zyon, Zyon! " I called still with closed eyes as I patted his hard chest.

"Hmm" he hummed.

"Shut your phone off " I said still with closed eyes.

"Huh?"he asked sleeply.

"I said shut your phone" I repeated with my hoarse voice.

"It isn't my phone baby, it's yours" he replied with his hot sleepy voice.

Baby?

"Who's ever it is just pick it up" I said.

My eyes were still closed but I could feel him sit and stretch his hand above me, near the nightstand and took my phone.

"It's a call from an unknown number" he informed.

"Tell that unknown number that Ashley is nowhere in sight" I said.

I guess he received the call, " Hello" he said. He was quite for a while as the other person on the line was speaking.

"Ashley!" He shook me " it's a call from Lucy Cole"

"Who, Lucy Cole?" I asked still with closed eyes.

"Who Lucy Cole?" He asked the person. Again he was silent and after a little while he called me. " She's saying she is Julia Cole's daughter in law"

"Who Julia Cole?" I asked as my eyes suddenly shot open as I recognised them. Lucy Cole as in daughter in law of Julia Cole. Julia Cole as in Mrs Cole.

I sat straight on the bed and took my phone from Zyon. "Hello"

"Hello,is this Ashley?" Lucy asked.

"Yeah it's me " my sleepy hoarse voice was now long gone.

"Mom told me that you would be accompanying me for the morning walk today onwards" she said and I internally groaned for accepting that offer.

"Yeah, I'm just on my way, where are you?" I asked.

"I'm standing outside your building"

"Just wait for few minutes, I'll be there" I said and disconnected the call.

I made my way towards the closet and removed one of my black hoodie for myself and one for Zyon.

I sauntered back to the room and saw Zyon cutely yawning and was about to lay down on the bed, when I tossed him his hoodie.

"Come on lazy ass, we're going for a morning walk" I said as he again sat up straight on the bed.

"But why me? She only invited you for a morning walk" he said rubbing his eyes with his calloused fingers.

"Look, if a girl is pregnant with your child,you don't say to that girl ,'that you're pregnant' instead you say ' we are pregnant' " I taught him some manners.

"But your not pregnant, right" he said yawning again.

"But I'm pretending this fake pregnancy just for you, right" I snapped. " And now just push this hoodie down your head and come " I said pointing to the hoodie.

He muttered something inaudible under his breath and got up, wearing the hoodie.

....

It was just quater to six when we made our way outside the building. " It's too cold" I was shivering even after wearing that hoodie.

"Yeah it is" Zyon said as he pulled me closer to him.

And walking further we spotted Lucy Cole. She was a blonde woman with a baby bump on her petite figure and she was wearing a gym outfit while I was in my pajamas beneath my hoodie.

"Good morning" she greeted.

"Morning" I greeted back.

"Let's go" she said as we both followed her.

Fifteen minutes later,

"Zyon I can't walk anymore" I was panting heavily while Zyon and Lucy were staring at me in disbelief.

Surely Lucy must be surprised, she was five months pregnant and walking fast without any tiredness and here I was, an unpregnant woman who can't even walk fast or worse, who can't even walk for few minutes.

"Ashley, come on we are just one metre away from our building" Zyon said gently rubbing my back.

I nodded and again started walking with a great difficulty.

As we reached our building, a huge smile was spread across my face as I walked for good half an hour. But Lucy usually walks for an hour but today seeing my state she just said that half an hour was enough.

After reaching our penthouse, my feet was wobbling, so as soon as I entered, I collapsed on the couch and heaved a contended sigh.

Zyon made his way towards the couch and raised my legs before sitting on the couch and placing my legs on his laps.

"My legs hurt" I groaned.

He slowly started massaging my legs with his hands and I slowly drifted off to sleep.

....

I was standing inside a huge hall all alone, when I felt someone kicking my stomach inwardly, I looked down to see a huge baby bump and suddenly a big gasp escaped my lips.

When did I become pregnant? Am I not a virgin anymore? Who is my child's father?

Fat sweat droplets were streaming down my forehead as I wiped them with my trembling palm.

Suddenly someone tapped my shoulders and I turned around to see a handsome man, who happens to be Zyon.

"How are you, baby?" He asked pinching my chubby cheeks.

"Is this your baby?" I asked with a horrified expression.

He just smiled and nodded.

"But how? When did we-" I was cut off as a sharp pain shot through my stomach and I felt wet between my thighs.

"My water broke" I said

" What?" He asked after which a loud scream escaped my lips.

"What happened Ashley?" This dumbass asked me again.

"The baby is about to come out" I said as again a pain shot through my abdomen. "Ahhh" I screamed.

"Are you having a labour pain? "

"Yes asshole yes" I cursed him in between my screams.

Suddenly my eyes shot open and the first thing I did was, check the couch to see, have I really peed on the couch and luckily I didn't.

I mean, in the dream I was feeling really wet in between my thighs and even the pain was feeling real.

Luckily it was just a stupid dream, I yawned and stretched my hands as my eyes shifted towards the wall clock, it was eleven in the morning. I looked around my surroundings and found a stick note on the coffee table, I took the note which read,

Good morning Ashley, I've prepared breakfast and it's on the microwave, do eat it and there are some boiled eggs and rice inside the refrigerator, have them as lunch and don't skip lunch, it's not good for our baby *wink*

I couldn't help but chuckle at his note, afterall Zyon is Zyon, he will never stop teasing me.

Chapter 36

"Oh my god! Oh my god" I was chanting as I was pacing back and forth in Zyon's room.

"Ahh" I winced as again a small pain shot through my abdomen.

I'm having my periods today and I just have a last peice of pad with me.

I thought I'm just gonna stay here for a week but I stayed for a month. I've been to mall thrice for shopping yet I didn't buy pads or tampons for myself.

How can I be so careless?

And now I have two options either call Zyon and ask him to bring me a pack of pads or I should go to the supermarket, which is just few steps away from this building.

I think the latter option is better.

I took my cardigan and my handbag as I marched towards the door and made my way outside.

After reaching the supermarket I bought myself a pack of pads as they were out of tampons.

As I reached out of the supermarket, I started walking towards my building. As I was walking on the busy street, I felt a pair of hands on my waist and in swift moment I was at the corner of the street and a man was infront of me wearing a black hoodie, his hair covered with the hood and his face was also covered with a black mask. The only thing which was visible to me was his eyes but sadly I couldn't see his eyes properly due to the darkness and panic.

It was evening and the sun was setting down.

The man's hand reached my neck and he started strangling me. Suddenly the adrenaline rushed through my veins and in an instant my hands reached his shoulders and I lifted my knees and kicked him hard on the place where sun doesn't shine. He took a few steps back, groaning in pain as his hand held his crotch.

I took it as my chance and ran for my life, I ran ,ran and ran until I reached my building. I was at loss of breath, the security gaurds of this building were staring at me weirdly. I ignored them and ran towards the elevator and still with my trembling hands I pressed the button to my floor.As the elevator dinged, I made my way towards the penthouse door and pressed the code after which the door opened revealing Zyon.

"Where were you?" He asked with a furrowed brows.

I couldn't talk, I was panting so hard.

"What happened to you?" He frowned.

Without answering him, I charged forward and collapsed on the couch. Zyon made his way towards me with a glass of water in his hands.

"Here, drink some water" he said and I took the glass and chugged the water down my throat.

"Now tell me what happened?" he demanded for my answer.

I was contemplating on whether to tell him about the attack or not. Last time when I was attacked, he was freaking out and I didn't want to tense him up.

I grinned, " Actually I have a good news "

"And what is that?"

" I got a call from Lucy, saying that she's going to stay with her in law's for a week, so that means we got a holiday from morning walk for a week,yay" I squealed as my insides were still trembling.

It's been a week, of us going to morning walk. I said Zyon not to accompany me as he has works to do in his office. Instead of accepting my offer, he refused saying that ' we are fake pregnant' saying this he comes along with me for the walk. And today afternoon Lucy called me, telling me that she wouldn't be accompanying me for a week. I was beyond happy but couldn't celebrate due to my stomach pain because of this damn periods.

"Just to tell me this good news, you ran from wherever you were to our house" I nodded and he shook his head in dismay. "By the way, where were you?" He asked.

"I went to the nearby supermarket to buy myself some things" I said and he nodded in understanding.

"Well even I have a news for you" Zyon said and seated himself beside me.

"Is it a good or bad news?" I asked.

"Well, you can decide it yourself, whether is it a good news or a bad news for you"

"Okay" I said pressing my lips together.

" Next week, my parents are throwing a grand party in one of the hotels as it is their wedding anniversary. Everybody will be present for the party, mainly the reporters and they also want to introduce you to the media as my girlfriend and tell them that, Carol and I broke up plus they even want to tell them that you're pregnant with my child" he completed and my face was blank. "If it is okay with you" he added.

"Is that Hobson's contract cancelled" I asked and for a brief moment he kept staring at me.

I waved my hands infront of him and he blinked, " No it's not yet cancelled but if you appear infront of the media as my girlfriend, it would be easy for us to cancel the contract as fast as possible."

I thought for a while, after which I said, " It's okay, tell the media that I am your girlfriend but don't tell them about the pregnancy thing"

He nodded.

....

Later at night I was in bed with Zyon sleeping beside me. I couldn't sleep due to the stomach cramps.

"Ahh" I winced as again I felt pain in my abdomen.

Zyon switched on the lights and turned towards me. " Is everything alright"

"Nothing is alright" I grumbled feeling the pain again.

"What happened?" He asked, worry lacing on his facial expression.

"I'm on my periods and my stomach pains like a bitch"

"Ohh.." he said sitting straight on his bed.

He took his phone from the nightstand, " What are you doing?" I asked.

"Calling my mom to ask for help" he said and I had the urge to knock some knowledge in him.

And I did give him knowledge but in a civil way, " When a woman is pregnant, she does not continue to ovulate and will not have periods. Menstruation only occurs when a woman is not pregnant"

"But your not pregnant" he smirked and I slapped my forehead.

"But for them, I am"

"So it means, we cannot call mom" he said and I nodded.

He tapped something on his phone and then got up from the bed and marched out of the room.

"Where are you going?" I asked but he didn't answer and just walked away.

After five minutes he entered the room with a heating pad.

"It will ease your pain" he said and handed me the heating pad.

I placed it on my stomach and it really soothed my pain.

After a while we were back sleeping, I kept the heating pad aside and Zyon turned off the lights as I was trying to sleep.

Suddenly Zyon's hand reached my tummy and he slowly started massaging it. I was enjoying his little massage until his hand slid inside my pajama top. As his calloused finger made a direct contact with my skin, a tingly sensation ran down my spine.

"What ar..e y..ou doi..ng?" I stuttered.

"Nothing, just giving you a little massage" he said as his hand was massaging my belly button area.

Well I was enjoying his skin to skin massage, so I didn't bother to reply and closed my eyes.

He kept on massaging my stomach like that until my eyes fluttered close.

Chapter 37

The week passed by and now I was getting ready for the grand party organized by the Rosington's. Zyon has already sent me a dress to wear for the party. The dress was beautiful and elegant, it was a nude colour floor length dress with a collar along with a long full sleeves. My skin was totally covered. But the thing is, the dress was beautiful, so no problem. Actually I do like wearing revealing dresses too.

After dressing, I applied a little bit of makeup after which I left my shoulder length dark brown hair open after straightening it.

I gave a one last look to myself through the mirror before exiting the room.

As I reached the lounge, my eyes met with Zyon who was wearing a black tuxedo and was looking devilishly handsome.

He extended his right hand out for me and I gladly took it. His hand perfectly fitted mine.

'Gosh! He is looking so soo handsome.'

As we reached the lobby of the building, I saw his white shiny car parked right outside the building. We made our way towards his car. The chauffeur, who was in driver seat drove us to our destination.

We reached the grand hotel, the Roosevelt's, where the grand party was organised. As we got out of the car, three bodyguards rushed towards us and were guiding us inside. We were making our way inside when different reporters popped up with different questions. Who is this woman? Is she your relative? Is she someone special Mr Rosington? Is she your one night stand or something? Blah,blah,blah....?

To which Zyon just replied,

We will introduce her to you'll later.

With great difficulty we entered inside the hotel. It was luxurious. The high ceilings to which a large golden colour sophisticated chandeliers were attached. It was exquisite, with all the golden tables on which there were beautiful red roses placed in a golden vase. Everything around me screamed richness, power and luxury.

Rebecca came towards us and greeted us with her warm beautiful smile. She was wearing a bottle green knee length dress and was looking gorgeous.

We three were standing and talking about our life, when Zyon excused himself and walked towards some other people to welcome them.

Rebecca also excused herself saying that she had to use restroom. I was all alone standing near the table sipping my apple juice.

I was sipping my juice and watching people around me, when Carol stood in front of me and I gulped.

Last time as I remembered, she cursed me and even tried to slap me. But this time she had a genuine smile plastered on her face.

"Hi" she smiled.

"Hi" I said back nervously.

" I am sorry for the last time.. " she hesitated and then smiled nervously " for my outburst, I'm really sorry, I shouldn't have cursed you aloud" by the look on her face, she was genuinely sorry " I .. I know Zyon loves you and I.. I... I'm sorry ,very sorry " she was flushed.

If she really loved Zyon then she shouldn't have slept around and especially with Liam.

" How is your pregnancy going on?" She asked.

"Huh?" I blinked and then I realised what she was asking "yeah, everything's fine, the baby is healthy" I said and I could also see a hint sadness in those beautiful grey orbs.

She excused herself and again I felt sad for her but she was also wrong, she shouldn't have cheated on him.

As I was busy thinking about Carol, I felt a hand on my shoulder and I jerked back and turned around to see who it was. It was Zyon who was smiling down at me.

"It's time for the announcement"he said.

I nodded and he placed his hand on my waist and guided me towards the stage.

"Ladies and gentleman" Thomas Rosington started and down the stage were all the reporters, who were clicking pictures and shooting videos. And on the stage were the

Rosington family, me, Carol and some others. " Today is a double happy day as today is our wedding anniversary" Thomas laced his fingers with Lily, who was standing beside him, " And also we are expecting our next heir for CTC" every guests eyes grew big including mine and everyone started murmuring.

Zyon laced his fingers with mine and charged forward, " People this is my girlfriend, Ashley Grayson" he said and murmurs got intense.

One of the reporters even asked, " Is she pregnant or Carol Hobson?"

Before Zyon could say anything, Carol butted in, " Ashley is pregnant, Zyon and I broke up a month ago,due to the incompatibility in our relationship ."

The reporters turned towards us and asked many questions like, When did you'll meet? When did you get pregnant? Blah blah blah?

I was quite nervous by being the centre of attention but with Zyon standing beside me gave me courage. But I did not answer to any of their questions, Zyon answered.

As Zyon and I excused the reporters, many other buisness men came towards Zyon to talk about business and I excused myself and made my way towards the small balcony at the corner of the hotel.

As I was standing there holding the railing and inhaling the fresh air, I felt a hand on my shoulder and I turned around to see who it was.

And it was none other than Liam wearing a black tux and grinning down at me. If I didn't know about the thing that he slept with his bestfriend's fiancé, I would have drooled seeing his handsome face but now as I know the truth, I wanna gag at his face.

"Hey, beautiful"

"Bye, Liam" I snapped and made my way towards the door.

"Whoa!" He held my forearm and stopped me " What happened ? Why are you so pissed?"

I pulled my forearm away from him and turned around to face him as anger swirled through me. "I can't believe"

"What you can't believe?" He asked as eyebrows dipped together.

" That you slept with your bestfriend's fiancé" I said and he was about to open his mouth but I cut him off, "Correction, ex-fiancé"

His eyes widened like saucers as he asked, "I WHAT!?!"

" Don't play stupid" I snapped, he's the main reason that I'm stuck here on the first place.

"Who said you that ?" He yelled.

"Nobody needs to tell me, I know you're a playboy" I shouted back.

"I agree I'm a playboy and slept with half the population of New York women but I disagree to this "

"To what?" I asked giving him a hard glare.

"That I slept with Carol Hobson"

"So you're telling me that you never banged Carol Hobson" I asked narrowing my eyes at him.

So did Zyon lie to me?

"No, I never slept with her" he gritted with determination. " Besides I agree I had a tiny crush on Carol but after what she did to Sienna made me hate her" he growled.

"Sienna?"I furrowed my brows

"Zyon didn't tell you about Sienna?" He asked.

'Act smart Ashley'

"Zyon did tell me about her and she twice visited our house also" I lied.

He narrowed his eyes for a moment and then said, "Miss Ashley Grayson, you know nothing about Sienna Maxwell" he stated and I looked down by being caught.

"Okay I don't know anything about Sienna" I confessed still looking at the floor and then took a deep breath and met his eyes before asking, " Is the Hobson's contract cancelled?" I asked as I wanted him to say no.

"Yes it's cancelled the day after Zyon announced you as his girlfriend and the mother of his unborn child" he said and I felt like a bucket of cold water was splashed on my face.

Another lie..

I pushed past him and exited the balcony, I heard Liam call after me but I didn't bother to turn back. I kept on walking, I pushed past the crowd of people when I heard Lily Rosington talking to her friends about Carol and that confirmed that Liam was telling the truth.

Zyon lied to me, everytime he lied to me. First with the amnesia,then taking my ID by lying to me ,then lying to everyone by telling them that I'm his girlfriend and pregnant, then that Carol cheated on him with his bestfriend, then about the contract and now who the hell is Sienna Maxwell? Everything about him is a lie. I hate him.

I don't know when I reached outside the hotel but I kept on walking. Tears were threatening to fall from my eyes but I controlled my tears. I kept on walking until I bumped into someone, when I looked up to see who it was, my face paled by looking at the person.

"Hello gorgeous, remember me" he asked with an annoying smirk.

' oh oh! I wasn't expecting to see him again'

Chapter 38

"What are you doing here?" I snapped.

"Oh! So you do remember me" he said still with that smirk. I wanted to wipe that smirk off of his face.

"Yes! Happy that I remember you" I snapped sarcastically.

"Well, you remember me it means, you also remember our half kiss in the club"

Anger swirled through me, " What do you want Mr blonde"

He took a step forward and leaned down to my ear, " I want you"

I pushed him but he didn't move. " What do you mean? and what about your girlfriend, huh?" I shouted.

"I mean, I want to complete that half kiss and I even want something more" he licked his bottom lip and I felt disgusted, " And about my girlfriend, she broke up with me because of you"

"Because of me!!?" I snarled.

"Yes, your the one, who initiated the kiss"

"And your the one who offered me the free drink" I snapped back. "And you even lied to me saying that you don't have any girlfriend."

"Despite of having a boyfriend,you kissed me right and the price I paid was too many punches on my face" he growled.

"We're equal, my boyfriend punched you and in return your ex-girlfriend slapped me" I pointed out.

Without any words exchanged further, he placed his hand on my waist and pulled me towards him harshly and was about to kiss me, when I was pulled away from him by someone.

It was Zyon with clenched jaw and suddenly his fist collided with that club guy's jaw. "How dare you even come near her and touch her" he growled.

Seeing Zyon's face made me mad as I remembered all his lies.

"Why are you punching him?" I shouted at his back.

He turned around with a scowl on his face, "What?"

"Who are you to punch him, huh? He was here for me and I can deal with him" I glared.

He charged forward and deeply looked into my eyes, "Your pissed because my father told the media about the pregnancy" he said still looking deeply into my eyes.

Before I could say anything, the club guy butted in, " YOUR PREGNANT!!!" he screeched.

We didn't bother to answer him as we were busy staring at each other's eyes, well I was glaring at him.

The club guy again started, "Such a whore you are, having a boyfriend and being pregnant with his child, yet you go kissing around different men, what a slut" he turned towards Zyon "dude I don't think she's carrying your baby, god knows whose baby this bitch is carrying, bit-" before he could continue, in a swift Zyon turned around and started punching him.

"How dare you call her a whore, slut and bitch" Zyon growled in between his punches.

The club guy was now on the floor and Zyon was kicking him hard on his stomach. He was groaning in pain but Zyon didn't stop neither I stopped him because I was infuriating.

Suddenly there were camera flashes and I turned to see all the reporters clicking pictures of Zyon punching the guy. Even Zyon saw them as he left the club guy whose face was covered with blood and bruises. He held my arm and exited the place.

....

As we reached his penthouse, he opened the door to his penthouse and I sauntered in, the whole car drive was silent, we both didn't utter a word.

"Ashley listen, I did tell my father not to tell the paparazzi about the pregnancy but he just blurted it out" he said in a pleading tone and I turned to him and let out a humourless chuckle.

"Seriously Zyon, do you really think that the pregnancy announcement pissed me" I again let out a humourless chuckle and his face was blank. "Your lies are pissing me Mr Rosington" I snarled.

"What?" He wrinkled his nose in confusion.

" how many times are you gonna lie to me,huh?"

"What are you talking about?"

"I am talking about you lies, liar" I shouted. "First, you lied me about having amnesia,then you took my ID by lying to me, then lied to everyone telling them I'm pregnant and your girlfriend, then you lied to me about the contract and you lied to me that your ex-fiancè cheated on you with your bestfriend" I shouted my lungs out and by now I was panting but I didn't stop, I continued, "Like seriously.." I scrunched my nose in disgust "...how could you stoop so low, Carol was solely in love with you and yet you hate her for nothing, I can't understand, she was nothing but nice to you yet you accused her of being a characterless woman. You know the Hobson's contract was cancelled the day after you announced me as your girlfriend and pregnant. How was it even possible to cancel the hard Hobson contract within a day, the reason behind it was Carol. She thought your happiness is with me,so she let her happiness drown. She let you go because she thought you love me and you're happy with me and she let her heart break into million pieces. She didn't want this fake baby..." I said pointing to my stomach "...to be raised by a single parent, so she let you go Mr Rosington. She let go of the contract along with you. In your eyes she might be a characterless bitch but in my eyes she's a great beautiful goddess in disguise" I said as I remembered Lily Rosington talking to her friends about the contract and Carol.

"You do-" Zyon started but I cut him off

" And who the hell is this Sienna Maxwell" his eyes grew wide for a moment and he was about to open his mouth but I beat him in that. "Why I am even asking you? You'll cook another story for me by stuffing all your stupid lies in it" I said and took a step away from him, when he grasped my forearm, I pulled my forearm, "DON'T TOUCH ME" I gritted " I hate you, I hate your lies, I hate everything about you Mr Rosington" I said with a pure hate in my voice and ran towards my room. I heard footsteps behind me but I didn't dare to turn. As I reached my room I turned to shut the door and saw Zyon standing at the threshold with his eyes welled up but I ignored him and shut the door on his face.

After locking the door, I sat on the floor with my back against the door. The tears I was holding back flowed down my cheeks.

I don't know why does it hurt so much.

Why does his lies hurt me so much?

'I don't know'

Chapter 39

"Tring! Tring" I stirred and winced due to the back ache because of sleeping on the floor, I got up from the floor and walked towards the night stand to pick my phone and again while walking I winced.

' ouch'

I picked my phone which was currently ringing and without checking the caller ID, I answered.

" Hello?" I said in my usual sleepy voice.

"YOUR PREGNANT, ASHLEY!!" The person on the other side screamed and I had to remove my phone from my ear and my once sleepy eyes turned big as I recognised the person on the other side.

"ASHLEY!!" Mom was still screaming.

I again placed my phone to my ear, "Yes, mom"

"ARE YOU REALLY PREGNANT?!!"

"Mom will you just stop screaming, my ears are hurting" I snapped.

"Are you serious, your pregnant and you didn't tell us about it, your dad is very disappointed in you" she snapped back.

"Mom, I really don't have any energy left in me to explain it to you'll, I'll explain everything to you later."

"Why not now?" She was annoyed to the core.

"Because I have bigger issues to solve mom"

"Ashley, I need you and your boyfriend to visit us " she paused for a while and then asked " where are you?"

I didn't reply

" Are you still in New York?"

"Hmm" I hummed.

"I need you and your boyfriend to meet us as soon as possible,is that clear" I hummed again.

"And why the hell your boyfriend is punc-" I disconnected the call as I was too stressed to answer all her question. I'll message her later saying that my phone died due to that the call disconnected.

I switched off my phone because I knew that I'm gonna get a dozens of call today.

I made my way towards the bathroom and freshened after which I took long soothing bath.

After the bath I wrapped myself with the towel and went towards my closet. I chose a yellow sundress to wear and after wearing it, I slightly combed my hair and reached the door of my room and threw it open revealing a messy looking Zyon.

He was still wearing yesterday's tux but the coat was off, his hair was fully disheveled and eyes were blood shot.

'Was he outside my door all night?'

Without acknowledging his presence I passed him but before I could take one more step,he caught my forearm,

" Please Ashley, just listen to me once, I'll explain everything to you, please and I promise I won't lie to you ever again" he was desperate.

I glanced at him and inhaled sharply, " Fine, but please do tell me the truth"

He nodded and we both made our way towards the lounge. I sat on the couch and he sat across me.

"Sienna and I me-" before he could say any further, there was a constant ringing of bell and we jerked our head towards the main door.

"Who could it be, whose ringing the bell like a maniac" I commented.

Zyon stood up to check but I stopped him as he was not presentable so I got up from the couch and made my way towards the door.

I opened the door revealing a very pissed off Thomas Rosington whose jaw was clenched .

" Is Zyon inside?" He asked in his authoritative tone, he was quite intimidating today.

I nodded and moved aside so that he could come in.

"ZYON!! ZYON!!" I flinched as he shouted Zyon's name as he sauntered in.

I followed him and Zyon also came rushing towards his dad,

"What happened dad?" Zyon asked.

"What happened to you?" Thomas asked looking at his disheveled manner.

"It's...uh.." before Zyon could find any excuse, Thomas threw the newspaper which was in his hands at Zyon's face, to which Zyon flinched but somehow caught it.

"Read the headlines aloud Zyon" Thomas commanded.

Zyon's jaw clenched by reading that newspaper,

"Read aloud, Zyon" Thomas demanded, giving Zyon a deathly glare.

Zyon threw the newspaper on the floor, " It's not true, he is not innocent" he shouted giving an equally deathly glare to his father.

They both were busy glaring at eachother when I took a glimpse of the newspaper, lying on the floor. The headlines were,

'The current CEO of CTC company Zyon Rosington, was seen punching and kicking an innocent guy right outside the grand hotel,' the Roosevelt's' , Is this what the Rosington's are taught,? beating an innocent'

My eyes widened as I saw the picture of Zyon kicking the club guy and beside it, was the picture of the club guy with blood all over his face.

"Why did you punch and kick that guy to death?" Thomas asked still glaring at Zyon.

"It's none of your business" Zyon said nonchalantly.

And then in an instant, Thomas raised his hand and gave a hard slap to Zyon. Zyon's head snapped the otherside and I gasped, my hands covering my mouth.

His face was still tilted to the other side as his right cheek had turned red due to the hard slap and his body was shaking with rage as he balled his fist.

"Where are your manners Zyon?" Thomas snarled.

Zyon didn't utter a word and the next moment, he just walked towards the the stairs and ascended upstairs.

"Zyon! Get back here" Thomas shouted behind him but Zyon just kept walking without casting Thomas a single glance.

I just stared at his retreating figure until it vanished and then I turned my attention back to Thomas.

He sighed defeatedly before saying, " Zyon was never like this, he never got into fights, neither in school nor in college. Do you know why he beat that Peter guy to death?" He asked and I gulped. Sweat droplets formed on my forehead and slightly shook my head in no.

I lied.

He nodded and said, " Please make him understand,he loves you and he might listen to you, this is not good for his reputation" he pointed towards the newspaper.

I nodded and he gave me a small smile and left.

A wave of guilt washed over me as I again saw the newspaper. Everything was because of me. I was the one who kissed that club guy and I was the one he was searching for. But it ended up ruining Zyon's reputation.

Even I lied to Thomas Rosington because I couldn't say that I was the cause for everything. Maybe even Zyon lied to me for a reason. He was going to tell me the truth but my outburst stopped him from telling me the truth.

Another wave of guilt washed over me for the way I treated Zyon last night.

' well, I'm guilty.'

Chapter 40

It's total of three days since I last saw Zyon. After that morning when Thomas came and slapped Zyon neither I spoke to him nor did he spoke to me. I don't know who's avoiding whom.

Whenever I remember the slap that Zyon got, my eyes instantly wells up and my chest tightens in agony. I feel the mixture of guilt,pain, regret and all. It hurts so much ,that I was the cause for everything, specially for ruining Zyon's image.

I hate myself for what I did, for kissing that guy and then my stupid outburst.

I want to talk to him but whenever I try to dial his number,my hands tremble followed by a tight knot in my chest. I miss him, his comments, his cockiness, our bickerings, his hand around me, I miss everything about him. Without seeing him for three days is making me miserable, how am I gonna live in Florida without him beside me.

I don't know.

My phone dinged and I saw another comment but not on me, this comment was different,

'How could Carol just break her alliance with such a hot billionaire' it was a comment by a person,whose a fan of Carol.

From the last three days this was also a breaking news, Zyon and Carol's break up. However the club guy's case was concealed by Thomas. As Carol is a public figure with lots of follower on her social media, most of her fans cursed me by calling me whore, bitch, slut who seduced Zyon and snatched him away from Carol. But recently Carol has just posted that she was the one who broke up with Zyon because of their incompatibility, she also said to not interfere in mine and Zyon's relationship, it was her decision to break their alliance not Zyon's. She also requested her fans not to post any rude comments on me.

Most of her fans stopped cursing me but there were still some, who were commenting on my character.

Steve and Chase also called me to check on me but I didn't receive their calls, but just left a message saying that I was fine.

I checked the time and it was eleven in the morning, Zyon might have already left for office and I was really hungry. So I slowly opened the door and descended downstairs.

As I was making my way towards the kitchen, I stopped in my tracks as I saw a tall figure standing in the lounge near the huge glass window, his back facing me.

Again my eyes moistured, my chest tightened and there was an indescribable pain in there.

I slowly turned around towards the stairs and took a step when I heard him,

" Where are you going?" I slowly turned around to face him.

He was still standing near the glass window, facing me. Sweat droplets appeared on my forehead and my chest was heaving up and down.

"I... I..uh.." I stuttered and stopped as I saw him walking towards me.

He just stopped a few steps away from me and looked deeply into my eyes, I instantly lowered my gaze to the floor as my eyes again welled up seeing Zyon.

He gently cupped my chin and raised my head,so now I was directly staring into those beautiful green eyes.

"Why are you avoiding me? " He asked.

I swallowed the huge lump that was formed on my throat and shook my head in no as I couldn't speak.

"Are you still angry with me?" He asked and instantly all the tears which I was holding back streamed down my cheeks.

"Shhh, why are you crying?" He instantly pulled me in for a hug and I also hugged him back.

"I'm sorry" I whispered in between my hiccups as my tears were wetting his grey hoodie.

"Shhh,why are you apologizing, I'm the one who should apologise" he said still rubbing my back in a soothing way.

I cried and cried in his arms holding him tightly. I didn't want to let him go but however I pulled back and rubbed my eyes.

"Why haven't you still left for office?" I asked as he slowly stroked my cheeks.

"It's Saturday today" he answered still stroking my cheeks.

He took my hand in his and led me to the couch and I sat on it with him beside me. It felt great with him beside me.

"Were you avoiding me? " I asked as my eyes were fixed on my lap.

"No" he answered and I looked up at him.

"Then why didn't you come and talk to me?"

"I thought you needed some alone time as you were very sad and upon that those comments.." he faltered and I nodded in understanding.

I have to do this, I know I lo.., I like him but it's just an attraction and I'll forget him as soon as I reach Florida, I can't stay here, my life is in Florida. I have to do this. I want my normal life back because I can't bare this pain anymore.

I took a deep breath and braced myself, "Zyon!" I called.

"Yes" As my eyes met his green ones, instantly my eyes welled up and then unstoppable tears came streaming down my cheeks. "What happened?" He asked with a worry filled eyes.

"I..I.. I want to leave" I sobbed.

"What?"

I couldn't see his eyes anymore,so I hugged him tightly. " I want to go back to Florida, please Zyon I can't stay here, I want my normal life back, I beg you Zyon, please" I cried.

"But-" I pulled back and cut him off.

" Please Zyon, I want to go." I cupped his cheek and a layer of moisture coated his beautiful green eyes.

Without saying anything he stood and walked towards the staircase and ascended upstairs.

I sighed and wiped my tears, I knew he would never let me go. After ten minutes he returned and handed me my ID and I saw his face, his eyes were red, cheeks were flushed and nose puffed.

He was crying..

"I'll come along with you, to leave you. Please." he pleaded.

"No, I'll go by myself" he just stared at me for a while and then nodded and walked off.

' this is the end of our journey, goodbye Zyon'

Chapter 41

Zyon's Pov :

It's been two days since Ashley is gone and my home feels like a hell without her. I go home late at night and wake up early in the morning and leave that haunted house. This is my routine since two days. The home doesn't feel like home anymore without her.

I love her and I recognised it when we parted our ways in the airport. I knew I was falling for her when she was with me ,here in New York, but I didn't take it seriously, I thought it was just an infatuation. But now I can't live a single minute without thinking about her.

The door to my cabin opened revealing Liam,

"Zyon, where's Ashley?" He asked with worry.

"She left" I blurted out.

"What do you mean left?" He asked.

"Left means left" I yelled out of frustration.

"And you let her go?" He asked but I didn't reply. "Damn it, why didn't you tell her about Sienna?"

My eyes widened as realisation dawned on me, "You told her about Sienna,the contract and about.." I faltered as my next lie was about him and Carol.

He raised a brow, " About?"

"Nothing, about Sienna and the contract"

"Yeah, I told her, I know it's not my place to tell her but it just came out"

"What did you tell her about Sienna?"I asked.

"Nothing, I just told her the name and she asked further but I didn't tell her" he said. "did you tell Ashley that I banged Carol" he narrowed his eyes into a glare as his nostrils flared.

"What? You had a huge crush on her" I stated.

"That was before when I knew what she did to Sienna" he glared. "And why would you say that to her?" He asked.

"Because she was feeling guilty thinking that she and I both together cheated on her, so I said that, she was the one who cheated on me first" I lied.

He just shook his head in dismay, " But why didn't you tell her about Sienna?"

"Because I didn't want to"

"Are you serious, you banged her and then you put your baby inside her and then you hide things to her" my jaw clenched listening to him. "She deserves to know the truth" he stated firmly.

"I know she deserves to know the truth and I am going to tell her the truth" I said and stood up to leave.

"Where are you going?" I heard him call after me.

"Away from you" I spat and left the cabin.

It was evening and I was inside my car sitting silently, thinking about Ashley. Is she also missing me or is it just me? Why would she miss a liar like me, she might be happy in Florida with her friends and her normal simple life without any complications. If she's happy then I'm happy for her.

What if she gets a boyfriend and forget about me, The thought just caused an uneasy feeling in the pit of my stomach.

Suddenly my phone rang and my head snapped here and there insearch of my phone. I took the phone and checked the caller ID and groaned internally.

"Hello" I said in an disinterested tone.

"Hello son" dad's saccharine voice reached my ears.

After that day I never spoke to him.

"How are you?" He asked

"Fine" I replied dryly.

"I'm sorry son, I shouldn't have raised my hand at you" he said and I felt a pang of guilt inside me.

I heaved a sigh, " I'm sorry too dad, for disrespecting you"

"It's okay son, it happens" he said and a faint smile appeared on my face.

After a small talk about business, I disconnected the call and again my mind diverted to Ashley. God, I'm driving crazy.

A lone tear made its way from my eye down to my cheek. I miss her.

'I love you, Ashley'

Is it too late to tell her that I am in love with her. As the Seconds passed by more tears flowed down my cheek. I couldn't control it anymore.

To calm myself I drove the car to the park which was located near my parents old mansion.

After twenty minutes I reached there, tucking my phone inside my pants pocket, I got out of the car and made my way towards the park entrance, as I was inside the park, I sat on the far away bench were people were not around.

This place has many memories, specially Rebecca's and mine. This is Rebecca's favourite place in the whole planet, she says that this place is the most luckiest place for her and this place also calms her, she often comes here and plays violin for peace of mind.

I closed my eyes and took a deep breath to calm my nerves when suddenly my disturbing phone rang, cursing under my breath I took my phone out and suddenly my heart skipped a beat and a huge smile appeared on my lips.

Because the call was from Ashley.

'This place is indeed a luckiest place'

Chapter 42

"Come on Ashley, get up from the bed, you can't just hide in your damn blanket" Chase yelled and Steve started pulling my blanket off me.

"Shoo, go away you two" I growled

"It's been two days you left New York and look at you, from yesterday your wrapped around your blanket." Chase sighed.

"Ashley get up or I'm gonna throw a bucket of cold water on you" Steve threatened.

"Shut up what's with you guys-" I was cut off as both Steve and Chase carried me in bridal style, I was in between both.

"AHHHHHHH!!" I screamed.

"My ears Ashley" Steve snapped. " And what's that smell" he sniffed "ew you stink so bad" Steve gagged.

"Put me down" I wiggled.

"Chase I can't carry her, I'm gonna puke now due to the smell"

"Just carry her until we reach the couch" Chase said.

And as soon as we reached the couch, Steve and Chase both threw me on the couch. A certain memory flashed inside my head as they threw me.

Chase sat at the coffee table infront of the couch and Steve pulled a chair from dining area.

"I would have sat beside you but you stink really bad. When did you last take a shower?" Steve asked making a disgusted face.

"None of your concern" I muttered.

"Ashley, what happened to you? Your not the same Ashley who used to be with us. You've changed alot in two months" Chase was staring at me with worry filled eyes.

As he said I realised that I've stayed with Zyon for two months. And I kind of miss him. How is he? Is he sad? Or is he happy?

I don't know..

But why am I missing him. Suddenly Steve clapped his both hands and I flinched.

"What were you thinking?" Chase asked.

"I.. I-" I was cut off by Steve.

"She's busy thinking about Zyon"

"No, I.. I was thinking about the girl Sienna, who she can possibly be?" I said in confusion.

"Might be his old girlfriend" as Chase said that I felt a pang of jealousy inside me.

"Nah, I don't think so,he said to Ashely that he never had a girlfriend before"

"What if he lied to her" Chase gritted.

"Why would he lie about that?" Steve snapped.

"I don't know" Chase snapped back.

"Stop both of you,just...just drop the topic" I pleaded as they both nodded.

"So let's talk about your job in SDC" Chase chirped to lighten my sour mood. Unfortunately my mood was still sour. Even SDC name couldn't bring happiness to me.

As Zyon promised, the SDC company is willing to give me a job without any interview and they have asked me to join on Friday.

"The SDC company has asked me to join on Friday" I said dryly as they both just hummed and shook their head in dismay.

....

It was eight in the evening and I was sitting in my living room, hugging my knees. I don't know why but I feel sad, I feel like a huge part of me is missing. As if I left a part of me in New york. I can't help but feel sad.

Chase has already left saying that Clara was calling him and Steve was still here checking on me, saying that if he left me alone in here, I would end up committing suicide.

Like seriously..

Steve was nowhere around, so I got up from the floor and made my way towards my room to check on him, there was a pin drop silence and that tensed me because Steve was a loud guy.

As I reached my room, I opened my room door and saw that Steve was standing near my bed with my phone in his hand.

My both friends knew my password, so he easily unlocked my phone.

"What are you doing with my phone?" I raised a brow.

"I.. I was just scrolling through your contact list to find any girl's number but there are none. But as I was scrolling down my eyes caught this" he said and handed me my phone.

What caught his interest was, Zyon's name with two red hearts. As I remembered how he took my phone and saved his number and name. A faint smile appeared on my lips as I thought about Zyon.

"So you love him" I heard Steve's voice.

Do I??

"I do like him,but love I don't know" I shrugged.

"Ashley" he called and made me sit on my bed and then sat beside me. " Do you consider me as your big brother" I don't know why was he being all emotional today but somehow I nodded. " Then take a piece of advice from me" he paused then took a deep breath before saying. "If you love Zyon, admit it and don't push him away. I don't want you to regret later that you couldn't confess your feelings to him."

"It's of no use Steve,we are incompatible, look my name starts from letter A while his name starts from letter Z, see so much of difference." I gave him a stupidest reason and in return he gave me a look that said 'are you crazy'

" Seriously Ashley, it's a letter gap not an age gap that your reasoning about" he said.

"Okay fine I love him.." I blurted out without thinking and at that Steve smiled "but what about my life, my dreams, they are in Florida along with my family and friends and long distance relationship is not my thing" I growled.

"Who said that you can't live your life and fulfill your dreams in New York,huh? And about family and friends, you can keep coming to Florida once in a week to visit us and your parents" he said calmly and I couldn't talk further, so he continued. " You love him Ashley, you love him" he said and left my room.

Is Zyon ,the huge missing part of me?

Later, at night I was sitting on the couch staring at the wall, blankly. Steve left saying that I should talk to Zyon but I didn't have that courage to do so.

Do I really love Zyon??

As I was thinking about him suddenly I heard the sound of the doorknob turning and I instantly snapped my head towards the main door. I stood up and slowly took a step towards the door and when the door flew open, I gasped on seeing the person standing at the threshold.

Because the person was none other than Zyon.

Chapter 43

Zyon made his way inside and walked towards me until we were just inches apart. " Zyo-" I was cut off as Zyon placed his lips on mine.

I missed him, I missed everything about him, his touches,his kisses and all his annoying things and now I knew one thing for sure that I love him, as I saw him near the door I can't describe how happy I was, I felt like a huge missing part of mine was fixed. A sole tear rolled down my cheek and then one by one kept flowing down my cheeks. I was happy seeing him here.

Zyon suddenly pulled back and I internally groaned. "I'm sorry, when I just saw you I couldn't control myself, shit.. I should have asked you before kissing you, please stop crying" he said as he wiped my tears.

It's happy tears you fool, now kiss me..

"Ashley I'm so sorry, please stop cryi-" before he could say any other word, I grabbed his collar and pulled him towards me, kissing him fiercely.

He smiled between the kiss and then circled his one hand around my waist as his another hand moved towards the nape of my neck, tilting my neck upward to deepen the kiss. He kissed me in heart clenching pashion as his tounge slid inside my mouth devouring every nook and corner of it. I moaned in the kiss as hundreds of tiny butterflies erupted in my tummy.

We kissed and kissed for what felt like hours and then pulled back as he rested his forehead against mine.

It feels so good to have him here with me. And the kiss was mind-blowing. God, I missed him so much.

"I love you" Zyon said startling me. I abruptly took a few steps back and stared at those beautiful eyes, to check any sign of joke but those eyes were geniune. " I know you don't feel the same about me, as in your eyes I'm just a liar, who kept on lying to you. But I wanted you to know that I love you. I wi-" I didn't allow him to complete his long speech as I cupped his cheeks and again kissed and in no time he kissed me back. I took his lower lip between my teeth. This time I was the dominant one. I kissed him harder than the previous one and then pulled back as I was out of breath.

He touched his lips and then asked me, " What does that kiss means?"

I couldn't control myself anymore as he just confessed me about his feelings.

"That kiss means.." I paused.

"That kiss means?" He repeated it as a question.

"It means that.."

"That?" He again repeated.

"That, I love you too"

"You love me too?" He blinked twice in confusion and took in all the the words that I've said. As realisation dawned on him, his eyes widened and a huge grin broke out of his lips as he carried me and swirled me around.

"ZYON!!"

" You love me too, Ashley. I think I'm the happiest man alive in the world." He squealed as he slowly set me down on the floor. "Do you really love me? Please say those magical words to me once"

I chuckled, "I LOVE YOU ZYON" I said emphasizing each word.

"I love you so much, I love you too sweetheart" he pecked my lips.

....

I came out of the bathroom, Zyon was already on the bed waiting for me, I slowly made my way towards him and sat beside him,then took my moisturizer and started rubbing the moisturizer on my face. "You came here just to tell ,that you love me" I asked as I was massaging my nose with the moisturizer.

"Yeah, that's one reason and another reason is that Steve called me from your number and told me how miserable you were" he chuckled "and you know I can't see you miserable because I love you" I smiled and applied the remaining cream to his face and massaged it.

"Your skin is so dry, you should apply some, daily at night" I remarked.

"It feels so good " he sighed and rested his head on the headboard as I massaged his chin which was covered by a slight stubble. I was now on a lovey dovey mood, so...

My fingers went further down towards his neck and then towards the buttons of his shirt and he stilled. I unbuttoned the top three buttons of his shirt and touched his hard bare chest. He slightly relaxed but again stilled as my hands were replaced by my lips, I started kissing his chest and then moved upward towards his neck, I sucked his hard skin earning a groan from him, I pulled the collar of the shirt to a side and kissed his collar bone. Zyon's hand automatically rested on my hips and he pulled me closer towards him and leaned towards my ear and grazed my earlobe to which a shiver ran down my spine.

"I want to tell you the truth" he whispered to my ear as I stopped and pulled back ,then looked at him in confusion. "Everything, even about Sienna"

If it wasn't for the truth, I would have been pissed off at him for ruining the moment, but even I needed to know the truth,about who Sienna is, so I sat straight across him, waiting for him to tell me everything. I held my breath as he opened his mouth.

Chapter 44

Zyon's Pov:

2 years ago....

I was tapping my foot on the marbled floor impatiently waiting for Liam, when I felt a tap on my right shoulder. I turned around expecting to see Liam but it was Carol, with a ear to ear grin plastered on her face. "Happy Birthday!" I wished her.

She bit her bottom lips before replying, " Thank you"

Today was Carol's 24th birthday and her father Louis Hobson had thrown a grand party on their house. Liam and I were invited by Louis Hobson as we were an investor to their company.

"Thanks for coming" Carol blushed.

I don't know why she makes it so obvious that she has a crush on me. And on the other hand my bestfriend Liam has a huge crush on her. It's a kind of love triangle. But I don't feel the same about her. I mean she's gorgeous with those grey eyes and blonde hair but also I don't feel anything towards her. She's a famous model and half the country know about her. I must say, she achieved success at a very young age.

"HAPPY BIRTHDAY!!" Liam's voice boomed as he approached us and gave Carol a charming smile along with a red rose bouquet.

"Thanks" Carol took the bouquet from him with a small smile.

Liam's eyes were fixed on Carol and Carol's eyes were fixed on me. I felt like a third wheel, so I excused myself. I was walking in a hurry and suddenly bumped into someone.

"Ow!!" The girl groaned as the papers in her hand flew everywhere.

"I'm sorry" "I'm sorry" We both said simultaneously.

The girl bent down to collect her papers and even I crouched down to help her. I took a glance at the paper and it was greeting card which had Carol's name on it. I collected some and stood up.

The girl had some cards on her hand and I handed her cards which I picked, she raised her head and that's when I saw her face properly. She was a short girl with blonde hair and an ocean blue eyes.

"Thank you..." She raised a brow with a smile.

"Zyon.. Zyon Rosington" as I said my name,her eyes widened for a brief moment.

"Thank you Zyon" she smiled and was about to move away.

"And you?" I asked instantly.

"Sienna Maxwell, I'm Carol's bestfriend" " And your Caro l's.." she raised her brow mischievously.

"No, I was invited by Mr Hobson" I said and her round plump lips formed into an O.

"Sienna!!" Someone called and we both tilted our heads to the direction of the source.

Carol made her way towards Sienna, "I'm so sorry for being late, Carol." She apologized "and here, these our the cards from your fans" she handed her the bundle of cards.

I moved away from them and made my way towards Liam, who was still staring at Carol in awe,

"Isn't she looking hot in that hot pink dress" Liam said still staring at Carol.

I averted my gaze and fixed my eyes on the girl beside Carol, who was wearing a neavy Blue knee length dress and was looking beautiful.

"Hmm" I hummed.

....

"Rebecca I'm waiting, where are you?" I was outside the mall waiting for Rebecca, who went for a shopping today.

"Just gimme fifteen more minutes Zyon, I'm coming" I sighed frustratedly and said okay as leaned down on my seat before closing my eyes.

Somebody knocked on my window and I opened my eyes and saw Sienna on my window. I rolled the car window down.

"Hi" she chirped.

"Hi" I smiled.

"Waiting for someone?"

"Yeah, my sister"

"Oh! Wanna grab some coffee from Starbucks"

"Sure" I said and got out of the car.

She ordered herself a almond milk Latte and I ordered an espresso for myself. We took our seats near the window.

"So.." she started " you know Carol signed a new contract with those famous make up company for modelling, I'm so happy for her" she squealed and I nodded. "Carol is such a nice girl.." she kept on talking about Carol.

I knew she was trying to play a cupid here. I coughed continuously to get her attention and guess what, I got her attention.

"Are you alright?" She asked as worry lines appeared on her forehead.

"Yeah" I grinned. "Tell me about yourself"

"About me?" She said in a low voice.

"Yes, about you"

"Well, there's nothing about me, I'm just a simple girl who runs a bakery and loves to bake"

"You bake?"

"Ye..yes, my bakery is just few blocks away from here."

"I'm surely gonna visit your bakery and have a taste of you"

"Huh?"

"I mean taste of your cookies, because I love cookies"

"Sure" she grinned.

Suddenly my phone started ringing and without checking the caller ID, I recieved my phone, "Hel-"

"WHERE ARE YOU?" Rebecca's voice boomed.

"I'm i-"

"Your car is parked here but your nowhere in sight"

"I'm coming" I disconnected the call and stood up to leave.

"I should go now" I said in an apologetic tone.

"Yeah, I understand" I left the Starbucks and made my way towards Rebecca.

....

I don't know why I like seeing Sienna, after our last visit in Starbucks, I went to her bakery often to have a heavenly taste of her cookies. We got even closer as the time passed by. Sometimes we used to bake together and laugh, spending time with her was the most happiest thing for me in the world. And today again I'm going to visit her bakery.

As I reached her bakery and was about to open the glass door, I saw another figure inside the bakery, I moved aside from the door as I recognised the person. It was Carol, who was talking to Sienna,more like shouting. I couldn't hear about their conversation but Carol looked furious. Carol shoved her phone to Sienna and shouted again to which Sienna answered something. Carol raised her hand to slap her but stopped and closed her fist. She took her phone back from Sienna and stromed out of the bakery. In anger Carol didn't notice me outside the bakery as she kept on walking.

I made my way inside the bakery and saw Sienna, her ocean blue eyes were coated with moisture and she was sad.

"Hi" I said and she just stared at me blankly.

"Hi" her voice was low.

"What was Carol doing here?" I asked.

"She got a wrong idea about us, she thinks we are more than friends" her voice was shaking. "I think we should stop seeing each other" she said and my face twisted in displeasure.

"But I like you" I blurted out without thinking twice as she stilled in her position. "As a friend" I added quickly.

"I.. I have some orders to deliver, I think you should leave" she said and made her way inside the kitchen.

....

Since that day in the bakery, Sienna kept on avoiding me and that irked me. She avoided my calls, messages and whenever I visited her bakery, she used to lock herself inside the kitchen. I didn't want to be a harm to her business, so I used to leave.

I was still thinking about Sienna when Liam entered my cabin.

"Hey man yo-" I cut him off.

"You should make Carol fall in love with you as soon as possible" I said in one breath.

"What?" And then I said everything about me and Sienna and how Carol was being a hindrance in our friendship.

"Are you sure you both are friends" he asked and I didn't reply. "I think you should talk to her"

"But she's avoiding me" I reasoned.

"Ohh!"

Suddenly my phone rang with an unknown number. I looked at Liam and he gestured me to pickup. I did.

"Hello" I said.

"Hello, it's Sienna" I had a ear to ear grin by just listening to her voice.

"Yes" I said enthusiastically.

"I want to meet you" she said and now I was on cloud nine.

"Sure, when?"

"Now, I'm just closing my bakery, can you Come?"

"Yeah,yeah I am coming" I grabbed my car keys and pulled Liam along with me.

She disconnected the call and I sat on my car with Liam in the passenger seat.

"Why are you dragging me along with you?"

"What are friends for?" I said and he groaned in return before fastening his seatbelt.

I reached the bakery within five minutes and parked my car on the opposite side of the bakery. I got out of the car along with Liam.

I saw Sienna outside her bakery and when I was about to cross the road, she stopped me.

" Wait, my car is parked on that side" with that said she looked left and right and took a step forward to cross the road and I was grinning widely.

Suddenly my grin was replaced by a horrified expression as I saw a car coming towards her with a full speed and the next thing I heard was her scream.

She was underneath the car and the car passed by her body, everything happened in a flash, then again we heard a loud dashing sound. The car which hit Sienna was hit by a truck. All the people surrounded towards the spot.

"SIENNA!!" I screamed and went towards her and saw a body lying in the cement road covered with blood.

"Sienna, wake up" I was in panic, my hands were trembling as I took her blood covered head and placed it on my lap. "Sienna" I called. "Open your eyes, please" I begged.

My hands were covered with the blood as my eyes moistured seeing her state. "Please"

Slowly she opened her eyes with great difficulty "Zy.. Zyon" her voice quivered.

"Don't talk, everything's gonna be alright" Liam was calling the ambulance.

She cupped my cheeks with her blood covered hands, "I li..ke y..ou to..o" she said with great difficulty and then the hand which was cupping my cheek fell on her side and her eyes closed on their own.

I patted her cheeks, "Sienna!" No response.

I checked her pulse, and then her breathing, she wasn't breathing. "No,no,no,you can't..." A lone tear rolled down my cheeks. "Wake up Sienna, wake up" I screamed.

Liam came and grasped my shoulder slightly squeezing it. I looked at him and his own eyes were moistured as he shook his head in no.

....

Sienna's lifeless body was in front of me, nurses had cleaned all the bloods and also changed her clothes. Sienna's parents arrived to the hospital as soon as they got the message. Sienna's mom was crying and her dad was consoling her mom. I felt numb, I couldn't believe that Sienna was no longer with us.

Liam came and stood beside me, " It didn't look like an accident" he muttered.

I looked at him with a raised brow and thought for a while, the car was nowhere in sight and appeared suddenly when Sienna was crossing the road. My temper flared as realisation dawned on me, it was definitely not an accident, the driver intentionally hit her.

But the question was, why?

I straightened up, " Where's that driver?"

"He's under observation" Liam followed me, "Zyon, you can't..." His voice was cut off as I reached that driver's room.

A nurse came towards me, asking " Are you his family?" I nodded and she sighed "He's taking his last breath, you better see him and try to talk to him, he can't be saved" she said in an apologetic tone and again I nodded.

I sauntered in and saw his body lying on the bed, " Mom,d ad.." he called breathlessly " Bai..ley, h..ow is s..he?" his voice broke.

My jaws clenched as I made my way towards him, "Why did you kill her?" My voice boomed.

He was closing his eyes, " No, please why did you kill her" I pleaded breathlessly.

" Fo..r mo..ney" he was still breathless, his chest heaving up and down.

For money? bastard..

"Who offered you the money to kill her?"

He was breathing heavily, " C..aro..l Ho...bs..on's.." he lost his breath as he stopped his movements and I stared at him in disbelief.

He died...

Chapter 45

There was a brief silence between us, I couldn't believe that Carol bribed someone to kill Sienna, I can't even believe that Sienna is no more. How could Carol kill her own bestfriend for a man?

" Then the next day we were all standing infront of her grave, I saw Carol bawling her eyes out and I myself couldn't believe that she was the one who killed Sienna without leaving any proof,she even killed that car driver. " he paused " I hate her for what she did." " Then I vowed myself, that I would make Carol's life a living hell, I'll make her drown in her own misery, so I asked her hand in marriage" he gritted " Liam kept on telling me ' don't marry her' but I thought he told me that because he likes her. So when we both were engaged, the Hobson's made me sign a contract that said that if I ever call the engagement off, the CTC company has to offer it's 50 percent share to the Hobson's." I was still in shock with all truth as he continued.

"Liam kept on telling that I'm gonna make my own life a hell by marrying her, yet I didn't listen to him, I was blinded by rage. Then again Liam said me that I'm gonna lose against her by marrying her, all she want is to marry me and I was doing the exact same thing. So when I came to Florida for a buisness meeting, I was busy thinking about, how to get out of this mess. And that evening when you hit me with your car, I was still thinking about the contract and the mess I put myself into" he smiled. "And when I saw you at the hospital,my brain clicked and I saw hope. So I wanted to know you because of which I pretended to have amnesia" he said softly. " And when my plan was going well and when Carol herself cancelled the contract. I don't know what that conniving woman has planned this time." His jaws clenched.

"Was it Carol behind the attack that happened to me?" I asked and he nodded with clenched jaws.

"She's such a smartass, she never leaves any proof behind her" he gritted his teeth. "Even in Sienna's case, she didn't leave any proof, my regret in life is that I couldn't give justice to Sienna" he lamented.

"You know who that car driver was?" I asked, fiddling with my fingers.

"I don't know much about him but Liam told me that his name was Brian" he answered.

"What was his full name?"

He shrugged, "I don't know, all the formalities of the hospital was filled by Liam. I didn't pay much attention to that"

"So Sienna wasn't your girlfriend" I blurted out.

Oh shoot!! How can I be so stupid,, stupid Ashley..

"Um...uh.. I...I..-" I was trying to search words when he cut me off.

"No" he smiled slightly, " I liked her and she liked me too but things couldn't go any further as Carol killed her"

I don't know why? But I moved forward and hugged him tightly and in return he chuckled and laid down on the bed with me, as my hands were still around him.

"Goodnight" he whispered softly.

"Goodnight" I replied back.

....

Sunlight beamed through the windows as I sat straight on my bed and stretched my arms above my head. I rubbed my eyes softly and looked around only to find that Zyon wasn't here. I got up from the bed and again looked around and found a stick note attached to my night stand. I took the note which read,

'I know you're searching me, but don't search me. Breakfast is in the microwave, do eat it.'

What the..? Why shouldn't I search him? Where is he?

I made my way to the kitchen and there was another stick note attached to the microwave, which read,

'The breakfast is in here, and don't be angry. A hint : I'm arranging something special for you'

What is he arranging?

Oh god!it's so confusing.

I made my way towards my room and searched for my phone, where the hell did I keep my phone?

Ugh!!

Last I remember, I kept it on the night stand but now it's not there. I came out of my room and sauntered towards the living area, and there on the coffee table was my phone.

But I don't remember keeping it here..

Anyway I took my phone and on my phone was another stick note, which read,

'Please don't call me, sweetheart, I'm busy. Another hint for you to cool your temper down : tonight I'm gonna take you out as a date. So be ready and pickup the phone when I call you please *wink* '

Oh!! So tonight I have a date with Mr Rosington.

Date..

Chapter 46

"Oh my god! What should I wear tonight?" I groaned in frustration.

"You don't even have a proper clothes with you, all you have is jeans and shirts" Steve said as he was shuffling my clothes.

I could have gone to mall and buy myself a pretty dress but the whole morning and afternoon I was so dreamy thinking about the date. And now I can't even go to mall because it's already evening and I atleast need half a day to shop myself a proper dress,so instead of going to mall I called Steve and Chase to help me.

I sighed frustratedly and turned towards Chase, who was quite upset with me for not telling him about Zyon's arrival and about my feelings towards Zyon.

And on the other hand Steve was giving me a ear to ear grin as I told them about the confession. However Steve knew about Zyon's arrival as he was the one who called Zyon.

"Chase.." I kept my hand on his " I am sorry, I told you I myself didn't know about my feelings until I saw Zyon's face again."

"Cut the crap Chase, just forgive our little Ashley" Steve said, in an irritating tone.

Chase shot a murderous glare and that shut Steve down.

"Chase, please.." I gave him my pretty puppy eyes and slightly pouted my lips.

Chase sighed defeatedly and said, " I forgave you " I squealed delightly.

"Good! Now help me select a nice dress for my date"

They both started searching a perfect dress for me as I was pacing back and forth.

"How about this?" Chase asked as he picked up a royal Blue knee length dress with a collar along with full sleeves and with some laces on it.

"Nah Chase, she's gonna loose her virginity today, don't you think she should wear something sexy and revealing" Steve said with his signature smirk plastered on his lips.

"Typical Steve.." I grumbled as my lips twisted in distaste.

"How about this one?" Steve picked up a nude colour satin cloth with a spaghetti straps and it might reach just below my butt. " It's sexy" he commented as he rotated the dress.

"It's a nightgown, idiot" I snapped. I don't know when I bought that nightgown because I don't usually wear a night-gown.

"Oh.." Steve faltered " but it's sexy"

"How about this one?" I picked up a hot pink off shoulder knee length dress. "It isn't too revealing nor too covering" I pointed out and they both nodded in agreement.

After selecting the dress, I took a long relaxing shower and then after having a shower, I blow dried my hair and applied my regular makeup. After the makeup was done, I slid inside my dress, which fitted me perfectly showing all my curves and to mention, I was looking sexy.

Maybe I'm gonna loose my virginity tonight..

I left my room and made my way to the living room, where Steve and Chase were sipping their hot coffee.

"How am I looking?" I rotated myself. "Pretty! right"

"Drop dead gorgeous" Chase smiled.

"Aww, thank you Chase"

"I think the dress should have been still more revealing" Steve commented and in return I rolled my eyes. "But however you're looking pretty"

"Thanks Steve" I smiled sheepishly.

Steve charged forward and stood infront of me, "I want to give you a gift" he said and my lips tugged up.

"And what is that?" I asked in excitement as he took his wallet out from his pant pocket.

Is he gonna give me money?

And then he opened his wallet and took a small packet out and handed it to me.

"What is this?" I asked in confusion.

"It's a protection, I don't want you to end up being pregnant" he said and Chase spluttered with laughter.

My nostrils flared as I balled my fists in anger but before I could burst out, my phone started ringing inside my handbag. I opened my bag and threw that stupid packet inside it and took my phone out, it was Zyon calling me.

I sauntered towards the dining area and answered the call, "Hello!"

"Are you ready?" Atlast I got to hear Zyon's voice.

"Yes"

"Come down" with that he disconnected the call.

I turned around and saw Chase and Steve standing behind me, Chase was giving me his humble smile while Steve was giving me a thumbs-up.

I bid my goodbyes to them and made my way downstairs.

There was a white shiny limousine parked and a driver was standing near the door and as I reached the limo, the driver handed a bouquet of red roses with a card that said,

I love you, Ashley

-- Zyon

I smiled and got inside the limo as the chauffeur revved the engine.

....

I reached the destination and looked at my surroundings in awe. The dinner date was in a beach, which was impeccably decorated.

There was a beach house at the corner of the beach and near the seashore was a table and cushions neatly arranged with the fairy lights hanging beautifully.

I felt a tap on my right shoulder and I turned around only to see Zyon's handsome face, he was wearing a white shiny shirt with grey formal pants and he was looking incredibly handsome, and those piercing green eyes were sparkling delightly.

He leaned in, his eyes fixed on my lips and I also happily leaned towards him until our lips locked together, perfectly moulding, he kissed me in a heart clenching passion, I bit his lower lip and he gladly parted his lips. He didn't fight for dominance as I slid my tounge inside his mouth and tasted him.

He pulled back from the hot kiss leaving me for more, "I think we should stop, the dinner is getting cold" he said and I nodded. ....

After having a mind-blowing dinner with Zyon, we sat near the edge of the water as the water was hitting our legs, my head rested on his shoulder as his one arm was draped around my shoulder.

There was peaceful silence until Zyon cleared his throat, "Uhm..uh" I looked at him and he looked nervous.

" Everything's alright?" I asked.

He took a deep breath to calm himself, "Will you be my girlfriend?" My head left his shoulder and my eyes locked with his green ones as he added, "For real?"

Chapter 47

My heart was jumping inside my ribcage and a huge grin broke out my lips as I pulled his collar and kissed him fiercely. '

atlast we both are no more virgins.'

Our wild hearts thumping against our ribcage and our tounge dancing together as he kissed me back fervently. The kiss lasted for good one minute as we both pulled back at the loss of breath.

"Is th..at a ye..s, Ash..ley" he panted.

"Yes, yes!! I'll surely be your real girlfriend" I shouted in ecstasy.

He chuckled and got up and also asked me to follow him and I did. He made his way towards the beach house and I followed suit. He opened the door to the beach house and my god!! The interior was fantastic with all those large glass windows and doors. It was a total of glass House, even the roof of the house was glass and the view of the night sky was exquisite.

He again opened the glass door which led us to a bedroom, I followed him inside and made myself comfortable on the comfy bed as he made his way towards the closet.

He returned after 3 minutes with a big gift box in his hands.

"What's this??" I asked as my eyes were fixed on the gift box.

"It's a gift for my real girlfriend." He smirked.

He handed me the beautiful box and I quickly opened the box only to find a weird thing inside it.

"What is this??" I wrinkled my nose as I took that weird thing in between the tip of my two fingers. As I took it out of the box, I got clearer view of the thing, it was a kind of belt, a weird belt.

" As I noticed your now three months fake pregnant, I thought of buying you this fake baby bump belt."he pointed towards the fake bump belt and smirked.

I wanted to gag at the belt, yell at him and then burn this weird thing but I didn't want to ruin our first date so I plastered a smile, "Aww!! Thank you Zyon" I cooed

"You really liked this gift?" he asked as amusement was glistening in his eyes.

I nodded, "Good! But you have a good news" he said and I raised a brow.

"And what is that?"

"This is not your real gift" he said and slid his hand inside his pants pocket and took out a platinum keychain, to which a key was attached. "This is your real gift" he handed me the platinum keychain and thoroughly looked at the key and gasped.

It was the key of an expensive car which I was aiming to buy. But before I could refuse him, he said, " NO is not accepted here" he pointed to himself.

"But-" he again cut me off.

"No buts"

And before I could say any other word, he locked his lips with mine.

Mmh.. I moaned in the kiss as he tasted so good unlike that club guy, I feel like pulling my hair out for kissing that eww guy, he tasted so bad,eww..

He slowly pulled back and I smiled,

"Thank god you saved me that day when that blonde club guy was trying to kiss me outside the hotel" I blurted out as his face twisted into a scowl.

"You are mine" he stated firmly as I raised a brow at him.

"What if I go and kiss another guy?" I challenged and he smirked.

"I almost killed that club guy for kissing my fake girlfriend and now if anybody touches or kisses my real girlfriend, I'm gonna burn him alive"

"Possessive much?"

"Can't help it" he replied.

"Okay, enough of possessive talks, shouldn't we decide our love names"

"Love names?" His eyebrows dipped together and that sight was quite attractive.

"Like sweetheart, babe, baby, honey, love or anything" I explained.

"Uhm.." he pursed his lips as he thought for a while.

"How about I call you daddy??" I bit my lower lip flirtiously and winked at him.

"Why would you call me a daddy?" He wrinkled his nose and continued " I mean, it's not a love name and a person don't call their lover daddy. Fathers are called as daddy"

Oh! Zyon

He's so naive, innocent and the most purest man present in the whole world.

I didn't want talk further about daddy topic, so I just nodded.

We were sitting side by side on the bed with a peaceful silence and my mind was having some dirty images of Zyon and me in the bed,naked.

I looked at him and he also looked at me and smiled and even I smiled back.

I know he wouldn't initiate anything for sure, so it should obviously be me to initiate the thing.

Omg! I'm so horny right now.

And without any second thought, I jumped up on his lap and kissed him hard on the lips, for a while he was stunned but later on he gave in and started kissing me back with equal fervor.

I slowly pushed him back as his back landed on the soft mattress. I wrapped my legs around his waist, straddling him and he had a slight hue of pink shade on his cheeks.

My hands reached his shirt buttons as I unbuttoned his shirt revealing his toned chest and abs. I started sucking his hard skin with my lips earning a series of moans from his mouth. My hands reached to unbuckle his pants, when he caught my hand and stopped me.

"Are you sure?" He asked.

"Sure about what?" I asked back.

"Uh..that you wanna lose your virginity to me"

"Then to whom should I lose it? Huh? Ofcourse it's you because I love you and-" I stopped and narrowed my eyes at him. "Do you wanna lose your virginity to me?"

"Yes..ye..s " he stuttered.

"Are you ready to lose your virginity?" I asked.

"Yes"

"So can we continue?" He nodded.

I started unbuckling his belt when he again interrupted and I internally groaned.

"Uh..uh" he was blushing in all possible shades of red.

"What?" I asked softly.

"I.. I don't have any protection with me" he said.

"That's not a problem"

I got up from him and reached my handbag and pulled the gift given by Steve to me.

I handed the packet to him and his eyes widened. "You've come prepared" I blushed at his comment and chuckled shyly.

"Okay, so now undress me" I said.

"What?"

"I said undress me" I repeated.

"Are you sure?" He asked and I internally groaned.

"Are we gonna do the deed with full clothes on" I snapped and he shook his head.

He slowly brought his shaking hands towards my zipper and slowly pulled it down as my dress slid down leaving me in my undergarments.

I laid on the bed as he hovered over me. I closed my eyes as mixture of pain and pleasure took over me.

Chapter 48

I woke up alone in the bed as Zyon was nowhere in sight. As I was thinking about Zyon,all the last night event came crashing down to me. One thing was for sure that he didn't lie to me about him being a virgin.

He was busy kissing my soft spot as I moaned, his hands roaming around my bare belly and it slowly came up towards my chest.

"Oh! I'm sorry, I shouldn't have touched ther-" I cut him off.

"Shut up and kiss me" and my good blushing Zyon obeyed and started kissing me.

The only piece of clothing in me was my under garments and I wanted to get rid of it.

" Remove the remaining clothing Zyon" I commanded.

"What?!"

"Come on Zyon" And again with his trembling hands he removed my remaining clothing and took a good five minutes to remove it. As his eyes fell on my body, he instantly averted his gaze back to my face and his cheeks were now bright red. He was looking anywhere but me. "Zyon! Look at me" he slowly averted his gaze back to my face and my god that pinkish hue on his face was looking hot on him.

My hands reached the waist band of his boxers when he said, "I think we should turn off that dim light"

I looked the light which was barely giving any brightness to our room but I simply nodded and he turned off the light with me beneath him, naked. As he imagined.

Somebody cleared their throat and I looked at the door frame to see a smirking Zyon wearing a white tank top and shorts, holding a tray of food in his hands.

I slowly got up and took Zyon's white shirt from last night which was lying on the floor. I covered myself and looked at Zyon, who was blushing profusely.

He brought the tray and placed it in front of me in the bed. I stood up from the bed and took a step forward and I felt the pain between my thighs and I winced. "Ow!" I sat on the bed and Zyon sat beside me as the worry lines appeared on his forehead.

"Are you okay?" He asked.

"I'm fine" I gave him a small smile.

"I warned you about the pain" he said and I frowned.

"I knew it's gonna pain. That's the reason why I was a virgin in a first place." I snapped. " and however the pain is worth for the pleasure I got" I shrugged and again Zyon's cheeks turned red.

He stood up and bent down infront of me before placing his one hand under my thighs and another hand around my back, he carried me to the bathroom and set me down infront of the wash basin.

After brushing my teeth and washing my face,Zyon again carried me towards the bed and gently put me down before sitting infront of me and placing the delicious plate of pancakes with maple syrup and some fried sausages.

Yummy..

"I love you, Zyon" I said as I took the first bite of my delicious breakfast.

"Oh really! Last I remembered, you said 'I hate you, I hate your lies, I hate everything about you Mr Rosington' " he quoted my words with a teasing look on his face.

I chewed my food before swallowing it and said, "did I say that?" I asked innocently "Okay let me rephrase it for you, I love you, I love your lies, I love everything about you Mr Rosington "

He raised an amused brow "You also love my lies?"

"Your lies is what brought us close together " he smiled and we continued our breakfast.

My phone started ringing and I took it from the nightstand and checked the caller ID and internally groaned. I disconnected the call and the very next moment I got the message from my mom,

When are you and your boyfriend visiting me? :(

"What happened? Whose calling?" He asked.

"My mom" I said and handed him my phone, he took it and read the message, then started chuckling. "What?" I asked.

"We can visit her tonight "

"Are you sure you wanna visit my mom?"

"Very sure"

"Fine" I took my phone back and messaged her saying that we would visit her tonight.

....

This fake baby bump belt is quite comfortable,I slid inside my maroon sundress and looked myself in the mirror. I was looking like a pregnant lady with a slight baby bump.

"How am I-" Zyon was cut short as his eyes landed on my stomach. "Are you wearing that belt?"

I grinned " yes" I rubbed my stomach.

"You don't have to wear that"

"I have to, my parents think I'm pregnant" he nodded and a hint of sadness coursed his expression.

"I'm sorry, because of my lies you have to bare all this "

Aww..

I walked towards him and hugged him, " Actually, I love to wear this belt, it's comfortable " he looked at me and then started chuckling.

I pulled back, "Are you ready?" I asked.

"Yeah, how am I looking?" He was wearing a black shirt with grey formal pants.

I narrowed my eyes scanning his outfit from top to bottom, I scrunched my nose and looked at him.

"Is that a no?" he asked

"Your looking.. " I said this part in a disgusted way " damn hot" and this part I said flirtiously with a wink.

"Don't seduce me, I might rip your clothes off"

I scoffed "I think you should take classes from Steve to become good in that field or you can even watch porn"

"Your saying that I wasn't good in bed"

"I didn't say that" I shrugged my shoulders.

"It was our first time so I was going slow, tonight I'm gonna make you scream" he smirked.

"Make me scream without blushing" and again he blushed.

"I think we should leave, it's already seven pm" I nodded.

....

We were inside our house sitting in the lounge as my dad's eyes were fixed on the fake baby bump with his jaw hanging open and my mom glaring at Zyon.

"There's a thing called protection these days, you could have atleast used that" my mom snapped at him.

"I..uh.. I .." Zyon got tounge tied as sweat droplets appeared on his forehead.

"Mom, I wanted the baby, it isn't his fault " I defended him.

"It is his fault, he was the one who put the baby inside you" mom glared at me. "You know I was 27 when I was pregnant with you and your so young to have baby"

"I'm 24, and this is the perfect age to get pregnant " she sighed defeatedly.

"What's done is done, we can't do anything, right honey " she averted her gaze towards dad,who was still in daze. He looked at her and nodded in approval. "And you.." she raised her index finger at Zyon and Zyon gulped. "Look after my daughter and her baby" he nodded. "And if she ever comes crying to me, you're gonna face my wrath"

"I would never hurt her ma'am " Zyon answered with a smile.

"Good" " Come, let's have dinner and by the way sweetie, when are you leaving for New York "

"Um..tomorrow " I answered and she nodded before walking towards the kitchen along with dad.

I stood up to follow my mom, When Zyon came from behind and whispered, "If you want you can stay in Florida, you don't have to come to New York, I'll keep visiting you"

"No, I'll come with you, I can even live my life in and dream in New York "

He grinned " really?" I bobbed my head up and down and within a second his lips landed on mine kissing me but it couldn't last long as mom's booming voice reached our ears.

"What's going on there?" He instantly pulled back and I laughed and we both sauntered towards the dining area.

The dinner went well with some normal chit-chat and then there were some threats from my mom to Zyon. After a while we drove back to my apartment and the long night went on with some intimacy fun.

Chapter 49

I am back to New York and as usual Zyon left for work in the morning and I'm all alone in the penthouse. Staying alone is so boring, it has already reached the lunch time and I'm thinking of visiting Zyon in his office.

I thought of cooking some lunch for both of us and pack it but then I thought of going to a nice restaurant with Zyon to have lunch. I took my car keys and walked out of the house. As I reached the parking lot, I moved towards my car,which was gifted by Zyon and got inside before revving the engine.

I reached the skyscraper CTC building and parked the car outside the building property. As I was about to enter inside the large gates, I heard a horn and I turned around. There on the other side of the road was parked an ice cream truck.

I licked my lips as I was craving for the ice creams. I can even visit Zyon and go to a restaurant after eating ice cream, right. So I started walking towards the truck. As I reached the road, I lazily looked right and left and the coast was clear. I started crossing the road and when I was in the middle of the road,I heard an annoying noise of the horn, my head snapped to the right and there was a black car coming in my direction with full speed. I was frozen on my spot without moving an inch just looking at the car with wide eyes. As the car was about to hit me, I was pulled by someone and I landed flat on that someone.

He was underneath me and I instantly lifted my body off of him as he also stood up.

"What the hell are you doing here?" He shouted as he grasped my forearm and started dragging me away from CTC and even the ice cream truck.

He halted near the Cafe which was near to CTC. He opened the door and entered inside and took a seat in the corner.

"What are you doing here,Ashley?" He asked.

"I just came here to visit Zyon, Liam " I answered.

Liam's eyes traveled down my face to my stomach and was fixed on my fake baby bump. As now I'm in New York, I wear that belt everyday, because I can't predict when I'll meet whom. "And how's the baby?"

I grinned and placed my hand on my fake bump and said, "My baby is absolutely fine "

"I never noticed the bump before"

"Oh come on Liam, I just got the bump recently and you know what, my baby is getting bigger and bigger" I said and Liam stared at me for a while and then spluttered with laughters.

"You are different Ash!" He said in between his laugh " you were just about to get into an brutal accident and your not even scared, you're so cool" he laughed his guts out.

"Yes I know that" I batted my eyelashes as he regained his posture.

"Next time be careful" he said in a serious tone. " I don't want the history to repeat" he muttered but however I heard it.

"You're talking about Sienna, right " I asked.

"Did Zyon tell you about her?" I nodded. " good!"

"Are you sure that Carol killed her?" At this Liam's face hardened.

"I was there when that bloody driver confessed " he gritted. " Zyon was depressed when Sienna died, I agree they weren't in any relationship but the friendship they had was beautiful, I despise Carol for what she did to her own friend"

My mouth was itching to ask Liam about the driver, and this time I didn't hold it back I asked Liam, "Do you know who the driver is? I mean his full name or anything"

"Yeah, I know his name but other than that I know nothing" he replied.

"What's his name?" I was desperate.

"Brian.... Brian Vincent"

"Vincent?" I've heard this name somewhere but I don't know where.

My eyes widened as I recognised the Vincent's.

Does Brian Vincent belong to them?

"Liam! do you have any proof against Carol Hobson " he shook his head in no.

"I have a proof against her by which she can be punished for what she did?" I exclaimed.

"And what is that?" He raised a brow.

I looked at him and smiled, "I'll tell you but first I need your help Liam " "Will you help me" he nodded eagerly.

"I will "

Chapter 50

"Why are you still here? It's already half past eleven" I furrowed my brows as Zyon was still lying on the bed lazily with a sly smirk on his face.

"I'm not going to office today" he got up from the bed and I raised a brow.

"Why? It isn't Saturday or Sunday today, why aren't you going today?" I asked and he slowly walked towards me.

"Because I want to spend time with my girlfriend" he answered as he reached me and slowly started rubbing his palm up and down my bare arm.

Holy shit..

I've asked Liam to pick me up exactly at twelve, so that we can go to the hospital where Brian Vincent was admitted to check whether he's related to Evan Vincent or not. It can also be a last name mash-up. And today this Zyon isn't going to office, which is a big problem for me. I've asked Liam not to tell anything about the Vincents to Zyon. I don't want to drag Zyon into this unless everything is confirmed.

Zyon tucked the loose strand of my hair behind my ears and kissed my cheeks, tip of my nose and then bit my earlobe to which a shiver ran down my spine. He pulled back as his eyes were fixed on my lips and without wasting a minute he kissed me, on my lips fiercely, he took my bottom lips in between his lips and sucked it hard, earning a moan from me. He pulled back as his eyes darkened with lust. He carried me in his arms and took me towards the bed and gently laid me down as he hovered over me.

When did my timid Zyon turned this wild?

He again kissed me on my lips and then trailed kisses on my neck, sucking the soft spot as series of moans left my mouth. I was wearing a tight fitted pastel green colour knee length dress, his hands reached the zipper of my dress as he slowly pulled it down and when the zipper was on its midway, that's when I was pulled out of my lovey dovey mood. I wriggled underneath him and pushed him.

Focus Ashley, focus..

He got up from me and I quickly got out of the bed with rosy cheeks.

"What happened?" He smirked.

"Yo... you're ge..tting.. late for w.or..k " I stuttered with my face fully flushed.

"But I'm taking a leave today " he stated as he sat straight on the bed.

"Why? Don't you have any work to do today in your office " I snapped.

"I have tiny works which Gregor can handle " he shrugged.

"Oh my god! How can you be so cruel Zyon? How can you put all your work on Gregor's shoulder and sit here,huh?" He grasped my hand and pulled me on his lap, so now I was on his lap straddling him.

Oh! How I wanted to continue what we were doing minutes ago..

"Ashley.." he purred in my ears and again I shivered "Let's continue what we were doing " I shook my head and got up from his lap.

"You should leave Zyon, you shouldn't skip your office like this" he frowned.

"Yesterday you said that you wanted me to stay and take a leave from my damn office and today you want me to go"

"Forget what I said yesterday, today is a different day so you'll find a different Ashley" his frown deepened at my words.

"Your weird " he stated and my nostrils flared.

"How dare you call me a weirdo? Huh?" I yelled.

"I didn't call you a weirdo, I just said that today your acting weird " he explained as I shot him a deathly glare. "Fine.." he raised both his hands in surrender "I'm leaving for office" he said and I heaved a contended sigh.

He got up from the bed and sauntered inside bathroom, my phone started ringing and it was Liam, calling me.

"Hello!"

"Come down I'm waiting" Liam said from the other end.

"Just wait for a while,Zyon still hasn't left for office" I said in a hushed voice.

"Okay" he said and disconnected the call.

After a while,Zyon came out wearing a two piece white suit and was looking incredibly handsome like always.

"Bye" I grinned and waved my hand at him.

" I'm leaving for office only on one condition " he stated with a stoic face.

"And what is your one condition?" His once thin lined lips turned into a devious smirk.

"Promise me we're gonna continue what we left, tonight" he said and heat crawled up to my neck and I shyly nodded as his smirk deepened.

"Now go" I said in a low voice and he chuckled before blowing a kiss towards my direction.

As he left, I quickly took my fake bump belt and wore it before taking my hand bag and making my way out towards the parking lot.

As soon as I found Liam's car, I got inside and Liam jerked his head in my direction.

"I think I disturbed your quality time with Zyon" he smirked.

"What?" I wrinkled my nose in confusion.

He jerked his chin towards my neck and I quickly took my pocket mirror out of my handbag and checked my neck and there was three big hickey on my neck and by now I was fully red out of embarrassment.

ZYON!!!

I internally groaned as Liam chuckled and revved the engine. As we reached the hospital, we made our way towards the lobby near the receptionist.

"Hello, how can I help you ma'am" the cute redhead receptionist asked.

"Um.. I'm here for some information about Brian Vincent, who died two years ago in an accident" I crossed my fingers.

"Sorry ma'am, but we can't give you any information"

"Please he's dead and I'm his sister, the information is very important, please I beg you" I joined my hands infront of her and pleaded.

"But ma'am we--" I cut her off.

"Please" my eyes were pleading and she looked at me weirdly.

"I'm sorry ma'am but I can't help you"

"Ashley.." Liam called and I turned my attention to him " just go and wait there, I'll get the information"

"But how?"

"I'll manage" he smirked.

I obeyed and made my way towards the corner and sat on one of the chair looking at Liam, he was giving the redhead his charming smile and spoke to her for a while and then the redhead left and after a minute or two returned with a paper in her hand. She handed the paper to Liam and Liam gladly took it before blowing a kiss to her and making his way towards me.

"I'm impressed" I stated.

"You know, my charms" he winked and I nodded.

He handed me a paper,I looked at the paper which was a report and my doubt was confirmed.

Brian Joseph Vincent S/O Evan Vincent died in an accident on......

Chapter 51

"Ugh!! Where the hell is that man's house?" Liam groaned and hit the steering wheel out of frustration.

"Umm..you know, I... I don't remember roads" I said in a low voice.

"Oh God!!" He sighed heavily.

As we got to know that Brian Vincent is Evan Vincent's son, we quickly left the hospital and made our way to his house as I directed Liam to the main road but I forgot the direction to Evan's house.

"I never forget roads but you know that day when our car crashed, I was in panic mode plus it was dark since it was night plus I was tired to walk so Zyon carried me in his arms as I'm pregnant" I said the last part by rubbing my fake bump along with a slight blush. "These are the reasons why I forgot the route to his house"

And again Liam sighed and parked the car at the side before resting his head on the steering wheel as the other cars passed by.

"I'm tired" he muttered.

"If you want, I can drive the car" I said as his head was still on the steering wheel, it was a sunny afternoon so I'm sure that I will not crash his car.

"No thanks " he said in a low voice " this is my favorite car and I don't want you to crash it" he said as my face flushed in embarrassment.

He abruptly raised his head from the steering wheel and looked at me with a weird expression.

"I know what I have to do" he said as he took his phone out.

"And what are you gonna do?" I furrowed my brows.

He tapped on his phone as he said "I'm calling Zyon "

"NO!! yo..." I was cut off.

"Shhhh" Liam hushed me placing a finger on his lips as he put the call on speaker and on the fourth ring Zyon recieved the call.

"Hello" we heard Zyon's bored voice.

"Zyon!!" Liam called as he mouthed me to stay quiet and I nodded.

"What Liam?" Again came Zyon's bored voice.

"I want to know where is Evan Vincent's home?" I had horrified expression on my face.

"How do you know about Evan Vincent?" Was the question Zyon asked.

"I..I" Liam was at loss of words and then he looked at me "Ashely told me about him" he blurted out.

"When did you meet Ashely?"

"Yesterday, when you were in office"

"Why did you meet Ashley yesterday?" Zyon asked.

"I visited her because it has been a long time since I last saw her and I also saw your little baby growing" Liam said the last part cheerfully.

"Hmm" Zyon hummed and continued. "But why would Ashley tell you about Evan Vincent?" Zyon's question.

"Because.." he paused and looked at me with confused filled face.

"Because?" Zyon repeated.

"It just came out of her mouth while we were talking about random things and she also told me about his daughter..." Liam was interrupted by Zyon.

"She cannot move her legs and arms, so stay away from her" Zyon yelled.

"I know she's suffering from diplegia and that's the reason why I am calling you?" Liam grumbled.

"What do you mean?"

"I know you donated a 50 grands to him for his daughter's medication and even I want to donate some money for his daughter's medication as I really felt bad for him"

"Why you want to donate money to an unknown stranger?"

"I just want to be a good man, Zyon" Liam replied calmly.

"Why-" Zyon was cut off by Liam...

" STOP with the questions man" he snapped "I just want to help him and now without any question direct me to Evan Vincent's house, my car is on the main road so.."

"Fine..." Zyon directed to Liam to our destination and then disconnected the call.

We reached our destination which was Evan's stone cottage. I banged my fist on the door and after a minute the creaked door opened revealing Gloria.

"Ashley!!" She squealed " what a surprise" I just smiled. "Come in" she said as she opened the door wide for me to enter and as she did, she noticed Liam standing beside me and she looked at me with me confused glance.

"It's my driver" I blurted out and Liam's head snapped in my direction "I was getting bored in the house alone and Zyon was busy with his works, I don't even have friends in New York and your the only one who I know in New York "

"Aww come in sweetheart" she said as we both sauntered in.

As I walked towards the lounge I saw a beautiful girl sitting on the wheelchair who looked my age and as her gaze fell on me, she gave me a heartwarming smile.

"This is my daughter, Bailey" Gloria said with a smile. "Have a seat, I'll go and bring a healthy juice for you'll and Ashley, your small little baby bump is cute " she said as I blushed and chuckled weirdly.

She left leaving us with Bailey. "Hi" I greeted and she greeted back.

I saw a magazine in her hand and on the cover page was Carol Hobson's picture wearing a purple sun dress and looking up at the sky.

Bailey might have noticed the way I was staring at Carol's pics as she said, "I'm a very big fan of Miss Carol Hobson, I always aimed to be like her..."

Be like her, seriously. The one who bribed your own brother to kill an innocent girl for a man.

"She even organised a charity event for all the orphan kids, I wish I could be like her..."

Be like her means being a freaking murderer.

"So nice,so gentle. Modelling was always my dream but just an accident killed all my dreams" her voice broke while talking about the accident.

Wait which accident..

And when I was about to ask, "The juice is ready" Gloria came holding a tray of classes.

Bailey composed herself and smiled at her mother.

"Where's Evan?" I asked as I took a glass from the tray as I averted my gaze back to Gloria.

"He went to buy some groceries, he might return in few minutes,why?" Gloria asked.

"Just asked" I shrugged.

We waited for fifteen minutes and yet there was no sign of Evan.

Should I ask Gloria about her son?

I can't sit and wait for Evan, so I averted my gaze to Gloria,who was chatting with Bailey.

"Gloria!" I called and both the heads turned in my direction.

"Yes"

"Can I-" I was cut off as I heard the creaked door's opening sound. I turned my head towards the main door to see Evan holding a lot of paper bags in his hands and as his gaze fell on me, he smiled.

"What a surprise Ashley?" He chirped and I smiled.

"Can I talk to you in private" I didn't have any time left for chitchat as Zyon might come early today.

"Umm...why?"

"It's urgent" I pleaded as he nodded.

I looked at Liam and gestured him to stay,as I followed Evan to his room.

I closed the door behind us, "What is so ur-" I cut him off.

"Do you have a son named Brian?" His eyes widened as I said the name of his son.

"How do you know about him?" I ignored his question and asked further.

"Do you know that your son killed an innocent girl.." he looked down " just for money" I added as he fixed his eyes on the floor. "Did you know about it?" I asked as he was still silent. His silence gave me my answer, he was guilty. "You did know about it, right?"He looked up at me as his wrinkled eyes glistened with moisture. "How could he kill a girl like that, even that girl had a family member, parents, siblings and without even a second thought your son just agreed to kill a girl for money"

A lone tear rolled down his cheeks. "I'm sorry" his voice broke.

"Why are you apologizing?"

"As my son was the one who made a deal with...." His voice broke as tears were rolling down his cheeks.

I narrowed my eyes, " Why Brian made a deal with Carol Hobson"

He wiped his tears and looked at me with a confused filled expression. "It wasn't Carol Hobson, who gave money to kill that girl"

My mouth automatically parted and my eyes grew big.

WHAT??

it was not Carol who bribed them.

"Then who offered the money to kill that girl?" My voice was filled with curiosity.

I held my breath as he opened his mouth.

"It was ...."

Chapter 52

"It was Elena Hobson, Carol Hobson's mother"

I opened my mouth then closed it, I didn't know what to say.

It was Elena Hobson.

"But why did Brian mentioned Carol's name to Zyon?" I asked him.

"Did Zyon meet Brian?"

"When Brian was taking his last breath he mentioned that Carol was the one who offered him money" and again his eyes moistured. "But why did he kill Sienna for money?"

"Sienna?"

"The girl killed by your son?" My words were harsh this time and guilt was written all over his face.

"Bailey was going for her modelling auditions in New Jersey when the van she was in got into a major accident." His voice was trembling." As soon as we got the news, we made our way to the hospital, we saw her body covered with blood, we asked the doctor about her condition and the doctor said that she was critical, the hospital demanded us to pay the bill first before the surgery and the bill was lot more than we expected. We tried for loans but it got rejected and then we went near our relatives for help but none helped us. While insearch of money we met Elena Hobson whom we knew as Carol Hobson's mother, we didn't know her name or the thing that she was the owner of fashion minds, we knew Carol because of Bailey as she was a huge fan of her. Bailey always showed us her post on social media with her families or friends. Elena Hobson..." Again a tear rolled his cheeks but he quickly wiped it off "Elena Hobson was ready to offer us money but in return she wanted us to kill a girl, I disagreed to her condition but Brian didn't. He loved his sister more than anything and he couldn't see her in pain, he didn't want to see her die,so he agreed to kill that girl for money, I tried to stop him but he didn't. The amount was transferred to our account as we paid the bills and the surgery got started as Brian left the hospital to .." he looked down again as his hands were shaking. " I tried to stop him but he didn't listen. It's karma, he killed her and made her family suffer and in return he killed himself leaving us to suffer." He said in broken voice, he titled his face upward as his eyes met mine. "We saved our daughter but lost our son on the same day. The accident was brutal which caused Bailey to have diplegia. We couldn't even see or talk to our son when he was taking his last breath, we were tensed about Bailey, I regret his decision which caused him death."

I was at loss of words as he completed the truth. Everything was planned by Elena Hobson but we accused Carol. Brian killed Sienna to save his beloved sister and he died. Everything in here was messed up, I don't know what to do??

Carol wasn't the culprit, Bailey was right, she's an angel in disguise.

I looked at Evan,whose eyes were bloodshot. It wasn't his fault either, he tried to stop his son but he didn't listen. Brian wasn't a bad guy, he was just having a bad time. He wasn't evil, he only wanted to save his loved ones, but the way he chose to save his loved ones was wrong.

Elena Hobson was on the blame, she was evil, she destroyed everyone's life but the question was..

Why did she wanted Sienna dead??

"Why was she after that girl?" I finally found my voice

He slightly shook his head "I don't know"

"Do you have anything against her?"

"No" "Please don't tell this to Gloria or Bailey, they don't know anything about this. I don't want them to think anything low about Brian" he said.

I nodded " I think, I should leave" with that said I left the room. Liam stood up and we both sauntered out after saying a small goodbye to Bailey and Gloria.

As soon as we entered the car, Liam broke the silence, "So does he have any proof?" He asked desperately.

"No" I said in a low voice as he sighed. "It was not Carol who offered Brian the money" I looked up at him and he had a relieved look on his face as a small smile etched his face.

"Then who was it?" He asked softly.

"It was Carol's mom, Elena Hobson" he gasped.

"What? Why would she want Sienna dead"

"I don't know nor do they"

"So now what?"

"I don't know" I shrugged "I just wanna go home, please drop me back" I was tired of everything.

He nodded and revved the engine.

I reached the penthouse in lost mind, Zyon has not yet returned, I took a long relaxing shower to free myself from the day exhaustion and then after a bath I made myself comfortable on the bed as it was already late at night. As I was about to close my eyes I heard Zyon's voice.

"You're sleeping?"

"Yes, I'm tired" I mumbled in a tirey voice.

"What about your promise?" I wrinkled my nose in confusion.

"What promise?"

"You forgot your promise" he shook his head in dismay and continued " the promise you made me this morning about continuing what we left..." He faltered and I understood about which promise he was talking about.

"Ohh that"

"Yes that" he smirked.

"I'll make it up to you Zyon but not today, I'm tired" I pleaded with puppy eyes

"It's okay" he pouted and made his way to the bathroom.

I had so many things going on in my head because of which I couldn't even sleep but as I saw Zyon coming out of the bathroom, I quickly closed my eyes and pretended to be asleep.

I feel guilty for hiding things from Zyon.

'I'm sorry Zyon'

Chapter 53

"Na na na na na..." I was chanting a song as I prepared the sauce for spaghetti. "Zyon taste it" I handed him the spatula with some sauce after blowing some air on it to cool it down.

Zyon took the spatula along with my hand and dipped my finger on it and then licked my fingers which caused me to blush.

"Mmm tasty" he smirked as I blushed in different shades of red.

"Zyon!!" I smacked his arm playfully as he just chuckled.

It has been two days after my visit to Evan's house, I didn't tell Zyon about the real culprit but after a lot of contemplation I decided to tell him today, now itself that, Carol wasn't the one who killed Sienna but it was her mother. I looked at him with a serious expression on my face.

"Zyon" I called and he looked at me.

"Yes?"

"I want to te--" I was cut off as somebody rang the bell to our penthouse.

"Who can it be?" Zyon asked and I shrugged.

"Is it someone from your family..- oh god where the hell is my belt??" I ran up to our room and searched for it as Zyon followed me. "Last night I was wearing it and you removed it and threw it somewhere,now search" I snapped.

"Yeah I'm searching"

After a minute Zyon brought my belt and fixed it on my stomach. "Ready" he asked and I nodded.

We both descended downstairs as Zyon made his way to the door and threw it open revealing Carol.

"Hi" she greeted us. Zyon just gave a blank look while I greeted her back with a smile.

"Come in " I said as Zyon moved aside and Carol came in.

Her eyes were fixed on my fake bump but this time there was no sadness in her grey eyes. She looked happy.

" I'm here to invite you guys to the auction that is held by the Hobson's and the venue is the Hobson's mansion, please do come." She said with a smile.

"Sure" I smiled back at her without acknowledging Zyon.

"Thanks" she was about to turn back towards the door when I called her.

"Carol !!"

"Yes?"

"Come sit with us for a while" she hesitated for a while as her eyes switched between me and Zyon.

"Sure" she slightly bobbed her head up and down.

Without any word Zyon ascended upstairs as Carol and I looked at his retreating figure until it disappeared.

"Why does he hate me so much?" She muttered lowly but however I heard it.

"What?"

"Um.. nothing"

"Come let's sit and talk" I said as I directed her to the couch.

We both sat side to side on the couch,

"I can't believe I'm sitting beside the famous supermodel, Carol Hobson" I squealed to lighten the atmosphere in here.

She just chuckled, I took a selfie with her and after a small talk she left.

I ascended upstairs to our room and saw Zyon standing near the large window, his back facing me.

"We are invited to the auction held by the Hobson's tomorrow." I said and in return..

"Hmm" he hummed as his back was still facing me.

"I want to go to the Hobson's mansion tomorrow" I stated as he turned around.

"We're not going" he stated back.

"But I want to go"

"WHY?" he kind of yelled.

"Because.." I was searching for a reason "because I want to see the Hobson's mansion" I blurted out as he sighed.

"Why do you like Carol so much?"

"What do you mean?" I dipped my eyebrows.

"You know what I mean, Carol is so wicked and I'm scared that she might hurt you"

"Why would she hurt me?"

"Because she did the same to Sienna"

"Carol wasn't the one who killed Sienna" there was brief silence for a while as his facial expression changed slowly.

"What?" He wrinkled his nose.

"You heard me"

"What do you mean by saying, Carol was not the one who killed Sienna.?"

"It was her mom, Elena Hobson."

"What?" He got a lot more confused.

I started telling him everything that Brian was Evan's son, my visit to Evan Vincent's house and atlast the name of the real culprit.

He had a blank face and I couldn't understand what was he thinking.

"Zyon?" I called slowly as I placed my hand on his.

"Are you sure what Evan told you is true?"

"Why would he lie to me?"

"But why would Mrs Hobson kill Sienna?" He asked and I shrugged.

"I don't know, maybe she had some grudge on her."

"Are you sure Carol isn't the one..." He faltered and again I shrugged. "Why didn't you tell all this to me before?"

"I.. I um.." I was tounge tied. "I didn't want to tense you up" I looked down as a wave of guilt washed over me.

He came forward and hugged me, "Next time don't you keep secrets from me." he muttered and I slowly nodded and hugged him back.

"So tomorrow are we going to the auction?" I asked as I snuggled closer and inhaled his masculine scent.

He pulled back and stared at me in disbelief. "Why do you wanna go there?"

"I just wanna see who Elena Hobson is"

Chapter 54

I took a step forward to enter the massive mansion of the Hobson's. My hands were locked with Zyon's as we made our way inside.

The mansion screamed richness,power and beauty, the large staircase in between the lounge and the everything was decorated impeccably. The large golden chandeliers were attached to the high ceiling and everything looked exquisite.

"This house is beautiful, I didn't expect the Hobson's to have this beautiful house" I said in awe.

"Do you want me to build a house like this for you?" Zyon asked.

"Can you?"

"Ofcourse I can" he said in determination for which I just patted his shoulder and chuckled. " By the way you look beautiful"

"You've said that already"

"What's wrong in saying it again?"

I shrugged " well, my boyfriend is the handsomest man in the world"

"I agree" he smiled and I smiled back as Carol made her way towards us.

"Thanks for coming" Carol came and greeted us with her warm smile.

"Your welcome" I said and you won't believe that Zyon just smiled and greeted Carol back.

"How are you Carol?" He asked and Carol gave him a confused glance as she jabbed her index finger to her chest.

"Are you asking me?" She asked.

"Is there any other Carol here?" She slowly shook her head in no. "So how are you?" Zyon asked again.

"I'm... Fine" she was still in confusion as she blinked twice.

"Good to know" Zyon replied as Carol turned her attention to me.

"Well you look pretty in your dress" Carol complemented to me.

I was wearing a baby pink floor length dress with some work on the lower side of the dress and I was showcasing my fake bump to everyone.

Carol excused herself as she went to greet the other guest.

"Someone is very good to Carol today" I teased.

"She isn't the culprit, so why to behave rudely, huh" he replied.

I was about to reply when we heard a voice, "Hey son" Thomas walked towards us along with Lily and Rebecca.

"Hey dad" Zyon hugged his dad.

"Oh my god Ashley, you've got such a cute little baby bump" Lily squealed.

I just smiled as she came forward and touched my bump, "Your bump is soft"

Actually my baby is made of cottons.

I wanted to reply but right now I was ruining my makeup by sweating because I didn't know what to reply. I looked at Zyon who was equally tensed as me.

"Actually.." I paused searching for a proper reason "...my dress has a double layer cloth in it and so it kind of feels soft..., My bump" however I completed and Lily wrinkled her nose and nodded wierdly.

"I'm so happy, I'm gonna get a cute little nephew or a neice" Rebecca said as her green eyes were glittering with happiness.

And I felt sad, guilty, how are we gonna tell them the truth, that there's no baby inside me, everything was a lie. I think I should discuss it with Zyon and tell his family the truth.

While the Rosington family were chatting we heard someone clearing the microphone and all heads snapped in that direction.

An old short man in his late fifties wearing a two piece suit was standing behind the microphone along with a tall woman with blonde hair who looked young and she had somewhat Carol's features in her. I recognised them as realisation dawned on me. They were Carol's parents Elena Hobson and Louis Hobson. My eyes were fixed on Elena Hobson as she smiled gracefully to all the guests.

"Ladies and gentlemen thanks for coming to the Hobson's auction and the auction will start within an hour." Louis announced to everyone, but my gaze was fixed on the woman beside Louis, Elena Hobson who was now talking to Carol and laughing on something.

They all got down from the stage and gathered in the crowd of guests.

"Did you see Mrs Hobson?" Zyon whispered and I nodded, "Can we leave now?" He whispered again.

"No" I had a plan going on in my head, which I had to accomplish.

"No?" He repeated.

"I want to talk to her"

"What?" He wrinkled his nose.

"Wait here, I'll come back in a minute" I said and started walking towards Carol, who was talking to her mom.

"Wait..." I heard Zyon calling me and was about to follow me when Liam came and interrupted him as I kept on walking until I reached them.

"Hi, Mrs Hobson" I grinned and in return she shot me glare. "By the way I'm here to tell Carol that, Zyon is calling you" I turned to Carol.

"Me?" Carol asked and snapped her head in Zyon's direction, who was talking to Liam.

"Yes, you" I said and she whispered something in Elena's ear and sauntered in Zyon's direction.

And now I was all alone with Mrs Hobson.

"Bitch, how dare you come and show me your face after snatching my daughter's fiancè from her" she whisper yelled at me with a smile.

"Well, hello Mrs murderer" I murmured with a sweet smile.

"What do you mean by, Mrs murderer, huh?" she again shot me glare.

"Don't be so innocent, I know how you killed Carol's friend Sienna and even tried to kill me and you won't believe that I even have a proof against you" I smiled as she grasped my hand and pulled me to the corner, where there were no people.

"What proof do you have, huh?" She gritted.

I pulled my hand out of her grasp, "Oh! I have a video of you and a man and to mention that man Brian Vincent happens to be my cousin and my late cousin had recorded your conversation with him and somehow I got the video while visiting their house and I also saw how you offered him money to kill Sienna" I paused for a while " and to mention the video is very clear" her face showed a slight fear as I continued, " But don't worry I'm not gonna leak that video as I need something from you"

"What do you want in return?" She asked.

"I need money"

" money? How much?"

"Five million" I demanded.

"Okay I'll transfer it to your account"

"No, I need it in cash"

"Okay I'll give you"

"Good, tomorrow at 6pm, visit me at my house and don't worry, Zyon will not be there" I said as she nodded, " And don't forget, the cash" I waved at her and left.

Your gone, Mrs Elena Hobson..

Chapter 55

I was busy fixing the camera behind the photo frame by watching a video on internet and finally the camera got attached. As usual Zyon was not in home and it was quarter to six and I was waiting for Elena to come,so that I can put my plan in action.

I hope my plan works..

After pacing back and forth for good half and hour my doorbell rang and I quickly walked to the door revealing Elena holding a briefcase in her hand.

I moved aside, so that she could come in but she stood at the threshold holding the briefcase with a stoic face. "Here's your money" she threw the briefcase to me and while catching it, I hurted my fingers.

Rude much..

"Come in and have some coffee with me Mrs Hobson" I gave her my sweetest smile.

"I don't have any time to come in and have a coffee with you, give me the video" she spated harshly with a glare.

"Are you sure, you don't wanna come in and collect the proof of your crime by yourself" I smirked.

She shot me another death glare and sauntered in, and stood near the dining area.

" Come to the lounge and sit with me Mrs Hobson"

Because the camera is in the lounge not in the dining area.

"No, I'm fine here" she sat on the chair as she lifted her one leg and placed it on the other one. " Now, can you give me the proof"

Why is she so hard today?

I cleared my throat, " Do obey what I say Mrs Hobson..." I faltered as she groaned and stood up and sat across me in the lounge. "Good" I smiled. "Before I give you the video, I wanna know, why you killed Sienna?" I asked.

"It's none of your business" she stated with a void expression in her face

"Excuse me?" I raised one of my brow and in return she smirked.

"I know you don't wanna give me the proof and you wanna just play around with me" her smirk got deeper as she stood up in front of me. " Now get ready" she leaned near my ear and whispered and then pulled back with the smirk.

Before I could register what she said, I felt a stinging pain on my right cheek and my head snapped to the other side. "Bitch, did you really think that I'm scared of you, huh?" She yelled as she pulled my hair and harshly gripped my chin before tilting my face to face her. " I'm here to kill you" she laughed wickedly.

My scalp was hurting badly as she was pulling my hair with all her energy. I tried to free her hands from my hair but I couldn't so instead I held my palms out and reached her neck and started tickling her neck as she wiggled and let go of my hair and took a few steps back. " You're quite lucky slut, everytime I tried to kill you, you've always got a saviour who saves you, but today there's none, whose gonna save you bitch".

She jumped on me as my back landed on the wooden flooring and again she started pulling my hair, "You conniving crazy woman, let go of my hair" with all my might I pushed her and luckily she fell down beside me, I took it as a chance and got up and God..

My back hurts..

"I'm a karate champion" I swang my arms in karate style as she slowly got up, groaning and then..

She freaking smirked again, "Oh really!" She said as she raised her hand and she had a huge dimond ring on her right hand, she rotated the ring to her inner finger and walked towards me but before I could escape I got a hard slap on my cheeks but this time there was a small gash from which blood was oozing out.

I touched my cheek and saw a little blood on my fingers. "You crazy woman I.." I yelled but again I was cut off as she punched me right on my nose and again I fell down on the floor. "Oww" I whimpered as my nose was also bleeding.

"Today you're gonna die and BTW take the video along with you to your grave" she laughed. "Well, you're just like Sienna, a bitch snatching someone else's guy" she spated "Sienna was my daughter's bestfriend instead of bringing Carol and your boyfriend together, she got closer to your boyfriend and I was the one who saw my daughter crying day and night because of Sienna's betrayal and after I killed her, everything was fine my daughter was happy until you appeared along with your unborn child" her eyes were now fixed on my bump. "First, I'm gonna kill that thing" she pointed to my stomach as she grasped my forearm and pulled me up and then kicked hard on my stomach.

This crazy woman kept on kicking my stomach and finally I screamed my lungs out and again she punched my lips causing a busted lips.

"DON'T SCREAM" she screeched.

"There.. is n..o b..aby....insi..de ....me" however I managed to tell as the blood came out of my mouth.

She laughed again before kicking me hard on my stomach, "Did you hide your baby inside the locker,huh?" She laughed again as she pulled my hair and punched on my jaw.

I for sure know that now my face might be covered in blood. " You know it's time for your death" she opened her handbag and took out a knife which had a sharp pointed end.

"No...n..o...no" I pleaded with my eyes.

Am I gonna die?..

"Do you know how I'm gonna handle your death case" she smirked. "It's gonna be like some morons entered your so called beautiful house and killed you for money and even the security of this building couldn't save you, so sad" panic surged in me as adranaline rushed through my veins.

The sharp knife was getting closer as Elena was walking closer to me with a signature smirk plastered on her face.

As she got closer I pushed her and ran for my life, I ascended upstairs and got into my room and locked myself inside, my whole body was paining, I took my phone out of my pocket and dialled Zyon's number.

And at fourth ring Zyon received the call, "Hello"

"Zyon.." I called breathlessly, "Come home soon, I do.." he cut me off.

"Ashley this time your prank is not gonna work on me and by the way I'm in an important meeting so I might come late tonight" he said.

"Zyon, list..en to m..e, ahh" I said in a pleading along with a panic tone. " Elena Hobson is here.." my voice broke as fear overwhelmed me. "..please co..me hom..e I'm sca..red and ..." I was interrupted because of the loud banging on my door and the phone in my hand slipped out and fell on the floor.

"As I said, I've come prepared" she yelled as the banging got louder and louder until the latch broke and the door opened revealing two big men and in between them was Elena.

Elena came forward and reached me and I, in an instant pushed her and ran away from her, "Get her" she shouted and both men instantly came towards me and caught my arms.

Elena started laughing at my pathetic state and I couldn't help the tears that were wetting my cheeks.

"How pathetic you are?" She laughed and then grabbed my hair and pulled me downstairs and threw me on the floor inside the lounge. " Don't worry I'm gonna give you a very brutal death along with a gift also and that is your boyfriend's death. After you, I'm gonna kill him for breaking Carol's heart twice, for shattering her heart in million pieces, he's gonna pay for it." I didn't have any energy to reply nor to take anymore punches from her." I killed Sienna for her betrayal and even your late cousin Brian Vincent, who was having second thoughts on killing that bitch, Sienna" my eyes grew big for millisecond as I couldn't keep my eyes open.

She killed Brian also..

" How I wish Carol was more like me than her father, naive and stupid. You know what's the difference between me and Carol, Carol always forgives and forgets while I avenge and never forget" she held out the knife while I was still on the floor waiting for my impending death.

"First let me kill your baby properly and then I'll rip your heart open and chop your body into pieces." she smirked.

And then with full force she drove the knife in me, in my stomach area and the pain was unbearable as blood came out of my mouth, my breathing got ragged ,tears kept flowing down my cheeks as I loudly yet painfully screamed.

"Ahhhhhhh!!" The knife was still in me as I was adjusting to the pain while Elena was laughing.

Is there no humanity in her?

As I got slightly adjusted to the pain Elena pulled the knife out and again I screamed in pain.

"Pl..ea..se" I begged as she roared with laughter and kicked my stomach,where she just drove the knife. "Ahhhhhhh" she kept on kicking and the pain was undescribable.

She took the knife and aimed it towards my chest area as my eyes slowly got closed, waiting for my impending death.

But then I didn't feel the pain in my chest but instead I could hear some yellings, I tried to open my eyes but couldn't. Again I could hear some shoutings until my consciousness faded away.

Chapter 56

Zyon's Pov:-

I opened the door to my penthouse as I saw Ashley lying on the floor, covered with blood and Mrs Hobson was about to stab her when one of the officer shot the bullet up in air and Mrs Hobson's head snapped in our direction as she froze and the knife in her hand fell down. There were two men standing beside Mrs Hobson, who also had a horrified expression on their faces.

I walked inside towards the lounge and saw Ashley lying on the floor with blood surrounding her. My feet gave up and I abruptly kneeled down in front of her body. Looking at her lifeless body. Only One thing came in my mind and that was...

It was all my fault.

I was the one who brought her to New York and introduced her to everyone as my girlfriend. I lied to her and put her life in danger, I killed her. My throat pained as a huge lump was formed and it was difficult to swallow it.

"I was not in fault"I lifted my head only to see Mrs Hobson yelling at the cops.

As soon as Ashley called and informed about Mrs Hobson's arrival and then with all the breaking shattering sounds and yellings. I instantly called Liam and then the cops to come along with me.

"That bitch was blackmailing me and then committed suicide" she defended herself with her freaking lies.

"TAKE HER" my voice boomed as the cops took Elena and the two men.

I couldn't look at Ashley anymore, seeing her in this state breaks my heart as tears kept flowing down my cheeks, the world around me crumpled. Liam crouched down beside me and hugged me. "She can't leave me" I cried.

"Shh"

"I..." There was a movement in Ashley's body, " She's alive" I said and pulled back from him.

I took Ashley's head and placed it on my lap and then slowly patted her cheeks, "Ashley, you're gonna stay with me" her eyelids were moving. " Ashley!!" I patted her cheeks as a small smile formed on my lips.

She slowly opened her eyes and raised her blood covered hands towards a frame, a frame in which there was a defination of success. I looked at the frame but couldn't make out,

What was she trying to tell??

"Mr Rosington, we have to take her to the hospital, the ambulance is here" one of the officer said as three Ambulance attendants came carrying a stretcher in their hand.

The attendants slowly placed Ashley's body on the stretcher and lifted it.

I followed them to the ambulance as they slowly took Ashley inside and I followed suit. I held her blood covered hand mine, "You're gonna be fine" I whispered as the ambulance driver revved the engine.

....

Everybody were standing with me outside the hospital room, waiting for the doctor to come out.

As soon as Liam and I reached the hospital, Liam called mom and dad to the hospital and all of us were waiting for the doctor.

The door to the room opened revealing the doctor, who had a small smile on his face.

"She's okay, there was a big bad gash on her lower stomach which only required some bandages" the doctor explained and all of us heaved a contended sigh.

"Mr James" mom called the doctor and everyone including me turned to face her. "Is the baby alright?" She had tears in her eyes.

Shoot! I totally forgot about it..

Doctor gave her a wierd look as he said, "Yeah, about that I-..."

"DR JAMES" I yelled and grabbed his collar, " Don't tell me you couldn't save my child"

The expression on doctor's face was priceless, he was so confused. Liam came beside me and caught my hand, "Leave him Zyon" Liam whispered in a broke voice.

"I want to talk to the doctor, alone" I announced and pulled the doctor inside the room.

"What going on?" The doctor asked with furrowed brows.

"I'll explain everything to you Mr James, but first how's Ashley" I asked.

"She's fine but she's not pregnant"he exasperated. " And why was she wearing a fake belly belt?"

I sighed before talking "you see, Ashley and I are together since 3 years, we wanted a baby before our wedding.." I fake lamented "last year was a very happy year as Ashley got pregnant but the happiness didn't last long as she got into an brutal accident, she was fighting for her life and she won, she survived but we lost our baby.." I exhaled deeply and looked at Mr James,whose eyes were gleaming with sympathy as I continued "after the accident, she lost her ability to conceive, so we thought of adopting a baby but my family is a lot of traditional and blood matters to them as they didn't want us to adopt a baby and if they will ever get to know about Ashley's infertility, they will force me to break-up with Ashley and I cannot live without her because of that we had to plan all this fake pregnancy and in the end we'll adopt a baby and tell our parents that it's our own blood" I looked at the doctor and he was already looking at me.

Did he believe me?

"So Mr James, can you please lie to my parents that Ashley and I lost our baby" I said in a pleading tone. "I know it's hard for you to lie, but please help me out doctor" I pleaded as he didn't even utter a word. " I know what we did was wrong but we had no choice,we were scared that our parents might separate us" I still didn't get any response from him as I continued. "Please doctor help me out" I joined my hands infront of him.

"I'll help" Mr James concluded as I thanked him and then we both got out of the room.

I wish this will be my last lie..

The doctor stood infront of everyone, "We couldn't save the baby as the knife was directly drove to her lower stomach" the doctor explained and everybody nodded sadly. "Well you can see the patient, she'll be awake within an hour"

Chapter 57

The first thing I saw when I first opened my eyes was the white cieling, in confusion I looked around and saw Zyon looking at me with a huge smile on his face. "You.. ow-" I moaned in pain as I tried to move my arms.

"You're okay" Zyon sat on the stool which was placed beside my hospital bed.

"I'm fine" my voice was hoarse " but my whole body pains"

"Doctor said that the pain will reduce in 3 to 4 days" Zyon said.

"How am I looking, I mean my face" I asked touching my face as I could feel all the bandages around my face.

"You look beautiful" he said with a smile.

"Your saying that I look beautiful with bruised face and in a hospital gown"

"Yeah, your beautiful in every way"

"Aww thank you, well I wanna see my face"

"What?!" He asked with furrowed brows

"Pass me your phone, I wanna check my face" he passed me his phone and I opened the camera and checked my face, I had a black eye, nose and forehead covered with bandages and a lot of bruises. "Oh! I look so ugly" I scrunched my nose.

"No you don't" Zyon took his phone back and all of the sudden his face turned serious.

"Ashley I have to tell you something.........." He stated as he began to tell me how he had to lie to the doctor and also how he convinced the doctor to play along.

I nodded, all I could do was nod.

His phone dinged and he checked his phone and then looked at me and said. "Mom wants to see you, now" he said

"What??"

"Yes, act like a sad woman who just lost her baby"

"How am I gonna act, I'm not a good actor" I protested.

"Just think of something bad that happened to you"

"Something bad?" The only bad thing that happened to me was Elena and other than that, were my ex-boyfriends who only wanted my virginity and not me.

But none of these things were making me cry. So the one thing which always made me cry or bawl my eyes out was Stefan Salvatore's death and on thinking about that my eyes instantly welled up.

"What are you thinking?" Zyon asked as worrylines appeared on his forehead.

I sniffled and wiped one of my tears "I'm thinking about Stefan Salvatore's death, how he sacrificed himself for his brother, on his wedding day he died and how Caroline became a bride and a widow on the same day" I sniffled again.

"She lost her husband on the wedding day" I nodded. "Woah! Who was her husband BTW"

"Stefan Salvatore"

"What so Stefan was mar-" he was cut off as the door to my room opened revealing lily, Thomas and Rebecca. "Perfect timing" Zyon muttered.

"Oh Ashley!!" Lily exclaimed "Don't cry sweetheart, I know it really hurts to lose a baby" she hugged as her eyes moistured.

I sniffled and nodded, "I'll make sure that Elena Hobson is punished well for her doings " Thomas exclaimed as his jaw clenched and he balled his fists.

Lily kept on consoling me and Thomas kept on cursing Elena and Rebecca just gave me a sad smile.

After a while all three of them left leaving me and Zyon alone, " Zyon I have a recorded video of Elena confessing her crimes " I whispered.

"How?" He asked as his eyebrows dipped together.

"Elena didn't come home by herself yesterday I called her" I looked down onto my lap as I knew that he's gonna exaggerate it simply.

"You... how could you be so careless, you knew you could have died because of the stupid stunt you've pulled " as expected he's exaggerating.

"But I didn't and now Sienna can get justice and there are no more stalkers around who were a threat to my life." I chirped and he sighed defeatedly.

....

Its been two days since I'm in hospital and today is my discharge day and I'm really happy that today is my last day in this hospital.

The door to my room opened and I expected it to be Zyon, who went out to grab some lunch for both of us but it was Carol.

"Hi, how are you?" She greeted and there was a hesitant in her voice maybe she's guilty.

But why is she guilty?

"Hi" I smiled.

She walked towards the bed and sat across me in the stool. "I'm sorry for your loss" her eyes were fixed on my stomach.

I just nodded as she continued. "I didn't knew mom would stoop so low and try..." her voice broke as a lone tear rolled down her cheek. "...to kill you, hell I didn't even knew that she killed my best friend,Sienna" more tears rolled down her cheeks.

"I had a huge fight with Sienna because of a misunderstanding" she started talking about Sienna all of the sudden "I thought she and Zyon had a thing for each other, she tried to explain me that there was nothing but I didn't listen and that day I went home crying, mom saw me and I know mom loves me and she cannot see me crying. I told mom everything about Sienna and Zyon, mom was very disappointed and angry with Zyon and Sienna. I was miserable for weeks and then however I composed myself and thought that Zyon would never love me and I was just being a hindrance in their relationship. The day when she died, that morning I called her and told her that if she has feelings for Zyon, she should confess it and I was happy for her, that same day, that evening she died, I never suspected anyone, I thought it was just an accident, I never expected my mom to be behind all of this. I'm sorry, and again my mom is the reason you lost your baby" she hiccuped.

I placed my hand on hers and gently squeezed it, "It's okay, you're not in fault "

But she kept on crying and asked for forgiveness.

Chapter 58

"The owner of the fashion minds, Elena Hobson is guilty of her crimes, she killed an innocent girl named Sienna Maxwell and then even tried to kill Ashley Grayson, girlfriend of the current CEO of CTC, Zyon Rosington..." and then my photo was on the TV screen.

OMG! I can't believe I'm on television..

It's been a month since the attack and the news channels are still busy chattering about the owner of the fashion minds, the great Elena Hobson who is now behind the bars for the crimes she committed. The Hobson's tried and asked for many lawyers for help but none could help as my proof was strong enough as she herself confessed her crimes on that video.

Everything was set now, I don't have any stalkers around me who were a threat for my life as the main root of threat is in the prison.

Someone cleared their throat and I looked at Zyon who was wearing a shiny white shirt with black fitted pants and a charming smile plastered on his face.

"You took almost an hour to get ready" I pointed out.

Today, Zyon and I are going to a restaurant to have dinner, you can call it a date also. I was wearing a maroon colour tight fitted strapless dress, which Zyon gifted me.

"You look gorgeous" he complimented.

"Thank you"

"So let's get going" he said and we both sauntered out.

....

Zyon has booked a table at the top of the building and has arranged the area beautifully with some cented candles and flowers and the area was looking exquisite in the night sky with the star's shining above us.

"This is amazing" I exclaimed.

We took our seats as the waiter came and placed a bottle of wine and then took our orders and walked off.

"Ashley.." Zyon called and I fixed my gaze to him.

"Yes?"

His piercing green beautiful eyes turned all dreamy as he sighed dreamily, "I wish I could have approached you better"

I scoffed before saying, "Stop with the cliché lines, you could have never approached me better"

"You just had to ruin our moment" he narrowed his eyes.

"I'm just stating facts, I mean if you have approached me better, you wouldn't have lied to me in the first place and if you wouldn't have lied to me, we couldn't have been together" I said everything in one breath.

"I didn't mean it like tha-" I cut him off.

"You live in New York and I was living in Florida, it's another reason why you couldn't have approached me better" I grinned.

"I didn't mean it like that" he groaned "approached you better means, what if we both were living in Florida and we both met in a Cafe, where I by-mistakenly dropped my handkerchief and you picked it up as you return it back to me and as your eyes land on me, you ask me out..-" I interrupted his long story.

"Why I should be the one who asked you out first, huh?" I snapped.

"Fine, I'm the one who asked you out first and then you shyly say yes and then we go on our first date and then you ask me to be your boyfriend and I said yes and then- " again I cut him off.

"You were the one who confessed and asked me to be your girlfriend first " I playfully glared at him.

"Okay fine, I confess my feelings and asked you to be my girlfriend and again you shyly say yes-"

"I don't shy" I wrinkled my nose

"Okay you didn't shy, you boldly said yes and this is what I meant by saying 'approached you better ' understand"

Too much cliché..

I wanted to comment but I didn't want to ruin the moment, so I gave a curt nod as he smiled. Within the time the waiter came and placed our orders on the table and I licked my lips seeing the delicious dishes infront of me. Without wasting a second I digged in my food.

After having the deserts I wiped my mouth with the cloth and Zyon did the same.

"So shall we get going?" He asked out of blue.

"What? Why so soon?" I asked incredulously as he raised a brow in confusion. " I mean we can roam around for a while and then go home"

"Who said we are going home?" He asked.

"Then where are we going?" I asked with a furrowed brows.

"It's a surprise" he winked and got up from his chair.

....

"Where are you taking me?" I snapped as he took different turns on the road where I've never ever been before.

"Relax, I'm not kidnapping you" he said in a chilled tone.

"But where are we going?" I asked again.

"As I said it's a surprise"

"For your information Zyon, I hate SURPRISES!!"

"I'm glad that I knew it now and next time Ashley do remind me to wrap a cloth around your mouth, your so talkative" he shook his head in dismay.

"You stupid jerk" I bursted " how dare you call me talkative, huh?" I growled.

His one hand was on the wheel and the other hand, he placed it on his ear and groaned, " Your so loud Ashley" he commented.

Before I could respond to his comment he stopped the car infront of the large gates and the large gate automatically got opened.

"Woah!! Where are we?" Zyon however ignored my question.

He drove the car inside property and as my gaze fell on the property place, I was awestruck. He parked the car at the corner area and got out and opened the door for me and I also got out, still in awe.

There in front of me was a large garden which was neatly decorated with some fairy lights and in the middle of the large garden was a big mansion. Ahead of me was a cobblestone pathway which led us to a large mahogany doors.

Zyon pushed the door open and we both sauntered in as Zyon closed the large doors behind us. I couldn't see anything inside due to darkness, everything was dark in here.

"ZYON!!" I yelled as suddenly the lights turned on and there infront of me was a huge lounge decorated with red roses and on one of the walls was hung a beautiful banner and in the banner, there was four words written and reading those four words, my eyes popped out of their sockets, the four words were,

Will you marry me..

I looked down and there was Zyon kneeling down in front of me holding a neavy Blue velvety box in which there was a beautiful diamond ring.

"Will you marry me Ashley?" I was awestruck, I can't believe that this is happening. "Will you be my better half in everything, in happiness,sadness, richness,poor and-" I cut him off by jumping on him as he lost his kneeling balance and landed flat on his back and I was on top of him, hugging.

"YES!! I will marry you, Zyon" I kissed his cheeks.

"A little warning Ashley, before jumping on me" he said in a pained tone.

"Oops, I'm sorry" I got up from him and he also stood up groaning a little in pain.

"Oh my god!!" Zyon gasped.

"What happened?" I asked.

"You shouldn't have jumped on me" he showed the velvet box and the diamond ring was missing.

"You lost the ring?" I asked incredulously.

"I didn't loose it, it's just when you jumped on me, I lost my balance and the ring might have fallen somewhere.." he started looking here and there.

"That ring must cost millions" I bent down and started searching for the ring.

"Ashley" Zyon called but I ignored him as I was busy searching for the ring. "Ashley" he called me again.

"What??" I turned around, my voice was panicky.

"Will you marry me?" He asked holding the diamond ring in his hand and then suddenly started laughing on my face.

"You just did not lie to me " I growled as his laughters got loud. "How could you lie to me, I thought you stopped lying" I yelled.

"How can I stop lying after all your loving a liar" he shrugged and again started laughing.

"Liar, liar pants on fire" I yelled and stuck my tongue out but still he didn't stop laughing as my nostrils flared. "I will not marry you Mr Rosington" I bursted as he stopped laughing, he had tears in his eyes due to all his laughings.

"Oh come on Ashley don't say like that" he pouted.

"I'm angry" he took a step forward and kissed both of my cheeks.

"Still angry?" He asked.

"Yes" he smirked and then suddenly his lips landed on mine, kissing me fiercely and I melted in his arms, kissing him back.

"Still angry?" He asked after pulling back and I shook my head in no as heat crawled up my neck. "Okay let's do it properly" he said and I raised a brow in confusion.

He took a step back and kneeled down in front of me before asking, "Will you marry me, Miss Ashley Grayson"

I nodded shyly before saying yes and stretched my right hand out, opening my fingers.

Zyon stood up and gently placed the ring on my ring finger.

"So it's like dream come true for you" he said and I narrowed my eyes at him.

"Why?"

"You always wanted a man with green eyes to be your husb and.." he pointed his both thumb finger to himself and slightly shook his hips "...and see here I am, your future husband" I couldn't help but laugh aloud.

"Your funny Zyon" I commented still laughing.

"Whatever, now your officially mine and this ring.." he pointed towards the ring in my finger "...is an evidence and this house is for our family, you, me and our kids" with that said he hugged me tightly in his arms and I hugged him back feeling safe in his embrace.

"I love you" I muttered still in his arms.

"I love you more" he kissed the top of my head.

"I love you the most" I said as I snuggled closer to him.

Chapter 59

"I, Zyon Rosington, take you, Ashley Mary Grayson to be my lawfully wedded wife in happiness and in sorrow, in richer and in poorer, For better and for worse, in health and in sickness, to love and to cherish until death do us apart." Zyon took his vows as his beautiful green eyes were locked with mine, his hands held mine in a gentle manner and a huge was smile plastered on his beautiful face.

Holding my dad's hand, when I walked down the aisle and when my eyes landed on Zyon, waiting for me at the altar and when I reached the altar as my dad took my hand and placed it on Zyon's hand, I felt an undescribable emotion overwhelming me but whatever the emotion was, it was good, the feeling I felt while climbing the altar was good. I was happy, joyful and enthusiastic, however you wanna define it.

Wearing a beautiful white dress during my wedding has always been my dream and today I'm living it, and now infront of me is standing my soon to be husband who's eyes are glistening with adoration.

Someone cleared their throat and I averted my gaze to the priest, who gestured me to take my vows and I abruptly nodded and averted my gaze back to Zyon and gave him a soft smile before taking my vows,

" I, Ashley Mary Grayson take you, Zyon Rosington to be my lawfully wedded husband in health and in sickness, for rich and for poor,for better or for worse, in happiness and in sorrow, to love and cherish you until death do us apart " Zyon gave me a ear to ear grin as he gently squeezed my hand.

"Now I pronounce you both as husband and wife " the priest said as the ring bearer entered the hall with our wedding ring, we instantly exchanged our rings as the priest turned towards the congregation.

"And now I present to everyone who came here to witness the beautiful union, Mr and Mrs Rosington " the priest announced and the crowd cheered loudly. " now you may kiss the bride"

My favorite part..

Zyon cupped my cheeks as he leaned in and gave me a soft kiss on my lips which had love,warmth, protection and everything that I ever wanted.

He slowly pulled back and then we signed our marriage certificate before turning towards the congregation.

In the crowd I saw, my mom clapping loudly and grinning widely, my dad, who was busy wiping his tears, Chase was clapping and had a small smile on his face, Clara and Steve were giving a thumbs up and blowing kisses in our direction,

Zyon's mom and dad were drinking wine and celebrating the moment, Rebecca had a smile on her face, Lucy Cole was also invited along with Julia Cole, Julia was busy drinking wine with my mother-in-law and Lucy was sitting in a corner with a huge bump. Well Carol was my maid of honor as I don't have any girlfriends and Liam was Zyon's best man. Majority of people were coming in our direction to congratulate us.

"You look damn hot today" Zyon whispered in my ear.

"Your telling me that for the tenth time" I pointed out.

"What's wrong in calling my wife beautiful ?" He emphasized on the word wife.

"Nothing is wrong in calling your wife beautiful, husband " I emphasized on the last word.

"It's feels so good to hear it from your mouth, say it again"

"What? Husband?" I asked in confusion as he nodded. "Oh my dear husband " I purred in his ear.

"Oh my dear wife" he pinched my cheeks but I quickly swatted his hands away.

"Not here Zyon"

"What-" Zyon was interrupted by Lily.

"Ashley come soon, you have a bouquet throwing ceremony to do"

"Yes coming " with that said I and Zyon both walked towards Lily to the huge garden.

I had a beautiful white colour flower bouquet in my hand as I turned around from the crowd of girls who were standing behind me to catch the bouquet.

One. Two. Three.

With that count I threw the bouquet up in the air and turned around to see, who caught it. And the person who caught the bouquet was Carol, who was smiling seeing the bouquet in her hand.

"Wohooo" the other girls in the crowd cheered as Carol had a slight pink hue on her cheeks.

"Now it's time for garter throwing ceremony" somebody yelled and everyone gathered for the garter throwing ceremony.

I sat on a neatly decorated chair as Zyon came and kneeled down infront of me. He got into my dress, towards my thighs and slowly pulled the garter down using his teeth, butterflies spluttered in my tummy due to his actions.

He pulled the garter and stood up and stretched his hands out for me and I gladly took it as I stood up from the chair.

All the bachelor men gathered behind Zyon, wait, correction most of the men gathered behind Zyon including Liam and Steve who are the certified playboys and I knew the reason.

Because Carol was the one who caught the bouquet..

Zyon turned around as his back was facing all the men, within a second he threw the garter up in air and all the men's head snapped upward, eagerly staring at the garter, the garter was coming in Steve's direction and Steve was about to catch it but Liam interfered and pushed him away which caused Steve to fall flat on his butt on the floor and in process Liam caught the garter.

"What the hell man?!!" Steve growled at Liam as he stood up from the floor.

"Sorry man, but I needed it the most" Liam said as he spinned the garter in his index finger.

Carol sat on the decorated chair and Liam kneeled infront of her as the crowd cheered loudly.

Carol was wearing a knee length sky blue colour dress. Liam pulled the garter up her ankle using his hands and above her ankle, he used his teeth to pull the garter up and the action of him caused a pink hue on Carol's cheeks.

As the garter reached her thighs everyone in the crowd clapped and cheered loudly.

......

The night has fallen down and the same garden where are wedding ceremony was held is now decorated with red roses, lanterns and fairy lights.

It was our reception tonight and everything in our wedding went well.

Many of our guests, who were probably Zyon's buisness investors came towards us and talked to Zyon about business.

Like seriously, on his wedding reception..

With great difficulty I pulled Zyon away from them and took him to a corner.

"Oh my God!! Those stupid investors, how can they talk to you about business, specially on your wedding day" I exaggerated but obviously Zyon ignored me and pulled me towards him by placing his one arm around my waist.

"I love you" he murmured.

"I know you love me" I stated.

He pouted before saying, "Always ruining the moment"

"I love you more" I smiled as he kissed my forehead before hugging me.

"I love you the most" he muttered huskily still hugging me as I hugged him back.

"Aww" someone cooed as we both pulled back and looked at the person. "Mom is calling you both, for the couple dance" Rebecca smiled and walked away.

"Dance" we both said in unison and followed Rebecca towards the dance floor.

Many people joined us to the dance floor including Chase and Clara, Liam and Carol.

Wait, Liam and Carol are having a thing between them nowadays..

Zyon and I locked our one hand together as I placed my other hand on Zyon's mascular shoulder and Zyon placed his other hand on my waist. The music started and we both started moving along with the rhythm.

You're the light, you're the night, You're the colour of my blood, You're the cure, You're the pain, You're the only thing I wanna touch. You can see the world you brought to life, to life So love me like you do, la la love me like you do, Touch me like you do ta ta touch me like you do, What are you waiting for?

"My favourite song" Zyon said as he gently rotated me twice in his arms.

"Mine too" I whispered as I faced him and gently placed my forehead on his

Fading in, fading out, On the edge of paradise, Every inch of your skin Is a holy grail I've to find, Only you can set my heart on fire,on fire..

I looked at him, at his beautiful piercing green eyes which is the first thing I've noticed and loved the most, I couldn't believe that he was mine and I was his, everything was kinda surreal but if it's a dream, I would never wanna wake up. After all the storms we've encountered, we stayed together facing it and he was always there for me, for my better and for my worse, I knew one thing for sure.

Zyon is my man of dreams.

He's imperfectly perfect and I couldn't believe that this man is my husband, the man I love the most.

"What are you thinking?" Zyon asked still holding me in his arms.

I smiled and shook my head in no.

I leaned in and took his lips in mine, he kissed me back fervently and I poured all my love and affection towards him in the kiss. I love him so much.

Zyon is the best thing that has ever happened to me..

Chapter 60

It has been three months for our marriage and there was never a moment where I regretted my marriage with Zyon, every moment with him was beautiful and every single day my love towards him grew stronger and stronger. I still couldn't believe that this sweet loving man was my h u s -
band.

"Honey, where's the pepper?" Zyon called me from the kitchen.

"It's on the second cabinet on the right" I yelled back from the lounge.

We shifted to our new house, two months ago right after returning from our honeymoon, the house was too big for both of us but the atmosphere in here is peaceful.

Today is Sunday, so my sweet big honey bunny husband is preparing my favourite chicken lasagna with creamy white sauce for dinner and the aroma of food was mouth watering.

I walked towards the kitchen and on the right time Zyon wore the oven mitts and removed the chicken lasagna out and my god it smelled so good.

"Is it ready?" I asked as I licked my bottom lip.

"Yes, Mrs Rosington" He bowed like a gentleman holding the lasagna.

I took two plates and forks out of the crockery unit and we both sauntered out of the kitchen. I poured orange juices into two glasses, which were placed on the dining table and sat across Zyon. Zyon sliced the lasagna and placed a small piece in my plate and another small piece in his.

"I want a big piece of lasagna" I pleaded.

"Ookay" he sliced a large portion of it and then placed it on my plate.

We digged in our respective plates and my god it tasted like heaven, the taste was even better than the aroma.

After having our dinner we both made our way to our room, Zyon made his way to the bathroom to take a bath while I sat on the bed waiting for Zyon to come out.

Fifteen minutes later.

Zyon still hasn't returned from the bathroom, and I don't know what is taking so long.

Is he having a beauty bath..

Suddenly I felt a bile rising up my throat and I started feeling nauseous. However I swallowed it but again I felt the bile rising up my throat. I ran towards the bathroom but my bad luck Zyon was in there, I banged my fist on the bathroom door as I couldn't yell.

"I'm coming " he said as he opened the bathroom door.

I thought I would push him away and then run to the wash basin and puke on it but nothing went the way I thought, as soon as Zyon opened the door I couldn't control myself as I puked on Zyon's naked upper body and on his sweat pants and some drops of fluids even flew on his slight stubble. I threw my guts out on Zyon as if he was a wash basin.

After throwing all my guts out I looked at Zyon's face who had a worried expression on his face. "Are you okay?" He asked.

"Yeah" I replied breathlessly.

"You ate that lasagna like an elephant, that's why you threw up" he reasoned out.

"I didn't eat like an elephant and go take a shower again, you stink" I said as I walked inside the bathroom near the wash basin and rinsed my mouth.

"I just had a bath" Zyon pouted.

"Should I help you in taking bath again" I asked flirtiously with a wink.

" Gladly " he said huskily with a smirk, before closing the bathroom door behind us.

....

Oh my god why am I feeling nauseous today, from morning I'm feeling nauseous and now it's already afternoon.

Am I not feeling well??

Zyon is in his office and might return at night, I feel like my head is spinning and again I'm feeling nauseous.

Wait! nauseous, does that mean I'm preg-..

No no no, wait Google can help me, I took my phone out and tapped on Google as typed on the keyboard,

Symptoms of pregnancy.

And instantly Google gave me my answer.

- missing of periods. - tender, swollen breasts.. - nauseous with or without vomiting... - fatigue.. - increased urination.

I instantly opened my calendar on my phone and checked my last period date and I did miss my periods this month.

Oh God..

I need a pregnancy test kit, now.

....

Sweat droplets appeared on my forehead as I waited patiently for the result. It has already been several minutes, so I slowly checked the test kit and it had two lines on it which means,

I'm pregnant, for real.

....

I was pacing back and forth waiting for Zyon and exactly at half past six Zyon entered the house.

"I'm exhausted" he said as loosened his tie and laid on the couch, closing his eyes

Should I tell him?

Ofcourse I should, after all I'm carrying his baby for real this time.

"Zyon!!" I called as he opened his eyes before humming.

"Hmm"

"I.. I um.. I have a surprise for you" he sat straight on the couch with a raised brow.

"What surprise?" He asked.

"Come with me" he stood up from the couch and stretched his arms above his head before following me to the room.

I took two papers and two markers in my hand, I gave one paper and a marker to Zyon and I kept the other one to myself.

"What are you doing?" He asked looking at the paper and the marker oddly.

"Now turn around" I made him face the wall as his back was now facing me.

I placed my paper on his back and instructed him to place his paper on the wall.

"Now write, what I write on my paper, in your paper" I instructed as he nodded.

First I wrote a big I on my paper as he wrote the same on his paper. Then I wrote AM and he also wrote the same. Then I wrote PREGN- but stopped in midway as he abruptly turned around with wide eyes and mouth hanging open.

"Are we pregnant??" He asked incredulously.

He still remembers the manners taught by me..

"Ye...yes" I stuttered.

"For real?"

"Obviously for real" I snapped.

"Oh my god" he gasped and then a huge grin broke out his lips. He took his phone out but I interrupted him.

"Are you happy?" I asked with crossed fingers.

"Ofcourse, I'm more than happy" he exclaimed as he dialled his mother's number.

And on the second ring my mother-in-law received the call and Zyon put the call on speaker "Hello sweetie,what-" but Zyon cut her off.

"Mom we are pregnant" he exclaimed.

"What?"

"I mean, Ashley's pregnant" he exclaimed as there was a brief silence on the other side.

"Thomas!!" We could literally hear her screaming her husband's name. " Ashley is pregnant" with her voice we could make out that she was ecstatic. "I knew she would conceive soon after her miscarriage" she exclaimed and our faces got down as guilt consumed us.

But however after saying our small goodbyes we disconnected the call and Zyon carried me up and spinned me around. "ZYON!! I'm gonna puke on you again" he laughed richly and slowly set me down on my feet,

"We are pregnant, Ashley"

....

Seven months later,

After the scanning, Zyon and I entered the doctor's office and sat on the chair infront of the doctor.

Doctor nodded and took a pen and paper and wrote the gender of the baby on the paper and placed the paper inside the envelope before handing it to us.

As soon as we were out of the hospital, we quickly made our way towards our car and sat inside the car.

"Being pregnant is the most difficult thing in the world" I exasperated rubbing my huge real baby bump.

"Hmm" Zyon hummed as he also brought his hand towards my bump and started rubbing up and down.

"Which gender is it,? check quickly" I said.

"Shouldn't we go home and then open it infront of our parents" Zyon told me.

"Oh please, I can't wait" I pouted.

"Fine" Zyon smiled and opened the envelope.

"Is it a girl or a boy?" I asked

"It's a.." Zyon looked at me.

"It's a?" I repeated it as a question.

"It's a..." He did that again.

"Zyon I'm gonna slap you hard and then kick in the bal-"

"It's a boy" he cut me off and handed me the paper.

"It's a boy" I rubbed my bump softly again. "I was thinking of-" Zyon again cut me off.

"NO!!"

"What no?"

"I know what you're thinking" he replied.

How come he knows what I'm thinking..

"What I'm thinking?" I raised my chin up in pride.

"You want to name our son Stefan"

How come he knew what I'm thinking.

"What's wrong in naming our son Stefan.?"

"You're naming our son after a character"

"What's wrong in that?"

"No" he said sternly.

"Okay let's play rock, paper, scissors, who wins will get the chance to name our son" I bargained.

"Fine" with that said we started our game.

"Rock. Paper. Scissors" I was scissors and he was rock, so obviously it was him who won.

Zyon smirked on my defeat but I raised my chin up in pride and..

"What name do you suggest?" I asked with attitude.

"Umm.. I wanna name my son Arthur" he smiled and touched my bump with his eyes glittering with adoration.

"Arthur?" He nodded with a smile.

"Yeah" he replied.

"Fine" I rolled eyes.

' Arthur, not that bad'

Epilogue

Four years later :-

"PAUL!!" I screamed as I couldn't find him anywhere. "WHERE ARE YOU?" I could hear some soft giggles behind the curtain as I pulled open the curtains revealing my one year old son. "Caught you" I carried him up in my arms as he laughed cutely.

Someone cleared their throat and I looked at Zyon who was holding Arthur and Ian's hands.

"We're ready" he said as I saw him wearing a white shiny shirt along with a black formal pants, Ian and Arthur were wearing the same. "You lost again" Zyon stated with a smirk.

"You know among our three sons, Paul is the naughtiest one" I defended myself.

"But you were the one, who planned this competition in the first place" Zyon narrowed his eyes and wrinkled his nose as I sighed.

"Just give me five minutes we'll get ready"

"It's fine" he charged forward and took Paul from me "I'll take him and make him wear his clothes and you go and get ready" he said as he took Paul from me and sauntered out of the room.

Well after Arthur, I gave birth to the twins, Ian and Paul,they were identical twins with only one difference and that was their eye colour, Ian had green eyes like Zyon's while Paul had brown eyes like mine, rest everything was the same, nose, lips, hair colour, complexion everything.

I still remember how Zyon gave me the chance to name our twins and I was hell bent on naming them Stefan and Damon. But Zyon strictly prohibited those names for our twins, So instead of naming them Stefan and Damon, I named them Paul and Ian, the real names of the character Stefan and Damon. Foolish Zyon didn't get know that I literally named our son after Ian Somerhalder and Paul Wesley. He just said that the names were good and agreed with me.

Arthur also has green eyes like Zyon, so I held a competition saying that Zyon should look after the green eye kids while I'll look after the brown eyes one, but Zyon being the good father looked after the green eye kids properly while me being me couldn't even look after our one kid properly. Well among my three sons Paul is the most naughtiest and notorious one, so can't blame me.

In my second pregnancy when I got to know that I was carrying twins I was very happy but when I got to know that the two kids inside me were boys, I was kinda sad because I wished to have a girl, a little daughter but I don't have one. Among the twins atleast one could have been a girl.

I wish Paul would have been a girl.

My phone started ringing and it was Chase and Clara on the FaceTime. I answered the call and I was greeted with some soft giggles of Jasper, their two years old son. "Ashley don't forget to come to my wedding next month" Chase's voice bellowed from the other line

"Yes, you have to come" Clara insisted.

"Sure" I smiled.

"bring Zyon and your three sons along with you" Chase said sternly.

"Ofcourse I'll bring them, I just can't leave them here and come all alone to Florida " I said as they both chuckled.

After having a small chit-chat with them, I disconnected the call.

Steve was still the same, a playboy. He keeps saying that marriage and kids are just a burden and right now the life he's living is better than a married life.

I don't know when Steve's gonna change..

Today we had a small get together party at Zyon's parents house and we all were getting ready for that.

"My son's are ready to go" Zyon's voice bellowed as I gave a final touch to my makeup.

"Aww my sons are looking so handsome, come let me take a picture" all my three sons were wearing same clothes as Zyon's and all were looking so so handsome like their dad. I took my phone out and clicked a picture of my sons with Zyon. "You know sons, I can see future and you know what I see now?" I asked as I crouched down to their height with a grin.

"What you see mommy?" Arthur asked.

"When you guys will get older, girls are gonna be after you'll, to worship your body and kiss your fac-"

"Ashley!!" Zyon interrupted me by calling me with wide eyes.

"What??"

"Don't talk such things infront of kids"

"Fiiine" I stood up. "But my sons are so damn handsome "

"Just like you" I whispered in Zyon's ear and squeezed his ass.

"Ashley!!" Zyon glared at me as heat crawled up his neck and I just winked at him in return.

"Let get going babies " I said as I grasped Arthur's hand while Zyon carried Ian and Paul in his arms.

....

As soon as we reached our parents house, Arthur let go of my hand and ran towards his grandpa,

"Arthur, my grandson " my father-in-law carried Arthur in his arms and spinned him around as Arthur started giggling.

The twins ran towards their grandma and Rebecca, Rebecca changed alot in four years, she talks with me alot instead of just smiling and recently she dyed her hair into blonde and blonde suited her. I never knew that Rebecca was so sassy with Zyon until our marriage. Whenever we used stay here, there was always a tiny little argument going on between them.

"Hello guys" Liam voice bellowed as he entered the large lounge with Carol and his two year old daughter, Cara.

Oh how I wish even I had a daughter.

Carol and Liam got married, a few months after our marriage and now they have a two year old daughter, Cara. She got her mother's beauty and her father's charms, she also had a strawberry blonde hair and grey eyes like her mother. Cara was wearing a baby pink colour frock and was looking like a Barbie doll.

Aww, she's so cute..

"Dinner is ready" Lily called everyone and we all made our towards the dining area.

....

After having dinner everybody were busy doing their stuffs and I was busy feeding Ian and Paul.

"Paul baby, open you mouth" but Paul didn't open his mouth instead he snapped his head to the other side and shut his mouth into a thin line.

"Mum... ahhh" Ian called and opened his mouth widely as I smiled and put the spoon inside his mouth.

"My good son." I ruffled Ian's black hair.

As I finished feeding them, I washed my hands and made my way upstairs, while going upstairs I saw Rebecca descending downstairs, her eyes were bloodshot and nose puffed.

"Rebecca!!" I called her.

She looked at me with her moistured green eyes. " Marriage is not a game, we marry the person we love. You married Zyon because you love him. Marriage is about love, trust, belonging and companionship. I can't go and marry some stranger" she said all of a sudden in one breath as her chest was heaving up and down. "Uhm... I'm sorry, I was kinda depressed so it just came out of my mouth, I'm sorry" she apologized and descended downstairs in a hurry.

"Rebecca!!" I called again as she kept on walking.

I sighed as I knew why was she depressed, its about the arranged marriage. She don't wanna get married but my father-in-law wants her to get married to some guy.

Zyon and I tried to convince dad but he's not listening to anyone as he wants Rebecca to get married.

"Mommy!!" I was pulled out of my trance as Arthur called me.

"Yes baby" he slowly descended downstairs by taking baby steps.

"Daddy is calling you" he said.

"Where is daddy?" I asked.

"He's upstairs in his room" he said as he made his way downstairs and sauntered towards Ian and Paul.

I ascended upstairs to our room and pushed the door open. The room was dark as I closed the door behind me. I moved towards the switch board but suddenly I felt two arms around my shoulder and within a second I was pinned to the wall. My eyes got adjusted to the darkness as I could see Zyon standing boldly infront of me.

"Zyo-" I was cut off as Zyon's soft luscious lips landed on mine, kissing me fervently, our lips moulded together in a perfect symphony as I kissed him back.

Zyon is everything to me, my love, my partner, father of my three sons,my better half and sometimes even my bitter half but whatever it is I'm proud to have Zyon in my life,who loves and respects me for who I am. His beautiful green eyes which

I have always adored is the home my heart always seeks. He became my journey and we both built our destination.

"I love you" he said in between the kiss.

"I love you more" we pulled back as we were at loss of air.

"I love the most" he whispered as he rested his forehead on mine.

He is the man who appreciates to have me, scared of losing me, he's proud of having me in his life,and I'm proud to call him my husband, Zyon Rosington.

We will always stick together in better or in worse, in rich or in poor, in health and sickness, we will always cherish and love eachother until death do us apart.

CPSIA information can be obtained
at www.ICGtesting.com
Printed in the USA
LVHW081051070123
736479LV00014B/850